Fear No Evil

Brand of Justice
Book 9

Lisa Phillips

eBook ISBN:979-8-88552-254-0

Paperback ISBN: 979-8-88552-255-7

Library of Congress Control Number: 2024947867

Published by: Two Dogs Publishing, LLC. Idaho, USA

Cover Design by: Sasha Almazan and Gene Mollica, GS Cover Design Studio, LLC

Edited by: Christine Callahan, Professional Publishing Services

Fear No Evil

Chapter One

Friday, 10:55 p.m.
New Orleans, Louisiana

Darkness hung like a shroud over cobblestone and redbrick buildings, illuminated by yellow lights. Marketplace stalls selling anything from crystals and candles to small batch craft beer ran along one side in front of the ice cream shop, which was still getting plenty of foot traffic at this late hour.

The long line wasn't enough to keep Kenna from wanting ice cream.

Except she was in line for a taco truck.

Across from the stalls, customers flocked to a row of food trucks parked next to the courtyard—a meatball sandwich vendor, vegan food, and the one Kenna and Ramon were interested in. Tacos Locos was famous for its queso, but they weren't here for cheese dip.

They weren't even here for food, not really.

Ramon shifted beside her, sliding out his phone, which made him look like anyone else standing in line at a taco truck. Ignoring his date. Not that she would ever work to give anyone the impression that's what she was to him.

He pulled up the Tacos Locos website, scrolling through the menu. "The barbacoa tacos look good." He tapped on the About page and showed her photos of staff members. "He's not on here."

"You thought he would be?" Kenna said.

"It would save us taking the risk of getting food poisoning along with our guacamole."

She rolled her eyes. "Nobody is forcing you to eat."

Though, over the past few months working together, she had noticed he didn't eat much. Given how their occupation could be physically demanding on occasion, she figured the guy needed a whole lot more carbohydrates in his diet.

Just another item on the list of things she was planning on getting him to work on. All part of training him to be a private investigator, which was better than him being a mercenary for hire—although that was probably more suited to his skill set.

She might be a lifelong investigator—and they'd been at Quantico, training for the FBI together—but their career paths had diverged drastically after that. Ramon had gone undercover in Mexico, been burned by his handler, and spent years working for a cartel. He was now back in good standing with the FBI. The handler who had burned him was dead, and her whole family and their conspiracy had been shut down.

Kenna might have been instrumental in clearing his name, along with the new assistant special agent in charge of the FBI's Phoenix office, who happened to also be her boyfriend.

But she wasn't entirely sure Ramon cared to live on the right side of the law now, working with her to bring bad guys to justice.

Whether he stuck with it or not, Kenna would do what she could to help Ramon live whatever life he chose. Just as long as he wasn't hurting anyone or breaking the law. If she needed to add any stipulations or take any away, it would be on a case-by-case basis.

Ramon peered over the head of the person ahead of them. "If we get to the front of the line, I think I might be able to see inside far enough to confirm it's him in there."

"If you can't, we might have to improvise." Kenna blew out a breath.

Who knew what Ramon would come up with to achieve his end. He tended toward Lone Ranger tactics, but they'd settled into a decent rhythm after some weeks of working with her. Hopefully, he knew her well enough now to realize they were in this together. Or at least wasn't planning to go off on his own.

She was the boss, and he knew she called the shots.

"I don't have any Molotov cocktails handy, but I'm sure I can find something to throw into the taco truck."

Kenna shot him a side glance, one eyebrow raised.

He lifted both hands, his palms toward her. "Kidding."

Sure, he was. "No fires. I'll figure out a way to get inside the truck."

Noise broke out above the general buzz of music spilling from a bar on the far corner, a two-story structure with plenty of people on the balcony having a good time. Half a dozen teens, several of them on skateboards, entered the courtyard, and one brushed an older couple Kenna had pegged as tourists.

She frowned. "He just..."

"Pickpockets?" Ramon asked. "Pretty normal in a place like this. They're probably bored."

"That doesn't mean they get to rob people."

Ramon clapped a hand on her shoulder. "One case at a time. Isn't that what you drilled into me? Total focus on the mission at hand. Which I believe should in fact involve cheese dip. Right?"

"Find me a case that doesn't involve cheese dip, and I'll work it."

He smirked. "But you'd be miserable the entire time."

The people in front of them dispersed, having already given their order, and Ramon and Kenna stepped up to the window.

The guy at the counter was in his thirties, dark skin and short cropped hair. Given the disparity between them standing on the ground and him being inside the truck at a much higher level, she couldn't have said how tall he was.

He smiled. "What can I get you guys?"

Ramon looked at Kenna.

"Two shrimp tacos and a bottled water."

The guy tapped his iPad. "Anything else?"

"Four barbacoa tacos, an empanada, and a horchata," Ramon said. "Large."

"Got it."

Kenna handed over her card, then turned to Ramon. Now he decided to eat? "You're going to bankrupt our expense account."

"Then you should've listened to me about taking the other case as well."

Kenna grabbed the water bottle from the guy and followed Ramon over to the forks and napkins. "What were you just saying about one case at a time?"

"Anytime you wanna take the training wheels off, I'm ready to go."

"Just tell me whether or not you ID'd him."

Ramon's dark brows drew together. "I couldn't get a good look. But the guy cooking the food in there definitely fits the parameters. He's the right age, race, and body type. If he shaved off his mustache since the photo was taken, it's the same guy."

"What about his hair?" In the mugshot they'd been given, taken when Garth Sanders was booked into the local county jail, he had a ponytail mullet.

"Grungy baseball cap."

"Darn." Kenna shook her head.

"Not quite how *I* would've put it, but I share your sentiment."

Yeah, Kenna had been planning on addressing that as well. Not that she required the guy to be healed and redeemed in order to meet the standard for working with her. But she wasn't going to stand by and not address the elephant in the room—her faith and his lack thereof.

"Time to make a scene, I guess." She downed half the water, recapped it, and handed it to him. Then turned around and called out, "What's taking so long?!"

She stomped around a bit, acting like she was frustrated. Probably hangry.

Kenna was pretty sure Ramon told someone near him that she was on her period.

She spun to him and the person he'd been talking to, an older guy, who backed off quickly and tossed his empty wrapper in the trash before skedaddling.

Time to be obnoxious.

She wandered to the window, squeezed past the customer at the front of the line without touching them, and hammered on the window with the palm of her hand. "Get a move on! How long does it take to make tacos?"

"Give it a rest, lady," the customer said. "We're all hungry."

"I got here earlier than you!" Kenna shouted. "I've already ordered."

She was so unused to adding that much sarcasm into her tone in a way that wasn't humorous, she wasn't sure if she'd managed to pull it off. Going undercover had never been her thing. She had no idea if she was good at it or not.

She turned to the guy inside the truck. "Do I have to come in there and make it myself?"

It was the only way she would be able to get close enough to ID the chef.

She peered over the shoulder of the guy taking orders. "No wonder you guys are so slow. You've got some skinny gringo back there making Mexican food. Is this some kind of exchange student program?"

Kenna wasn't going to let on how much people who acted like she was right now irritated her. But it was enough to make her stomach flip over. With nothing in it, she just ended up feeling nauseous.

Maybe she really was hangry.

"I guess I have to get in there and cook the tacos myself." She stomped around to the back of the truck and yanked on the handle. It swung open, and she came face-to-face with the guy taking orders, barring her entry.

"Get out of my way!" She set her hands on her hips, in full Karen mode. "I'll just do it myself."

"No way." He folded his arms across his chest. "I'm canceling your order. No refunds."

"You can't do that! That's stealing. I'm calling the police!"

Behind the guy, the chef turned to her, and she got a look at his face.

Bingo. We've got a winner.

"This is unbelievable!" She spun away from the guy, stomping off to find Ramon scratching his chin. Probably trying not to laugh out loud. "These tacos probably aren't even *worth* it!" she screamed, realizing too late she didn't want to draw that much attention to herself.

In a crowded courtyard bustling with people and the music at a decent volume, hopefully not many would notice her.

She got close enough to Ramon to whisper, "It's him."

"Great. But I'm still hungry."

"Good thing we have snacks in the car." She shoved him toward the parking lot end of the courtyard.

He groaned, sounding a whole lot like the teenager Kenna knew. Probably because she'd used a mom voice to say that.

She said, "I guess Karens talk to everyone like their children."

"I thought it was Susan now." He glanced over. "I heard that Susan is the new Karen."

"Is it?"

Ramon slung an arm around her shoulders. "Good thing you have me, or you'd never know these things."

"I'm sure that information will save my life one day." She beeped the locks on her car and slid into the driver's side.

He got in the passenger seat and grabbed a granola bar.

Kenna tapped the dash screen and dialed Maizie's number. The call connected after a couple of rings.

"Banbury Investigations."

"Are you in the surveillance feed yet?" Kenna asked. "We confirmed it's him inside the taco truck."

"It's giving me trouble," Maizie said. "Something about

the server isn't letting me in. But not because it's high-tech. More like it's glitching and kicking me out every few seconds instead of refreshing.

"Keep working on it." Kenna shifted in her seat, watching the courtyard. "We'll go back and get close enough to keep an eye on him if we have to. We can wait until he leaves. No point doing this in front of a crowd when we can wait until he's alone and lock him down then."

According to Maizie's intel, Garth Sanders was a squirrely drug dealer with a penchant for using knives to get himself out of trouble. One of the two previous bounty hunters who'd taken the contract for this guy had nearly lost his eye because Garth didn't like being detained.

Ramon swallowed his mouthful of granola bar. "Any indications his coworkers know who he is? Maybe they're business partners...or they have no idea he's dealing out of the truck."

"From their social media, they seem like a pretty tight-knit family group." Maizie paused. "Garth isn't in any of the photos."

"Copy that." Ramon shoved another chunk of granola bar in his mouth.

"Maybe after we detain him, those guys will give us our food." It was possible they wanted Garth out of there. Maybe Kenna and Ramon would be doing them a favor.

Ramon handed her a granola bar.

If her boyfriend, Jax, had been here, he would know full well that she needed more than a snack right now. After all that Karen angst, she was pretty frustrated and hungry. Then again, these days as a Christian, she was supposed to exercise self-control, instead of being led around by her belly—or any other desires or needs. Even if that meant tying herself in knots, ignoring the thing she really wanted.

"Call me if you have anything, Maze."

"Got it," the teen said, and the call ended.

Kenna pushed her door open. "Let's go bag this guy."

They walked back over to the courtyard, sticking to the far side where they could see the taco truck. Those guys inside wouldn't know they were being watched by the crazy lady who'd lost her patience.

Ramon eyed her. "Maizie would like to see a place like this. Don't you think?"

Kenna shrugged, moving to sit on a low brick wall. "Maybe. I haven't really asked her how she feels about traveling. Mexico didn't go so well for her, but we got her back."

"Could be good for her to get out and see the world."

Kenna glanced over at him, then back at the taco truck. "Did she say something to you?"

"Not in so many words." He shook his head. "But it's not exactly normal for a kid to spend every waking hour holed up in front of a computer."

Maybe, like Maizie, Ramon hadn't had that much experience with the real world.

Kenna sighed. "The fact she spends all day on her computer and doesn't go outside much might be the most *normal* thing about that teenager." Apart from the fact that Maizie worked for Kenna, and most of what she did online was research and even occasionally hacking computer systems. The girl was a genius.

"Still..."

"If she wants something, she knows she just has to ask me. Doesn't mean I'll say yes. Nor does she need my permission. But she gets to feel things out for herself and widen her boundaries anytime she wants. She's the one who sets the pace."

For a while, when Maizie came to work for her, she had expressed an interest in working with Kenna side by side in the field. But at that time, she'd been barely weeks out of the traumatic upbringing she'd been raised in. These days, Maizie was doing amazingly better, but any little thing could cause a setback in her recovery.

Kenna didn't want to be the cause of something like that. Not if she could help it.

She needed to talk to Jax about the balance between working together and keeping Maizie safe. Confirm she was doing the right thing or come up with a new plan. But what she wasn't going to do was jump the gun in a gut reaction.

Two men moved through the crowd, their mannerisms and body language different than the people milling around. Both wore jackets, and the crowd surrounded them, obscuring Kenna's view. No way to see if they were carrying weapons.

She stood up.

"Blue Jackets?" Ramon said. "They're headed for the back of the truck."

His instincts had never been the problem.

"Let's get closer." She motioned with her head.

He followed behind her as they wove through the crowd. The two men reached the back of the truck, pulled the door open, and yanked the order taker guy out onto the ground.

She spotted a pistol a second before two shots rang out. A moment later, one of the guys dragged Garth from the back of the food truck.

The two men hurried him toward an alley off one side.

Kenna started running after them. "Cut them off." She waved at another exit from the courtyard, and Ramon raced in that direction.

She tore down the alley, toward the street at the end, where the two men shoved Garth into a pickup truck.

The engine revved, and the driver pulled away from the curb.

She sprinted to the sidewalk and nearly collided with a big guy walking with his buddies. All of them over six feet easily. She'd have bounced off the guy and landed on her butt if she hadn't noticed him in time.

She offered a breathy, "Excuse me" and stepped around them, spotting Ramon.

As soon as she got close enough, Kenna said, "He's gone."

Chapter Two

"The police are reporting one dead and one injured at the taco truck." Maizie's voice came through the car speakers, connected via Bluetooth.

Ramon glanced over at Kenna. "It could have been a lot worse than that."

"Doesn't mean it's okay." She pressed down on the gas, headed north on a busy city street-turned-highway. "We need to catch up with them."

"The police helicopter is still tracking them," Maizie said. "But according to the dispatcher, they're headed into a wooded area."

"Maybe trying to lose them in the bayou?" Ramon said.

Kenna didn't like the sound of that. "Have you ever been there?"

He shook his head.

"Great." She looked back at the road. They were headed into unfamiliar territory. "Do the police have any idea who the kidnappers are?"

Maybe they could make some kind of arrangement with law enforcement after the murderers were taken into custody.

Then again, the cops would take one look at Garth and realize who he was.

Bye-bye payday for Kenna and Ramon.

The contract they had taken from the bail bondsman was worth nothing if the cops were the ones who brought in a fugitive.

Ramon shifted in his seat. "They looked like enforcers to me. Whoever their boss is, he wants Garth. Probably so they can kill him before he gets arrested. Which means he's a liability to them."

"Seems like the cops are just trying to keep an eye on these guys," Maizie said. "Later, when they have them in custody, they'll be able to figure out who they are."

"Except if we knew who they were, we might know where they're going." Kenna tapped her index finger on the steering wheel. "Which hopefully isn't somewhere nondescript so they can sink Garth into the mud where no one will find him."

"Nah. The alligators will get him before he sinks into obscurity."

"There had better not be alligators." Kenna groaned.

Maizie chuckled. "If you see an alligator, make sure you take a picture for me."

She opened her mouth, but Ramon said, "Sure thing, kiddo."

Kenna just hit the gas and shut her mouth. It was good for Maizie to have healthy acquaintances to converse with. To show her that most people in the world were nothing like the man who had raised her.

Maizie said, "The cops are reporting the pickup pulled off the highway. There's a marina on that turnoff. Maybe they have a boat there?"

"With the helicopter above them, maybe it's easier to lose

the cops in the bayou than it is on a street." The trees certainly would give more cover than these guys found on the highway. Kenna continued, "We might not be able to follow them. But we can at least keep tabs on the police activity. Do an end run later and grab our guy."

"Where's the fun in that?" Ramon said. "I'm sure there will be someone in a boat who can give us a ride. You have cash on you, right?"

"Some. How about you?"

"You're the one with an inheritance."

"It's a trust fund." Kenna huffed. "And you aren't going to use it as bribery."

"Wouldn't we be making the world a better place?"

"The wheels of justice aren't going to be greased with my money."

Ramon chuckled. "Calm down."

Maizie gasped over the phone line. "Did you just tell a woman to calm down? Stairns told me that's a terrible idea."

Maizie lived under the care of Kenna's former boss, who was also the reason she no longer worked for the FBI. Stairns was retired now and helped Kenna out on occasion. His wife, Elizabeth, was a counselor who regularly worked with Maizie to smooth her transition into the wider world.

Right now, Maizie was working on her GED. After that, she planned to take some online college classes. The girl was smarter with computers than most college graduates, but if she didn't have the qualifications to prove it, she would be stunted in her career path, for sure. Not that Kenna would mind if the girl worked for her for years. Maizie just needed to know she had the choice to do whatever she wanted.

"Just tell me if I'm approaching the turn." Kenna glanced at Ramon. "That way we can stick with this the job and hopefully complete it sometime soon."

"You really should eat something," he suggested. "Jax told me it isn't pretty when you get hangry."

"Take the next exit," Maizie said.

Kenna held out her hand, easing off the highway with the other. "Just hand me an apple, or something."

Maizie directed her down the side streets toward the Marina, a small outfit with three or four docks that could be accessed from either side. A handful of boats, some with engines and some without, lined the wooden gangways.

"That must be them." Ramon pointed to a boat headed away, churning the water underneath it. He looked around. "I'm gonna go talk to that guy."

He left her alone in the car, and she gathered some things, sliding them into a backpack.

"Are you really going into the bayou after these guys?" Maizie paused. "It could be pretty dangerous."

"Ramon and I can watch each other's backs. That's why we're working together." It sounded convincing enough that she trusted Ramon implicitly. In reality, she was going to watch her own back and see what he did with the little bit of trust she was giving him.

"Comms?"

"I'll dig them out and text you." Kenna hung up the phone and dug in her backpack for the case containing her comms earbuds.

She didn't blame Maizie for wanting to stay in contact without having to call or text—something that could get anyone killed if it happened at the wrong moment.

She parked the car and caught up with Ramon, slipping one earbud in. "Put this in."

He took the earbud. "I rented a fishing boat from the guy who owns this place. At least, I hope that guy owns it, and didn't just take my money on a scam."

The smell coming off the water lapping at the underside of the dock had a kind of rotten egg tinge to it. Thankfully, there was a cool breeze blowing across the water, moving air around despite the humidity of this evening.

Ramon took her backpack and set it inside the little boat with two flat bench seats and a motor. He held out his hand to her, and she climbed in and settled on one of the benches.

Before she could ask if he even knew how to drive one of these things, he fired up the engine and steered the boat away from the dock.

He called out to her over the din of the motor, "I bet you're glad I'm working with you right now."

"Just don't make me regret it."

She meant it as a throwaway comment but caught a look on his face that she hadn't been expecting. This guy might be a maverick with many of his tactics, and a morally gray area everywhere else, but she got the impression that he wanted her to believe in him. Maybe he even needed it. Ramon was here to prove himself.

"By tipping this boat and plunking us both in the water," she added. "You know how I feel about alligators."

"Hold on." He flashed a grin in the dim light. "We need to catch up with them."

Kenna leaned over and grabbed the edge of the boat, digging out her gun with her other hand. No sense being completely unprepared, even if they were basically sitting ducks exposed on the water. "Maizie, do you copy?"

"Loud and clear," the teen responded in her earpiece. "Ramon?"

"I got you," he said. "The helicopter is circling around trying to find these guys, but we're catching up to them."

Kenna scanned the dark water. They turned a corner, and she spotted the boat up ahead. "That's them?"

As she asked, the boat motored left out of sight.

Overhead, the helicopter was too far and likely didn't see it. But if they followed the boat, it could lead the cops to these killers. Assuming they got there just in time for Kenna to detain her guy and leave.

Not something she was going to pray for. Even though God cared about her enough to work on her behalf, this did seem like doing an end run around local law enforcement.

Generally their run-ins with the law went okay—until the police or feds realized who she and Ramon were. Then, they'd want to interrogate the two of them about everything that had happened over the last year or two. Usually, they made it sound like a friendly chat, but Kenna didn't feel the need to make nice with everyone she met. It only made the job take so much longer.

Ramon slowed the boat, reducing the noise considerably. They eased around the corner nearly completely silent except for the displacement of the water around the boat. "That looks like a bar to me."

Shrouded in trees, the squat structure stood above the water on tall stilts. A porch in front of the building had a flight of wooden steps down to the dock. In both front windows, neon signs flashed in the darkness. At least half a dozen boats were tied up at the dock.

Even from this distance, Kenna could smell the distinct tang of recreational good times floating on the air.

"Can we even get in there?" she asked. "Looks pretty crowded." She scanned for movement around the building but couldn't see anything. They had to have gone inside already. Assuming they stopped here. "We don't even know this is where they went."

"You see anyone else out here?"

She frowned. "Good point. I guess it being so popular means we could blend into the crowd."

Ramon simply snorted.

Fine, she was kidding herself. Two outsiders who were unfamiliar with this area and had never patronized this establishment were going to stick out whether they liked it or not.

Ramon steered them into a tiny gap and tied off the boat. "I'm gonna look around."

"You're going to let me go in there by myself?"

"A woman who looks like you is gonna fit in a whole lot better than I would."

She stuck a stun gun in the back of her belt, glad she had worn her thin jeans. Converse and a short sleeve T-shirt over which she'd tugged a white shirt completed the ensemble. No one needed to see the scars on her forearms, or the spot where she had tucked the weapon. Plus, Maizie had said this shirt looked cute on her.

"Don't go too far." Kenna headed for the steps and the front door. "Going in."

In her ear, Maizie said, "Copy that. The police are still searching."

She pushed the door open and was greeted by a wall of sound, the music coming from a jukebox to the left by the tables. The bar was to the right, and in front of her at the far end were a couple of pool tables. At least fifteen people occupied the room, but she didn't see the two guys or Garth.

Kenna looked back at the boat, just to make sure Ramon hadn't ditched her and gone to find them himself. But the boat was still tied up by the dock.

"Come on, girly," someone called out in a low voice from the other side of the room. "Don't lose your nerve now."

Someone else seemed to think that comment hilarious, along with several others.

Kenna shut the door and turned to the room. She shrugged, aiming for a nonchalant expression. "I could use a drink."

She headed for the bar, where the bartender just kind of stared at her. The guy had a scratchy face and bald head. He wore a grimy white tank top and faded jeans, a gray towel over his shoulder.

He blinked. "What'll it be?" He tugged the towel off his shoulder. "And don't tell me you're here looking for some deadbeat ex."

Kenna set her forearms on the bar. "Something cold, before I tell you all about my six kids and how their daddy don't come 'round no more."

The corners of his mouth curled up as he plunked an open bottle on the bar in front of her, already sweating.

She raised the bottle to her mouth, about to sip, when someone closed in on her left, looking her up and down. Two teeth missing from his grin. Leather jacket, no shirt.

"A woman like you?" He whistled. "I can tell you now, that guy is a darn fool."

"That's very sweet of you to say."

Another man, who had closed in on her right—the two who had been playing pool a minute ago—said, "I ain't seen you 'round here before."

She figured she should talk the talk and said, "That's 'cause I ain't never been here before."

"You're lookin' for somethin'." He eyed her. "I can tell."

"Aren't we all lookin' for somethin'?" She gave him a second, then said, "Right now, I'm lookin' for a game of pool and a couple of cold drinks. Whaddya say?"

He didn't answer right away. Seemingly the more thoughtful of the two of them. Though, they acted as one another's wingman when needed. At least, if they were playing pool, she wouldn't be locked between them. She'd be able to walk around a little while she waited for one of those two guys or Garth to show themselves. One trip to the bathroom was all she needed to search the back rooms.

"Sure." His expression betrayed a little of the predatory nature beneath the surface.

"After I pee, of course. It was a long trip over here." She looked around. "Please tell me there's a ladies room in this place."

He held her elbow. "I'll show you where it is."

"Just point me in the right direction. I'm sure I can find it."

"A girl like you shouldn't go walkin' around in a place like this." His meaty hand shoved a swinging door open. He led her into the hallway beside the bar where she spotted restrooms on one side and closed doors on the other.

"Thanks. I really do have to pee."

"Sure, darlin'. Just one thing before you go in there..." He yanked on her arm hard, shoved her against the wall, and put that meaty hand around her throat.

Kenna held her breath against the pressure, purposely not trying to breathe through her constricted airway. At the same time, she dug in the back of her belt, slid out her stun gun, and pressed it to the soft flesh of his abdomen. She realized too late that she'd hit leather and slid the crackling weapon between the open edges of his jacket.

He hissed out a breath between gritted teeth that almost sounded amused. She didn't let go of the button. The fingers around her neck tightened reflexively, thanks to the voltage going through him.

In her ear, she could hear Maizie yelling to Ramon that she needed backup.

He had a free hand, but so did she. When he grasped her

elbow, Kenna wrapped her fingers around his arm, locking them both in place. She lifted her knee and planted it on target.

His fingers slipped from her neck, and he dropped back from her stun gun, landing on the floor in a heap.

Kenna stepped over him, going to the closest door. Just a closet with cleaning supplies and kegs of beer. She shut that one and tried the next, reaching for the handle a second before she heard a roar behind her.

Some two hundred fifty pounds of angry redneck slammed into her back.

Kenna hit the door first. It splintered, and they tumbled into the room, landing on pieces of door. The big guy glanced off her hip and shoulder and ended up going to the side, cursing a blue streak.

She lifted her head. Two men and an older woman stood around a guy tied to a chair—Garth.

All around the room, bundles of drugs, stacks of money bound with rubber bands, and rows of guns had evidently been used for décor.

The big guy sputtered, swearing all over again at what they'd landed in the middle of.

The two men waited for the older woman's instructions. She sneered at Kenna and the guy, hands on her hips.

"Well, gentlemen. I suppose we have to kill all three of them now."

Chapter Three

Kenna slowly eased to standing and brushed off her pants as she took in the room around her. *No big deal,* she told herself, trying her best to remain nonchalant.

With three guns pointed at her—one from the older woman and two from the guys who'd been beating Garth—Kenna listened to Maizie and Ramon yelling in her earpiece. It was loud enough she wanted to reach up and take the earbud out, but that would immediately let these people in on the fact she wore comms.

In her ear, Ramon said, "Maizie, calm down. Remember?" Bringing up the prior comment the teen had made about telling a woman to calm down served to break the tension enough for him to continue, "I'm outside. I'll figure out what's happening."

"Well, isn't this interesting," the older woman finally said. Her fluffy red-blonde hair had been hacked at rather than cut, close to her shoulders. She wore a long denim skirt with a tan-colored shirt over it, the collar open. She had a gold chain around her neck, rings on most of her fingers, and purple eye shadow. Both her forearms were covered with sleeves of tattoos that were visible where she had rolled up her shirt to her elbows.

Kenna lifted both hands. "I didn't mean to disturb you folks." Or find them in a room full of contraband that was no doubt illegally obtained. Not to mention their possession of it was also illegal. No need to mention anything.

Just by looking at this woman and the two men, both of whom had the same build as her and wore similar clothes, she could tell something about them. Though the guys wore jeans instead of a skirt. Kenna figured they were a mother and her adult sons.

The mother said, "Well then, I guess you had better explain what you did mean to do here. Cause I ain't never seen you before."

Bud, the guy who had crashed into her, groaned and rolled over on the floor, sitting up. He blinked at the occupants of the room and then let out a sharp curse. "I tried to stop her getting in here, Momma. She zapped me with a stun gun and kicked me."

Momma seemed to consider that hilarious enough she snickered. A second later, the humor disappeared, and in a flash she looked aside sharply at one of the sons. "Claude, take Bud out back and explain what happens when you let an outsider in here."

Bud inhaled sharply through his nose. "I didn't mean it. I wasn't gonna let her in here. It was an accident."

Kenna winced inwardly where no one would see it. "Far as I can see, no harm was done. I'll be going."

Momma ignored her. "Claude, get to it."

The guy snapped to attention at his mother's instruction and hauled Bud up to his feet. He marched the guy out into the hall while Kenna remained standing there with her hands up. Having them raised even this long was making her fore-arms, and those old injuries, ache.

Garth looked at her like she was some kind of savior, though she'd made no effort to get him untied from that chair. He might think she was here to rescue him, but as soon as she slapped cuffs on him and turned him in at the nearest police station, he would realize she was operating as a bounty hunter.

"The lady from the taco truck," he muttered.

Great, he recognized her.

He blinked. "Karen, is that you?"

The only way she could play this off was to pretend they did know each other, so she gave an exasperated smile and shook her head.

To this Momma person, she said, "Garth is my cousin. He likes to get himself into all kinds of scrapes. It's my job in the family to pull his butt out of the fire every time and bring him back home. That's why I'm here."

Thankfully, neither Momma nor the son looked at Garth, because he looked pretty confused hearing that she was his cousin.

"His cousin?" Momma looked at her with one eyebrow raised.

Uh-oh, maybe they knew him well.

"I'm from a distant part of the family," Kenna said. "We don't live around here."

The other son looked her up and down. "You from New York, or somethin'? Is Garth in the mafia?"

"Don't ask ridiculous questions, Georgie." Momma huffed. "Go find out what's taking your brother so long. We should have heard a shot by now."

Kenna tried not to seem overly interested in what was on the shelves or their casual discussion of murder. All she needed was Garth, and she could get out of here. "I'll just take my cousin off your hands. Save you the trouble of having to deal with him." She waited a beat, then added, "Don't worry. We'll take care of him."

If they thought she was some mafia hit person who had come here to clean up the mess Garth had made by burying him in a swamp so that he was never found again, she wasn't exactly going to disabuse them of that notion. They could believe whatever they wanted. Meanwhile, she would turn Garth in to the cops and get the bail money payout.

"I'm sure you'd like that," Momma said. "But Garth owes me a whole lot of money. You gonna pay his debt?"

"How much does he owe you?" Kenna tried to look suitably exasperated, as if she was the one left to deal with this burden on the family. And apparently, it happened often.

Ramon was supposed to have come in here by now to find out if she was still alive. Or he knew she was alive, because he could hear her talking. But then what was he doing?

Was her associate the reason why the brother hadn't returned quickly?

Come on, Ramon.

Momma said, "Fifty thousand."

Kenna blinked because anyone in that situation would have after hearing that amount of money. "I'll have to make some calls for that kind of repayment."

"I guess it's not as simple as you would think."

"I guess not," Kenna said.

Momma waved. "You want to pay me my money? You can take Garth off my hands."

And completely invalidate the payday Garth represented to Kenna? She wasn't interested in only breaking even. She said, "How will you get the money from him if it doesn't come from me?"

Maybe Momma wanted Garth in prison so he could do some kind of job for her on the inside. In which case, Kenna would be more than happy to deliver him to jail for her. She might even be inclined to split part of the payout.

Was that the kind of dirty deal this woman would be willing to make?

"I'll think of some way he can repay his debt to me." Momma put her hand on Garth's shoulder, suggesting something Kenna didn't exactly want to contemplate.

"And when he's repaid his debt, would you return him to the family?"

Garth looked from Momma to Kenna, wide-eyed.

Momma shrugged. "Depends if you make it worth my while."

Kenna didn't want to ask what that would entail. She just needed a resolution—some kind of deal she could renege on immediately after they got out of here. She smiled. "I'm sure we can come to some kind of arrangement."

"And I just take your word for it that none of this is going to be reported to the authorities?" Momma gestured to the shelves with her gun.

"You're a businesswoman. I am as well. There's no reason we can't part ways with an understanding. And no reason my business should interfere with yours—unless you gave me a reason to bother you. Or you become a nuisance."

Momma stared at Kenna, assessing her.

She was fairly sure only cops in situations like this felt the need to state emphatically that they *weren't* cops. So she left it to mean she hadn't even contemplated that fact.

Momma said, "You pay me, I'll hand him over. Just like that? No fuss."

As long as it wasn't money exchanging hands.

Kenna needed a different plan.

"Maybe instead of information, I could give you some helpful advice." After all, there could only be a limited amount of time before this all went sideways. Thankfully, there wasn't enough time for Kenna to make a call and have fifty thousand in cash delivered to this bar.

"And what might that be?" Momma seemed to find this whole exchange amusing, although Kenna could see lines of worry on her face. Now neither son had come back.

Thanks to Ramon?

Kenna said, "Your boys caught the attention of the cops when they shot a man and took Garth."

Her expression shifted, and anger flashed in her eyes.

"It's probably worth a whole lot more than fifty thousand for you to know that the helicopter outside, the one circling this area?" Kenna paused. "It's the cops looking for your boys. It's only a matter of time before they kick the door down and come in with guns blazing."

Momma moved away from Garth, strode past Kenna to the door, and leaned out. "Liam! Batten down the hatches. Now!"

Kenna had a quick mental image of shoving the woman and somehow securing the broken door shut, after which she and Garth would need to find a way to sneak out the window.

A door slammed down the hallway.

Momma looked the other direction, away from the bar and down to the end of the corridor. She gasped. "What happened?"

Kenna moved far enough she could see over the woman's shoulder out the door and peered around the opening. A little closer to Momma than she would have liked, but she wanted to see what was happening.

At the end of the hallway, one of the sons stumbled in,

blood streaming down his face. "There's a man." Claude gasped. "Outside."

Then he stumbled and hit the floor.

Momma swung around to face Kenna. "This is your doing. Who is out there?"

Kenna tried to feign innocence. "It has nothing to do with me. Maybe it's the cops."

Momma didn't seem satisfied, but she also didn't argue. A stream of men came down the hall from the bar, into the room, completely ignoring her and the prisoner.

Kenna went to Garth and helped him get to his feet but didn't cut his hands free. At least they hadn't tied him to the chair. She didn't need to let him go so he could run from her and these people. Instead, she walked him to the hallway and made him stand against the wall.

Momma watched the men, a queen ruling over her domain. Each one slid a stretch of wall paneling from between two shelves and fit it over the front of the recessed shelving. Within just a few seconds, the room looked like it had plain walls with just a couple of pieces of artwork on the walls and a map of the local area tacked up in one spot.

Someone else came in with a spray canister. The guy flicked out a wide stretch of plastic-looking material into a full-body suit and slipped it on. What on earth... He looked like a crime scene tech.

Everyone else left so the guy in the protective suit was alone in the room.

Momma backed up to the door and watched while the guy fitted a face mask on and started to spray down the room.

Kenna glanced at her. "To disguise the scent of your product from the nose of a police dog?"

Momma nodded. "My own invention."

"Impressive."

She strode past Kenna, moving as if to completely dismiss her. The older woman rolled Claude to his back and kicked him enough he roused, blinking up at her. "Nobody makes you bleed but me." She crossed her arms. "Tell Momma who did this, boy."

"A guy out there." He gasped, touching his side and wincing with the pain. Never mind the blood streaming down his face. "He's crazy."

Ramon.

Kenna was going to kill him if he was out there taking out Momma's guys one by one. She wanted to roll her eyes but fought the urge down.

Garth made a sound in the back of his throat. Kenna turned slightly toward him.

She felt more than her movement behind her as the guy who had been spraying down the room was done and coming their way. Before she could turn back, someone slid her gun from the back of her belt. The sensation was enough to disorient her.

Kenna turned but not soon enough to disarm him and get her weapon back. She didn't even know where her stun gun had ended up. Not entirely defenseless, she just didn't have a way to defend her life that wouldn't involve her getting shot in the process.

He pointed the gun at her, not Garth.

Neither of them moved.

Momma spun around. "Bring them both." She motioned to Kenna and Garth, then headed for the back door.

The guy in the clean suit nudged her with her own gun.

Kenna got Garth in front of her, and they followed Momma to the back door while Claude glared up at them from the floor.

Garth glanced back over his shoulder and said to Claude, "You should get that looked at. It could get infected."

"Shut up." Kenna shoved Garth out the back door onto a porch.

The porch was almost bigger than the bar inside, with screens on the upper half of the wall all the way around to keep the bugs out. String lights hung from wooden beams overhead, illuminating the tables that were spread around. If she didn't believe she was about to be shot, Kenna would have told Momma this was a "nice space."

Momma wove between tables, past a small dance floor area and a raised stage to a screen door at the far corner. She didn't go through the door, but turned and addressed the man behind Kenna. "Dispose of them. And don't make any noise, because the cops are almost here."

"Yes, ma'am." He nudged the gun into Kenna's back again. "Let's go. Outside, both of you."

Garth whimpered. His legs started to give out, and Kenna reached for him on a reflex. Pain arched up her forearms, and she let go, dropping Garth to the wood beams on the floor.

The gunman said, "Get him up. Now."

"I can't," Kenna said honestly. "My arms can't bear that much weight."

"You expect me to believe that?"

Did he want her to show him her scars?

"I'm good." Garth got to his feet. "Let's go."

Momma called over to them, "Eager to die?"

Garth sniffed. "Sounds like you're about to get raided by the police. I don't wanna be here when that happens." He pushed out the door, and Kenna caught it before it snapped back on its hinges.

She went out after him, hoping to put as much space as possible between them and the man with the gun. At some point they would have to try to overpower the guy. Or make a run for it through unfamiliar terrain in the dark.

The relentless croak of frogs swelled in the night air. A wash of sound that disoriented her because it seemed to be coming from everywhere, and now she'd noticed it, the whole volume seemed far too loud. If they could get ahead of this guy with her gun, the sound of nature at night could disguise them making a run for it.

And then the ATF would raid this place and find a gun registered to McKenna Banbury. They would know she'd been here.

Assuming Ramon wasn't about to show up and help them out.

The guy in the white suit stomped down the steps behind them, making the wood creak.

Garth stepped off the bottom, and Kenna did the same after him, her shoes sinking into the soft earth.

She kept her hands where he could see them, making a plan based on what she would be able to grab within reach. Though, the likelihood of her being able to toss a knife in his direction before he shot her wasn't high.

"Go." The gunman walked them for a good five minutes, deep into the woods.

Far enough away that the cops might not hear the gunshot? He would kill them soon. Kenna needed to figure out a plan that actually had a chance of working.

A low moan emerged above the croaking of the frogs, coming from in front of them in the trees. Something in the dark approached their position. A branch cracked, and leaves rustled.

It came into view, a hulking figure that stumbled from the shadows into the light of the flashlight the man had produced.

Their gunman aimed the beam at the man—covered with netting and foliage. Like a hunting blind.

Kenna bit her lip. Was he supposed to be some kind of bayou monster?

Ramon swayed, stumbled, and almost went down.

Kenna used the second of distraction to rush the gunman and tackle him. The guy hit the ground, and she landed on top of him in the dirt.

Something small but with long legs skittered past her hand, tickling her skin.

The gun discharged.

Someone screamed. "You shot me! I've been shot!"

Kenna ignored whatever that was and grabbed her gun from the man she had tackled.

Ramon rushed over and kicked the guy in the head, rendering him unconscious. He held out his hand to her. "Okay?"

Kenna lifted her elbow for him to grab. "Thanks."

"I always wanted to be a mythical creature in the bayou." He helped her to her feet. "I can cross that off my bucket list now."

"You're living the dream." Kenna sighed and turned around, rolling her shoulders.

Ramon snorted. "Let's get this guy secured."

Garth blinked. Ramon grabbed one of his arms, and Kenna took a second to get the flashlight off the ground so she could see where she was going.

She shone it at Garth's face.

Kenna frowned at the odd look he had. "What? You'd be dead right now if it wasn't for us."

"I thought you were my cousin here to make a deal." He hung his head, seeming almost sad to discover she wasn't related to him.

Kenna rolled her eyes. "You're going back to jail. And this time you're going to stay there."

Chapter Four

22 YEARS AGO
NEW ORLEANS, LOUISIANA

The woman's heavy hands weighed down Kenna's shoulders. "Children, this is Kenna. She's new to town, and she'll be staying with us for a while."

The kitchen smelled like the time Kenna had tried to make pancakes for her dad's birthday with a cast-iron pan. Eight kids were seated around a long table, with an older man at the far end. As for the woman, she had a soft figure and kind eyes, but there was a tiredness about her that said she was more than a little exasperated with some of the kids sitting around this table.

Given the fact at least three of them were older teenagers, Kenna figured they probably didn't want to be called children.

"Kenna, you can sit right here"—the woman motioned to an empty seat at the nearest corner of the table—"close to me."

She'd said her name was Madeira, but Kenna didn't plan on being here long enough to get used to saying it.

Madeira reached for the backpack Kenna was clutching. "I can hang that up for you, if you'd like."

Kenna took a step back. "I'll keep it."

"So she can speak." The man at the far end of the table lifted his chin.

Kenna ducked her head and slid into the chair. She shoved the backpack down between her knees and squeezed it tight between her shins.

No one said a prayer over the meal. Kenna had seen a family do that on TV recently and had been curious about how it worked. Apparently, this family didn't want help or blessing.

Serving bowls were passed around her, and someone dumped rice with pieces of sausage and chili beans into her bowl. It smelled weird, but her stomach growled, so she ate.

Halfway through the bowl, she realized the boy beside her kept staring at her. He had to be at least thirteen, and twice her size. One day maybe she would be tall, but right now she was eight and couldn't even carry more than three shopping bags at a time.

On the other side of the table, a girl a little older than her, but kind of scary looking, stared at her.

An hour later, she found out that the girl slept in the bunk below the one they'd given Kenna. Not that she even spoke to Kenna at all. So Kenna lay there clutching the backpack to her front. She kept her eyes closed, wondering when the doorbell would ring and her father would show up to pick her up.

Kenna's eyes burned hot, but she wasn't a baby, so she wasn't going to cry. All she was going to do was protect the information her father had given her, tucked away in her backpack, and wait for him to come and get her.

He'd told her to be strong, and she would be.

Two days later, they had enrolled Kenna in the local school, and she had to walk there and back by herself. That was the best part. Pretending she was back to normal, and going to the trailer where her father would be.

She'd been keeping the backpack close, just in case her dad found her at the school, and they had to leave quickly.

Today the sun was high in the sky as usual. The sticky air around her made her hair cling to the back of her neck. She didn't have any hair ties in her backpack, and they never let her go back to the trailer to get some things so she couldn't even put it in a ponytail.

This had to be a mistake. She'd tried telling the police she could take care of herself until her father came home. Then she met a nice lady who told her she was a social worker. At least, she had seemed nice until she poked Kenna too hard trying to get her into Madeira's van. But they hadn't listened— they just sent her to the home for children who had nowhere else to go.

Not even her teacher had listened when Kenna tried to explain it.

She knew how to take care of herself. She *had* somewhere else to go.

Kenna turned the corner into an alley that led through to the neighborhood where the house was. Yesterday she got lost, but today that wasn't going to happen. Her teacher had printed out a map, and she was going to follow it.

She wished she could tear up the map and walk all the way back to the trailer, but it was too far and she didn't know the way.

Her nose tickled, so she sniffed and rubbed at it. Then she had to swipe the tears from her cheeks.

She kept walking, the backpack hugged close to her front.

Someone snickered behind her.

Kenna glanced over her shoulder and saw two of the boys from the house. But it was too late. They ran up to her and knocked into her back, shoving her to the ground.

Her knee slammed onto the sidewalk, and she cried out. One boy grabbed the backpack and pulled it from her arms, making her cry out.

"Give that back!" she shouted.

He dug into her bag, pulling out case files. "Dude, check this out."

The other kid went to look at her father's notes. Photos. "Those are sick."

"I knew there was something wrong with her." He dumped her backpack and ran over, kicking her in the side.

She cried out.

He kicked her ribs and then her hip. "You're sick! I bet you're the one who did this. Didn't you? I bet you're a killer!"

"It's not mine!" She wasn't one of those people her father hunted.

She curled up, her arms over her head. He kept kicking her. "You're sick! We should kill you right now for what you've done!"

The other kid joined in, kicking her front. He even stomped on her thigh.

She screamed, crying at the pain.

A disgusting crack sounded to her right. One of the boys fell to the ground.

Kenna looked up and saw her bunkmate swing a piece of wood and hit the second boy in the chest.

He stumbled back and fell in the street.

The girl came over, still clutching the wood. "Come on, we have to run before someone sees us."

Kenna gathered up her papers and shoved everything

back in her backpack. She managed to climb to her feet and raced after the other girl.

When she had finally caught up, she said, "Thanks."

The girl looked over, something in her eyes. Like she enjoyed what she just did. Maybe those boys had kicked her, too.

"You owe me now. And I plan to collect."

Chapter Five

Present day

Under the table, Kenna rubbed her fingers over that old scar on her knee. The restaurant had been here for decades. High-backed wood booths lined one wall opposite the bar. Down at the far end, rows of pool tables were occupied by some pretty rowdy college-age guys.

Ramon might have wanted to hustle someone for cash, but she preferred privacy with her steak salad and fries. And probably a brownie with ice cream for dessert, if she was honest with herself.

Being back in New Orleans was probably throwing her off. Making her think about those couple of weeks she had spent here in foster care so many years ago.

"Why do you look like you're sad?" Ramon took a huge bite of his burger. Around the food, he said, "We're supposed to be celebrating. We found Garth, brought him in, and got paid."

Kenna sipped her drink. "I'm not sad, I'm fine."

"What time does your boyfriend get off work anyway? It's been a whole day since you spoke to him."

Kenna rolled her eyes. "This isn't about Jax."

"Of course, it is." He shoved a fry into his mouth.

Given Ramon had been living in Mexico for years as a disgraced FBI agent, working for a cartel, she was going to give him the benefit of the doubt on his living life to the fullest these days. But maybe he didn't need to enjoy it with his mouth open quite so much in front of her.

He said, "Show me the check again."

"Why don't I just take a picture of it with my phone and text it to you? Then you can look at it as much as you want." She had already shown him the cashier's check from the bail bondsman more than once.

"Too bad the bank was closed by the time we got the check." He shook his head. "Now we have to wait until Monday morning to cash it."

Kenna eyed him. "Are you planning on joining the real world and getting a bank account?"

He shot her a look she figured meant no.

"If you plan to work for anyone else, or ever have a credit history, you might want to think about at least starting with a checking account."

He shrugged. "When I want to buy something, I'll just have Maizie come up with a credit history for one of my aliases."

"And you didn't understand why the police gave you the cold shoulder?"

"They just haven't experienced my charming personality the way you have."

Kenna said, "Right."

She wasn't even sure she wanted him to change. A lot of

his instincts were going to keep him alive, and she wasn't the kind of person who would fully trust a law enforcement officer or federal agent at face value either. Except Jax. And now that she was thinking about her boyfriend, she did want to call him.

Kenna pulled up the app they used to locate each other—something that would come in handy if one of them was kidnapped and still had their phone on them—and saw that he hadn't left the FBI's Phoenix office yet. He wasn't done at work for the day.

No point bothering him if he was busy.

"I don't need to win over every cop I meet," Ramon said. "I just need to do my job, and anyone that cares to look will see I'm on the level."

Kenna at least agreed with that tactic. For now, anyway. "You might not ever change someone's perception of who you are. Far better to just focus on who you're going to be."

The server brought them a couple of refills, then walked toward the bar. Behind her, a local news channel played on the TV. And the headline scrolling across the bottom—"Breaking and Entering Trend Turns Deadly"—caught Kenna's attention.

"Do you know anything about that?" She pointed at the TV with a fry.

He nodded. "I was watching the news earlier and they were talking about a gang who has been breaking into houses and stealing people's stuff over the last few weeks. But they usually only do it when the person is out for the evening."

"Looks like someone got hurt this time."

"You need a new case already?" he asked.

"Not when the local police are all over this." She shook her head. "And if they need help, they'll contact local federal agents. I'm not sure there will be anything left for us to do."

"Good," Ramon said. "Because bounty hunting pays better than sticking our noses in police business."

She grinned, helping him play it off. He wanted nothing to do with the cops.

The cops at the precinct where they had turned in Garth Sanders had gotten to him. Not that Ramon was a people pleaser. He was far too solitary for that. But when he did venture out into the world, he wanted to be treated with the same respect as everyone else. Not painted with the brush that a dirty FBI agent had used to tar his reputation in the worst possible way.

She was dead now. Ramon was free of her, and he could have been reinstated into the FBI if he wanted. Instead, Kenna had agreed to train him as a private investigator.

Ramon shoved a couple more fries in his mouth.

Kenna ate her salad in silence, contemplating the fact it was easier to work with Ramon than Jax for the simple fact she wasn't attracted to the guy across the table from her now.

With the last case she worked with her boyfriend, it had been pretty hard to concentrate—although there was nobody she trusted to have her back the way that she trusted Jax.

Ramon continued, "Are we leaving town as soon as the check is in the bank and we have our money?"

Kenna shrugged one shoulder. "Neither of us has spent much time here before." But did she actually want to reminisce?

"You mean zero time," he corrected. "I've never been here before."

She tried to remain nonchalant. "Might be nice to look around a little before we leave. Do some sightseeing."

Ramon stared at her. "Why do you look like that's the last thing you want to do?"

"I'm just tired. We've been going full throttle for a few

days, and I'm ready for a rest. Plus, I got tackled by that huge guy, and all you did was coldcock a couple of people."

"That old lady was a piece of work. Did Maizie come back with any information on her?"

Kenna shrugged. "Why don't you text her and find out." She dropped some cash from her pocket on the table and slid to the end of the bench seat. "I'm going to get some fresh air and then head back to my RV. I'll touch base with you in the morning."

"Just don't make it before ten. I need my beauty sleep."

Kenna rapped her knuckles on the table and walked to the front door of the restaurant, where she pushed out onto a busy sidewalk.

She did like the amenities of a big city, but there was nothing like wide open sky and green grass. Mountains and nothing but space for miles around. The kind of place where she could sit and look at the stars after dark. Or drink coffee and watch the sunrise after a bad night where memories seemed close to the surface.

She sent Jax a text asking him to call her when he left the office, since she was done with her case.

They tried to connect every day, but it didn't always happen. Given the fact he had only been recently promoted, she was trying to offer space for him to get a steady foundation as the Assistant Special Agent in Charge of the FBI's Phoenix office. His colleagues didn't need to see his girlfriend—the private investigator with a tendency to cause trouble, sticking her nose into his work life as well as his personal life.

Most FBI agents these days knew her as the woman who had shot the former FBI director. The fact that the guy had been chasing her and also happened to be a predator meant she was justified in shooting him to defend herself when he tried to kill her.

But she didn't exactly want to have that as her reputation. Kenna's life was about justice—even if the way she brought that to the world was her own and no one else's.

She wandered down a street lined with three-story brick houses and wide concrete steps. An older man nodded and said good evening, which Kenna returned.

At the end of the road, she realized she wasn't far from the courtyard where the taco truck had been parked. That scene had to have been cleared away now, and the cops would have plenty to go on to find the killer, so she didn't feel the need to revisit the place.

Her phone rang as she eased to a stop and hit the button for a crosswalk. A picture of Kenna's dog flashed on the screen with her name, Cabot.

Kenna slid her thumb across the screen and put the phone to her ear. "Hi, how's it going? Did Ramon ask you about the background on those people we met?"

"I'm texting him back now. I'm still working on the profiles."

"No rush. I'm mostly just curious if they belong to a wider organization or if they run a solo operation that is kept in the family."

"I do know from the police band that they never techni-cally raided the bar. It sounds like they walked around inside but didn't find any reason to dig deeper, so they just left." Maizie sounded disappointed.

"They're probably taking what evidence they have from what they saw and going to a judge to get a search warrant." Kenna paused. "Even if they didn't see anything, no cop who walked around in there would believe there was nothing going on."

Momma had conveniently covered up everything, had that guy spray whatever. But any cop worth their badge would get the vibe she and her sons were up to something.

"That's good," Maizie said, sounding relieved. "Listen, you got a call from someone who says he knows you. Actually it was from his assistant, but she said he wants to talk to you."

"Okay."

"You know Preston Lightwood? I looked him up. Did he really go to prison for twenty years for the death of his wife?" Apparently, the teen had done her homework before she passed any message on to Kenna.

"He was in Arizona when Jax and I were there. I guess I never said anything to you about him. He actually got hit by a stray bullet, but he left before I could follow up with him. What did he say he wants?"

"He's in New Orleans because of a work thing, and he knows you're there somehow. He wants to meet up with you. Tonight actually."

"Does that mean he's keeping tabs on me, or did someone tell him where I was?"

She didn't like the idea of either of those things, but given her father's connection to Preston Lightwood, she wasn't completely worried.

The man she had met in Arizona was nothing like the person who went to jail more than twenty years ago and served his term. He had written an autobiography since being released about how he found Jesus in prison. Most people who read the book didn't seem to have noticed that part. They were too busy commenting on the many chapters where he had laid out why he was innocent in the first place.

What he'd told Kenna was that her father had been the one who brought him to justice. Preston hadn't trusted anyone else to bring him in safely. He had presumed the police would shoot him on sight and he would never see a courtroom.

These days, he seemed to feel their connection with her father gave them some kind of bond. Kenna hadn't thought much about the guy since Arizona.

"Well...," Maizie began.

Kenna's steps faltered. "Maizie, how does he know where I am?"

"I might have added a feature to your website that says what part of the country you're in at any given time," the teen said. "Just a general range, nothing specific. So that people can see if you're nearby and ask you to work a case for them."

"Send me a link to the page. I want to look at exactly how general it is."

"Okay." Maizie sounded choked up.

"I'm sure it's fine, though."

Maizie cleared her throat. "So Preston wants to know if you'll meet him in the Broadway Hotel bar. Apparently, he's there with some associates, but he wants a minute of your time so he can ask you a personal question."

Kenna turned the corner at the end of the street and looked up at the sign indicating where she was. "How far is that hotel from where I am now?" She had been going in a circle, effectively. But she might still be able to walk straight to the hotel from here rather than going back to her car.

"Two streets west of where you are," Maizie said, "and then about a fifteen-minute walk south. But there's a streetcar you can get on that leaves in two minutes and will save you seven."

"Does the hotel have parking?"

"The website says there's a valet."

"Thanks, Maizie." Kenna hung up.

A couple of seconds later, her phone pinged with a text message that contained the address of the hotel and Preston's phone number.

"I guess I have a date."

Chapter Six

The lobby of the Broadway Hotel stretched up in an expansive arch, at the center of which hung the biggest chandelier Kenna had ever seen. A yellow glow permeated every corner of the room, from the reception desks along the wall on the left across the entrance to a restaurant and the lounge bar next to it. All the way to a small shipping center storefront, a coat check closet, and the small lobby for the elevators.

She picked out several groups of conference attendees all wearing matching badges. Lines of people waited at the reception desks, rolling suitcases by their sides. A porter rolled a cart stacked with suitcases and duffel bags toward the elevators.

An older woman chased a toddler by the center sitting area that included sofas and a couple of round couches where occupants sat practically back-to-back all the way around them. The woman scooped him up and set him on her hip, looking more exasperated than the kid even realized she was toward him.

Kenna headed across the lobby toward the lounge bar where Preston Lightwood requested she meet with him.

As soon as she crossed the threshold to the lounge bar, the atmosphere changed. Music played in the dim light, where just a few feet earlier she'd heard nothing—a trick of quality acoustics that kept the sound contained to the lounge bar.

Just inside the room, over at the end of the bar, she spotted a couple of suit-wearing police detectives, a male and a female, speaking with a woman dressed in a skintight tiny silver dress and sky-high silver heels. She had teased blonde hair that barely came down past her ears and a tiny purse over her shoulder with the long strap that dangled it down by her hip.

As Kenna approached them, she heard one of the detectives use the word *coma* and slowed her stride. They might be talking about the breaking and entering that happened recently. She remembered the victim was in a coma from the TV broadcast at dinner just now. One in a long string of break-ins. But this one was different.

She had done some quick research earlier that morning over coffee, digging into local crime over the past few months. It was why the TV had distracted her the way it had, because she'd already looked into it a little.

So far there had been nearly a dozen reported break-ins where various items were stolen, including jewelry and even a Lamborghini. The most recent crime, the one on the TV, was the first time the home occupant had been present during the incident, resulting in an attack that left the man unconscious and almost dead.

Kenna looked around the room, not working overly hard to find the person she was looking for. The place was decently crowded, but she was interested in the conversation.

She stepped to the side and leaned against the wall at the

entrance, where she pulled out her phone as if she was waiting for someone. Content to hang by the door until the other person arrived.

She was pretty sure Preston Lightwood occupied a booth in the far corner, and she had clocked at least two people she would presume to be private security. She had no idea if they were connected to Lightwood. It could have something to do with why he had asked her to meet him.

Kenna pulled up her running text thread with Jax and sent him a quick message.

Meeting Preston. I'll let you know later what he wants.

One of the cops, the guy, said, "But he came to see you regularly?"

The blonde replied, "He was one of my favorite customers."

"How often?"

Kenna scrolled on her phone, looking at nothing in particular. Then at the woman when she could do it without the cops noticing.

"Once a week. Sometimes twice." The blonde sniffed and rubbed at her nose. "Damien was such a nice guy. I don't understand why someone would want to hurt him."

The female detective said, "That's what we're trying to find out. Was he supposed to come and see you that night?"

"It isn't like he made appointments. He knew how to find me." She shifted on her heels. "I didn't have anything to do with what happened to him. So don't go tryin' to pin anything on me. I have a kid to support. I can't do that if I'm in jail because you decided to make my life miserable."

The male detective said, "If you didn't have anything to do with it, why would we bother you?"

"Great. Then I guess I don't have to answer any more of your questions."

Instead of going to the bar, the blonde turned and strode out of the lounge into the lobby of the hotel. Talking to two cops was probably bad for business.

The detectives followed the woman, but only for the sake of heading in the same direction—outside. One glanced at Kenna on the way out. She gave him a pleasant smile that she hoped was unassuming. There was no reason that her presence there meant anything to him.

A second later, a tall, wide-shouldered man in a dark-gray suit with a pale-blue tie approached her.

Kenna lifted her gaze to his eyes, which were smiling at her. "Bear?"

She had never used his real name, and he'd never told her what it was. His people called him "boss."

She grinned. "I didn't even see you in my scan. You're here with your guys?"

She hadn't seen them since Mexico.

"You were busy eavesdropping on a police interview." He grinned back and opened his arms. "I could see how that would make you distracted."

Kenna gave him a quick hug. "How are you?"

He stepped back. "Good. Working a gig for Lightwood. Six-person team, but only four of us are here tonight."

"Anything I need to be aware of?"

"We have it covered. But if Mr. Lightwood wants to explain the situation, that's up to him."

Kenna would have answered the same if she had been on a job for a client. She had respected this Miami-based private security agency since she had called them from Mexico and asked them to come and protect her family. The fact they had a helicopter hadn't hurt and meant they could get there quickly. When it came to Maizie, Stairns, and Jax, Kenna wasn't going to take any chances. Things in Mexico had reached a breaking point, and she had been far too exhausted to do anything but pay good money for top-notch protection.

She figured she could at least clue him in. If he was unaware. "Anything to do with Avery Masonridge?"

Bear frowned. "The Florida senator? I heard she was dating that musician guy."

Kenna made a face because she had no idea.

"Are you on a case?" he asked her. Probably because of the eavesdropping.

"Just finished one. Got paid."

Bear's eyes shifted slightly, his attention elsewhere for a second even though he was still fully aware of what was happening around him. Then his focus came back to her. "Mr. Lightwood is ready."

She smiled. "It's good to see you."

She hadn't spent much time with the guy but wouldn't mind catching up—or actually getting to know each other. Given the way he worked and how he carried himself as a professional, she could see them being good friends. The kind of people who passed each other referrals and called one another for help when it was necessary.

In her line of work, she couldn't have too many people she trusted that she could call when things got crazy.

Kenna squeezed his arm and headed for the far corner, where Preston Lightwood sat in a booth by himself. At least one private security agent stood nearby, and she lifted her chin. If she was anyone else than someone the boss knew, she would likely have been patted down or at least questioned.

Preston wore a lime-green shirt, open at the collar. He was pushing late fifties but didn't show much sign that he had spent twenty years in prison. Apart from one tattoo on the inside of his forearm, where he had rolled up his sleeves. He had a glass of something sparkly in front of him but didn't seem in a hurry to finish it. "Drink?"

"I'm good." She eased back against the padded seat covered in dark-red fabric. "How have you been?"

The scar on the side of his neck was new, but the last time she'd seen him was the day he caught a stray bullet. A sniper had taken a shot at them on the back patio of a resort in Arizona. She had assumed the bullet was meant for Jax but could never be sure that Preston wasn't the target. Either way, the case they'd been working was closed.

Preston lifted his glass and took a sip. "Can't complain. I've always liked New Orleans, but it's been a while since I was here the last time."

Kenna nodded. "Me as well." Before he could ask her what she was working on, she said, "What brings you here?"

"I'm working on some real estate investing, trying to get my business off the ground. I have capital, but I'm looking for partners and other investors."

"Sounds boring."

Preston laughed. "It's not as exciting as going after killers and bringing them to justice, but I'm hoping it will at least pay the bills."

"That's always a good plan."

"Honestly, what I'm really looking for is something not so different from what you do. Not the catching bad guys part. But being certain of my purpose." He stared at the bubbles in his glass. "God seems content to be silent on the subject. I'm feeling out this new path, trying to live what I believe."

"That's the best kind of purpose." And it sounded to her like he was on the right track.

"I feel like I'll know for sure that I've changed. Because I'll be making better choices."

"Maybe that's what the silence is about." Kenna paused.

"Seeing what you'll do when you're in charge of making your own decisions."

She didn't have a lot of experience with "God's will" and how it worked, but He had given her plenty of logic to utilize.

Hopefully, whatever he was going to ask her to do wasn't about some kind of scam he would want her to investigate. Real estate cases were as boring as financial ones. She much preferred missing persons or bringing killers to justice. Those just seemed to make a difference in the world way more than one sleazy guy scamming people out of money.

"For the record," Preston said, "I'm much too busy trying to get my business off the ground to worry about stalking you. But I'm glad you were in the neighborhood."

She had been planning on ignoring how coincidental it was. "Good to know."

"I'm sure you want to know why I asked to see you, and as much as I like to catch up with people who mean something to me, I do have a favor to ask."

"Does it have something to do with the protection detail?" Kenna asked. "Though, I have to say you chose well."

"That was your doing, actually. I had my assistant e-mail your office, and they referred me to Miami Security International. But I have an upcoming trip, and they don't have many agents available to go with me. They can spare a couple, but I'm headed to London in the new year, and I could use protection that can blend in as my traveling companions."

He wanted her to go to London?

"What's the threat?" Kenna said. "Why do you feel like you need a protective detail wherever you go?"

Preston sighed. "Unfortunately, despite the fact that I served a twenty-year sentence for something I didn't do, there are some who are still not satisfied that justice was served. But not because the real killer was never caught. My wife's brother has never kept it a secret that he thinks I should be as dead as she is."

Kenna caught the edge of grief in his expression. "You think he'll come after you?"

"He's been quite vocal about being prepared to pay anyone who could take me out. Aside from hiring a hitman straight-out, he's made it plain he will reward anyone who does the deed on his behalf."

"And that worries you? Surely if he intended to end your life, he wouldn't be so vocal about it." Usually, people try to hide their intentions.

Preston shrugged one shoulder. "Explain the fact the brake line on my car was cut two weeks ago. Before that, someone messed with the gas at my house and half the garage exploded. Thankfully, I was out of town for a couple of days at the time." He sighed. "I'm getting death threats online, and on at least two occasions, this security detail has deemed it necessary to rush me away from a particular location."

"Sounds like you made the right call keeping them around." Kenna thought about it for a second. "Rather than being part of the detail, wouldn't it make more sense for me to speak with the guy who wants you dead? Find out if we can shut him down?"

"I had a friend try that. My esteemed brother-in-law had security escort the guy to the front doors of his New York office, where they threw the guy onto the street. Evidently, the call already went out, and he claims there's nothing he can do to stop other people's actions. As if when inevitably anyone who tries to kill me in order to reap the reward shows up, he will deny being responsible for their actions."

So he had no intention of paying them.

Either way, Preston would be dead.

Kenna said, "I'd still like to take a stab at meeting the guy. My current associate can assist in that endeavor. He's not a guy you could easily throw into the street."

"You're working with Jax? I thought he got promoted after what happened in Arizona."

She shook her head. "I'm training another private investigator."

Preston's expression shifted. "Did you guys break up?"

"Jax and I are fine." She lifted her fingers and waved off his concern, not that her relationship was any of his business. "I'm helping someone else get started. He might be able to do some digging with your brother-in-law. And I can have my associate in the office take a look at anything on the internet, find out if there is actually a hit out on you."

"And while they do that," Preston said, "you're willing to at least consider coming with me to London?"

She stared at him for a second, then said, "I'll think about it."

The man across the table from her had known her father, but Kenna didn't have much of the information on how. Just that in a time of crisis, Preston had known her father was the one person in the world he felt could help him and keep him safe at the same time. She wanted the chance to ask Preston more about their friendship. Spending a bunch of time together on a trip would give her the chance to do that.

He eyed her. "You do have a current passport, don't you?"

After what happened in Mexico, and the trouble they'd had coming home, Kenna had since made a point to have a valid passport. "I'm good. It's been a while since I traveled to Europe, but I enjoyed going there with my father." Her dad had consulted more than once with Interpol. She'd been to Belgium, France, Germany, Austria, and over to the UK.

They had ridden trains across Europe, moving between countries while he worked to find a dangerous killer.

"I'll send everything I have to your office e-mail so your people can get on it."

Kenna nodded. "Send it, and I'll make a determination if we want to take on the case."

"Fair." He grinned. "How long will you be in New Orleans?"

"The case I was working is finished. So maybe only a few days. Unless something else crops up."

"How about dinner? If you think Jax wouldn't mind me boring you with my business plan."

Kenna slid to the end of the bench seat. "Have your people call my people, and we'll set something up."

She had always wanted to say that. And apparently Preston appreciated it, because he laughed.

It helped that these days she had people.

Gone was the solitude of the years between the FBI and meeting Jax. These days, she had a whole family.

If anything or anyone was going to put them in jeopardy, they'd find out pretty quickly how far she would go to protect the people she loved.

Kenna was willing to go so far as to hire a protection detail of her own.

Chapter Seven

Kenna slid into the front seat of her car just as her phone started to ring. She turned on the engine to get the air-conditioning blowing. Despite the fact it was after dark, it was still pretty warm. Doing that allowed the call to connect through her car's Bluetooth so that when she answered the phone, she heard the caller's voice through the car speakers.

The number on the screen belonged to the bail bondsman's office who had given them the contract for Garth Sanders.

"What can I do for you, Reggie?"

"You can tell me why there's a pregnant girl in my office asking for you. I ain't no secretary."

Kenna frowned, but not at the couple who wandered past the car holding hands. She didn't have anything against that. In fact, holding hands was more underrated than giving someone a hug.

And the whole sequence of thoughts just made her miss Jax.

"Someone's looking for me?" Kenna said. "Who is it?"

"Like I said, I ain't no secretary."

She pulled up her maps app and put in the address of the bail bondsman's office so she could figure out how long it would take to get there. "Does it look like she's going to bolt in the next ten minutes?"

"Seems more like she's gonna wait here for you until she goes into labor."

Kenna winced at the frustrated anger in his tone.

"Do not let her have that baby on my floor."

Kenna sighed. "I'll be there as quick as I can."

She pulled out of her parking space, turning onto a road lined with bars spilling out with people enjoying their evening. Plenty of pedestrians, so she kept her focus on the road until she got past the busy social area of the city.

Then her thoughts inevitably returned to Jax, and everything she was working on right now. Despite the fact she had no open cases, that didn't put her at a loss for things to do—or mysteries to solve.

She called Maizie and explained what Preston had asked her, giving her teenage assistant the information she needed. "I want a full workup on Preston's brother-in-law so we can determine the threat level."

"Are you really going to London?"

"I'll at least think about it. Nothing wrong with considering a job." Kenna paused. "Would you want to come with me if it works out?" She waited, not filling the silence with more chatter. Wanting to know how Maizie felt about taking a step like that into the real world.

"Who would take care of Cabot If I was gone for however long?" Maizie asked. "Stairns thinks he knows about dogs, but he's really clueless."

"It's a good thing you're there to take care of her."

That was all Kenna would say about that. She'd rather let

Maizie think about the opportunity to travel and realize that for all her logical reasons why she needed to stay in Colorado, the fact was that there was a world outside the trailer she lived in. The teen never had to step one foot outside of the US, or even Colorado, if she didn't want to. Which wouldn't mean she hadn't lived a full life. If Maizie wanted to explore the world, they could do so in a way that meant she was kept safe.

Like going with a protective detail led by Bear. Probably at a different time than Preston's trip, when Kenna could focus fully on the teen.

Maizie stayed silent.

"I'm at the bail bondsman's storefront." Kenna parked the car around back in the staff parking lot. "So I've got to go. And you have work to do."

"Try not to get kidnapped and taken into another country again, bye."

Maizie hung up, laughing. Which in itself was a huge sign that she had overcome a lot of her trauma. The fact she could make jokes about something like that after what had happened to them both in Mexico was a positive sign.

Kenna knocked on the back door and heard footsteps inside, a second before the door eased open a couple of inches. Reggie confirmed it was her and then swung the door wide.

She stepped inside. "No baby yet?"

"Make it fast. Just in case."

"I think babies come when they're ready. So far as I know."

Reggie said, "I have two kids, and I still don't wanna know."

She headed for the front of the office, down a dark hallway lined with wood panel walls where he had hung the occasional framed print she could only describe as "biker art." Reggie couldn't possibly weigh more than a hundred twenty pounds, and he always wore slacks and a silk shirt. Loafers on his feet and a gold chain around his neck. He slicked his dark hair back with product that doubled as cologne.

"If you have some time, I've got a couple of contracts you can look at," Reggie said. "One of them is a real sicko. Right up your alley."

At the end of the hallway, she glanced over her shoulder. "Send it to my e-mail."

He grinned, then ducked into his office.

The girl in the waiting area had turned around, probably when she heard Kenna's voice. She stared. "Are you her?"

The girl couldn't be more than nineteen. She wore a forest-green oversized man's T-shirt, the sleeves hanging past her elbows. The front of her abdomen pushed out the shirt, and her shorts were barely visible under the bottom hem. She had a tattoo on the front of her right thigh and her hair pulled back in a messy bun. Flip-flops on her feet, and no other belongings that Kenna could see.

"I'm Kenna Banbury." She walked over and held out her hand.

The girl put a smaller clammy hand in hers, and they shook. "Nora Thibodeaux."

"What can I help you with?" Kenna motioned to one of the hard plastic chairs along the wall. "Do you want to sit down?"

"Garth told me all about how you saved him from the Landrys. He said you were his guardian angel, and that you would protect me from Momma Landry."

As long as he didn't actually think she was his cousin. "You spoke to him since he was arrested?"

Nora nodded. "I know you were the one who brought him in. He said you saved his life." The girl set her hands on her swollen belly. "He said you'll protect us as well. That you'll do the right thing."

"Protect you from what?"

"Momma Landry knows she won't get her money from Garth if he's in prison. She's trying to find me so she can sell my baby to pay off his debt. She said the sins of the father should be transferred down to the son." Nora shook her head. "But she doesn't know I'm not having a boy."

"It's an expression," Kenna said. "And she's using it wrongly."

"Does that mean you're gonna help me? I don't want to have my baby stolen by the Landrys, and I'll never see her again."

Kenna was glad Maizie couldn't hear this conversation. "Something similar happened to a friend of mine. But she wasn't the mom, she was the baby."

"The Landrys did this to someone else?" Nora gasped.

Kenna shook her head. "It was far away from here, a long time ago. But I'm not going to let that happen to you. I'll help you get somewhere safe where you can have your baby and not have to worry about the Landrys."

The girl reached out and clasped Kenna's hands. Tears rolled down her face. "Thank you so much. I was so scared when my friend told me they took Garth from the taco truck." She sniffed. "They killed my brother. He was working in the truck with Garth."

"I'm sorry for your loss."

"I'm not really crying about my brother. He hit me with a frying pan once, and I think he was stealing from Garth's tips." The girl let out a breath, seemingly relieved by the turn of events.

Kenna would rather the police arrested that whole family when they'd gone into the bar. This girl might have enough information that the police would be interested in protecting her—maybe even getting her into witness protection. She could touch base with the cops and find out if they wanted to talk with Nora Thibodeaux.

"Do you have somewhere you can stay tonight where you will be safe?"

The girl shook her head. "I didn't even have time to pack. I was going home, and I saw them outside my apartment, so I just drove around trying to figure out who would help me."

The Landrys were out looking for her already.

Kenna said, "I can get you tucked away at a motel for now, or even on a bus with some cash and a few things to tide you over. Is there anyone close to you that doesn't live in New Orleans that you could go stay with?"

"I have an aunt who lives in Durango, but she doesn't like little kids, and her dogs are mean."

Kenna said, "Okay, I'll think of something." She twisted to look over her shoulder.

Out the window two cars pulled up to the curb. Thanks to the low light in here, whoever was out there likely couldn't see them inside. "Reggie!"

Kenna walked to the blinds and looked out. She tugged one blind slat down just enough to see multiple guys get out of the cars, each of them holding a pistol.

"Did you get your business sorted?" Reggie said.

"Any reason why a group of guys is approaching your front door with guns?" How else would they have known to find Nora here if it wasn't for Reggie? But had he actually tipped them off? She wouldn't put it past him.

Nora whimpered. "They'll kill me and cut my baby out."

Reggie paled.

"That's not going to happen." Kenna grabbed the girl's hand and tugged her toward Reggie. "We need a way out."

"I can check my cameras and see if any of them came around the back way." He turned and went to his office, shaking the mouse of his computer so the screen came to life.

Kenna wasn't entirely sure they had time for that. She tugged out her phone and quickly dialed Maizie. "Get Ramon here. I need backup. Now." She ended the call as soon as Maizie confirmed.

Kenna stowed her phone and pulled out her pistol, taking off the safety.

Nora whimpered.

"We need to get to my car." Kenna turned to Reggie. "Call 911, but you can leave it off the hook. Someone will show up and find these guys in here."

"They just smashed the front door," Reggie said. "No one is out back."

"Let's go." Kenna tugged on Nora's hand with her free one and hurried to the door where she looked out at the waiting area. They hadn't made it into this office, just the lobby of the small storefront. "Quickly and quietly now."

She heard the ratchet of a shotgun, but it was Reggie. "I'll hold them off. You guys get out of here. I'll just tell the cops I was defending my place of business, and they won't be able to arrest me."

"Thanks." Kenna and Nora scurried to the back door, where she twisted the handle and eased the door open a little the same way Reggie had done. She didn't see anyone out back but leaned out to double-check, glancing both ways. "Come on."

Reggie yelled, then the shotgun exploded. Followed by the sound of buckshot punching tiny holes in the drywall.

Someone let out a manly yell.

Kenna hurried across the sidewalk to the parking lot with Nora in tow. As they ran, she beeped the locks on her car, and

Nora rushed to the passenger side. Kenna covered the back door of the business with her weapon until Nora was in and the door was shut, then slid in and turned the car on.

She shoved it in Reverse and hit the gas just as the back door of the bail bond office flung open and a man stumbled out. Not Reggie. The man had blood running down his face and a gun in his hand.

Kenna said a silent prayer for Reggie's survival and swung the car in an arc so that her side of the car faced the man. As much as she might want it, there was no time to roll the window down and fire off a couple of shots. She shoved the car into Drive and hit the gas again, peeling out in a spray of gravel.

The man fired at her car, multiple shots pinging off the back quarter panel. Nora screamed and ducked her head but couldn't get too low because of the baby.

Kenna focused on getting them as far away as she could, as fast as she could. "I'll have to ditch the car now. They've seen it."

"We also have another problem."

She turned the corner, and they bumped up onto a side street, heading into a residential area where they could lose any pursuer. "What's that?"

Nora sat up, brushing strands of hair back from her face. "My water just broke."

Chapter Eight

A heart-wrenching scream ripped through the air, torn from the throat of a woman in the kind of primal pain that only comes from childbirth. And that was *with* an epidural.

Kenna eased the door closed, not sure why she made a point to shut it so quietly.

Ramon stood in the hallway, where he'd told her he was waiting.

"I've changed my mind," she said. "I never want kids."

Another scream ripped through the air.

Ramon's expression hardened in a way she'd never seen before. He glanced one way, up the hospital maternity ward hallway, and then the other. "It'll be hard to guard the baby when they start moving him—or her—around for tests and stuff, and so the mother can sleep."

"Nora asked us to help her keep the baby safe." Kenna folded her arms. "That means no matter what, none of the Landrys gets anywhere near her."

"I know." His expression turned to something hard as granite. A determination she'd never seen in him. Though, she realized it might have been similar to how he'd been with the young woman he'd met in Mexico. Kenna had helped the same woman in Colorado. All of it was a long story, but the gist was that she'd realized they were on the same side.

Neither of them was prepared to allow an innocent person to suffer if they could do something about it.

He continued, "I'm just thinking through logistics when they start running tests and checkups."

"Maybe they'll come to Nora to do it here, and we can keep them together where things are locked down," Kenna said. "We can explain the situation." She looked at her watch. "I've got the head of hospital security coming up."

Never mind that it was not yet five in the morning, she'd rousted security to talk to them. Neither Kenna nor Ramon had a badge or any authority, but who would argue with a vulnerable woman in danger? A woman who believed someone wanted to steal her baby from her. No one would want to stop that from happening.

"You really don't want kids?"

She wanted to make a quip about him not telling Jax that, but the look on Ramon's face stayed her tongue. Instead, she said, "Anyone who thinks having a baby is no big deal should be forced to stand out here and listen to that."

Ramon almost smiled.

A nurse passed them and said, "Can I help the two of you?" She probably thought they were next of kin.

"We're waiting for the head of security. We're with Ms. Thibodeaux." Kenna pointed her thumb at the door.

They took up flanking positions, their backs to the door. The way two cops would when they were on protection detail —whether that meant protecting the world from whoever was with the doctor, or the other way around.

The nurse didn't seem completely convinced, but evidently decided to reserve judgment.

Just then, an older dark-skinned man in a white shirt marked SECURITY, black slacks, and rubber soled black shoes stepped off the elevator. He clocked them right away, which wasn't surprising. Their interaction with the nurse left them in protection mode.

They stayed where they were, on either side of the door, as he approached.

When he got close enough, Kenna held out her hand. "Makenna Banbury. I'm a private investigator. This is my associate, Ramon Santiago."

"Clive Badeau. Nice to meet you both. I know your names." The guy shook both their hands. "My wife loves those true crime podcasts. They love to pick apart cases, and people's lives." He gave Ramon an assessing glance. "You guys ever guest on any of them? She didn't remember either of you being on one."

"No," Kenna said, "but if we're in town long enough, we'll have coffee with her. If she wants."

Clive's whole demeanor changed. "She'd like that."

And in return for the promise of coffee with his wife, they would get a whole lot of goodwill with this guy.

Small price to pay as far as she was concerned.

Kenna told him, "The patient, Nora Thibodeaux, is concerned for the safety of her child. She believes another family may try to abduct the child from her care. One of us will remain with the baby at all times."

Given how he'd reacted, she figured Ramon would be the one to do that for now. Kenna could switch off with him later when he needed to rest. She wanted to go to the bail bondsman's office and make sure Reggie had survived the run-in with the gunmen who had chased her out of the back.

"You need any of my people up here?" Clive asked.

Ramon answered before she could. "We've got this."

Clive eyed him.

Kenna smiled. "We appreciate you allowing us to keep the patient and her baby safe."

"My team is happy to stick to business as usual, and step in if either of you require backup." The way he said *either* reassured Kenna he didn't take Ramon's intensity the wrong way.

Which was good.

She wasn't going to ask him to be less intense. This time. If Ramon intended to give all of his energy and skills to protect an innocent baby, she was fine with it.

After all, it could mean the difference between success and failure.

"And if this goes beyond our combined skills?" Clive rocked back and forth on the soles of his shoes. "What happens then?"

It was a test. Asking if they were prepared to get involved with other people would tell Clive if Kenna and Ramon worked on the right side of the law—or another side entirely.

"If the situation goes beyond our ability to control, we would welcome the help of local police or federal agents," Kenna said. "The last thing we want is for innocents to get caught up as collateral damage. Or for anything to happen to that baby."

Ramon said, "I'm not interested in getting into a gunfight in the middle of a hospital, but I will do what it takes to keep them safe."

"To keep everyone here safe," Kenna added.

Except the Landrys. If they were going to come in here, they would find out pretty quickly that Kenna and Ramon weren't going to roll over and show their weaknesses.

Clive nodded. "Keep us on speed dial." He tugged a radio off his belt and handed it to her.

They watched him walk away.

Kenna turned to Ramon, about to speak when a baby cry sounded from the other side of the door. She took a second to listen, the corners of her lips curling up.

Ramon said, "What were you saying about not having children?"

She looked at him. "Do *you* want kids one day?"

He shrugged. "Who'd want to get into a relationship with me?"

"If you've already decided no one can take on what you'll bring to the relationship, then whoever she is...you already made the decision for her." Kenna eyed him. "Doesn't she get to have a say? Or the chance to prove you're wrong?"

Before he could answer, the door opened, and the doctor stepped out. To the woman's credit, she looked like she'd worked a long day, but a good one.

"Everything went okay?" Kenna asked.

The doctor had shaken her hand earlier, but they hadn't talked much past introductions. Now, she said, "I'll leave Nora to fill you in."

Which meant, *It's not my business to tell you*, Kenna figured.

"Go," Ramon said. "I've got this." He tipped his head in the direction of Nora's room.

Kenna eased inside, where one of the nurses was cleaning up the baby and doing some preliminary tests to the left. The baby was a squirming set of pink limbs and dark-brown hair in the bassinet.

To the right, in the hospital bed, Nora watched intently. She looked spent, her hair matted to the sides of her head and her face flushed. She didn't take her attention off the baby with the nurse.

Kenna didn't walk between them, so Nora missed nothing. She grabbed the closest stool and rolled it past a couple of machine monitors to sit by the bed.

"Everything good?" She meant the delivery, mom and baby's status, and the nurse tending to the child.

Nora said, "Look at her," wonder in her tone.

"That's a pretty amazing thing you did, Mama." Kenna squeezed her hand.

Nora beamed. "I did do that."

"What is Garth going to say when he sees her?"

A laugh erupted from Nora's throat. "He isn't going to know what to do."

Neither of them mentioned the lingering question of whether Garth would be a free man when he met his daughter. He might be in prison for most of her childhood. Right now, they didn't know much other than that he wasn't getting out of prison anytime soon.

The nurse wheeled the bassinet over to the far side of the bed, then scooped up the baby. "Ready for her?"

Nora held out her arms, one of which had an IV and a hospital bracelet. There was a matching bracelet on the baby.

The nurse laid the child in Nora's arms. "I'll be back to see how you're doing after you've had some time with her. Do you want anything to eat?"

"Yes, please," Nora said.

"All right, I'll go find you a menu." She gave them a kind smile and headed for the door.

"You probably need to rest, so I won't take much of your time." Kenna explained who Ramon was and how he'd stay with the baby at all times when she wasn't with Nora, and when she was he would be at the door. "You only need to yell, and he'll come running." Kenna tugged a panic button from her pocket. It looked like a key fob. "Hit this if you need us. Don't wait until it's an emergency. If you even get a weird feeling, I want you to press it."

"Thank you." Nora looked a little teary-eyed, but Kenna figured that was mostly hormones.

Kenna gave the girl a few moments to stare at her baby. Then said, "She's beautiful." She wasn't going to say it aloud, but she felt good knowing she'd had a hand in this baby being born safely.

Whether it was enough for Nora to call the girl Kenna was another matter. How would it feel to know there was a child named after her somewhere in the world? She knew now why guys called their kid "junior," and it wasn't just hubris. It was also about connection. The soul deep understanding there was another human in the world who would always carry a part of you, no matter what.

"Did you name her?"

Nora smiled down at the baby in her arms. "We said we'd call her Elvira, after Garth's mother."

Kenna bit the inside of her lip. "That's a nice name."

"It's terrible, but we can call her Ellie. Elvira Makenna Sanders," Nora said. "I heard you tell the doctor your name."

Kenna smiled. "I'll leave the two of you to rest. I want to go back to the bail bondsman's and check on Reggie. Make sure he's all right."

Fear flashed on Nora's face.

"Your job is to rest and take care of this little one. Don't worry about anything else. I've got this. All right?"

Nora nodded.

Kenna patted her arm and headed for the door. As soon as she closed it, Kenna said, "You've got this?"

Ramon didn't flinch. "You doubt me?"

Kenna just said, "Good," and stepped away. "I'll be back soon."

She took the elevator down to the ground floor and found her car in the parking lot. As soon as she slid in the front seat, she let out a long breath.

Kenna cranked the car to get the air-conditioning going—and try and disperse the odd smell. After she checked on Reggie, she needed a shower and a change of clothes, as she'd likely be on a long shift watching Nora and Ellie so Ramon could get some rest.

They'd also need food.

She dialed Jax, then pulled out of the parking space. The phone rang a couple of times, then a warm voice said, "Jaxton."

"Sorry. I didn't look at the clock." It was two hours earlier there than in her time zone. "I woke you up."

"I'm glad you called." He groaned a little as he stretched. "I should get a little single cup coffee maker and put it in my room so I don't have to get up. I'll leave a bottle of water by it. Then I can just roll over and make coffee before I even get out of bed."

Kenna chuckled. "Wanna hear about my night?"

"Depends. Will coffee be enough, or will I need something stronger?"

"You won't have to call a US Attorney and plead my case. Not yet, at least."

She started with Garth getting kidnapped, hit the highlights of the Landrys, and ended with news about Reggie and Nora.

"I'm on my way to check on the bail bondsman now and..." She gripped the steering wheel. "How would he have survived that? At most, he took out a couple of Landry's men before he was killed. I don't see how he could be alive."

"He told you to go," Jax said gently. "He knew the risk, and it was his choice."

"I still don't like it."

"Because you don't believe anyone should give their life to save yours. But this was about Nora and that baby." Kenna wasn't sure Reggie had been that altruistic in the moment, but she didn't know. Maybe it had only been about a child at risk. He might not have thought it over. Just reacted in the spur of the moment. "It's not that I don't think I'm worth it."

"I know," Jax said. "You value life. Enough that you believe every single one is far more precious than yours."

That, and not having the choice taken from her. If someone died protecting her, that meant she hadn't been able to save them. At some point, she'd have realized it was futile. The cost of them choosing to die for her had to be worth it. She had to know she'd done everything she could to save them.

To fight for the best outcome.

"Did you think about what you want to do for Thanksgiving?" he asked.

Kenna smiled to herself at the change of subject. "You're trying to catch me off guard so I'll agree to something I wouldn't otherwise."

Jax just chuckled. It sounded nice, even coming out of the car speakers.

She sighed. "You're taking the week off, or just a couple of days?"

"I'll take the week. My sister said she wants to meet you."

Which meant Kenna would be roped into meeting his mother. She shouldn't have put it off so long.

Jax continued, "She can get a cabin in Aspen for the week and come down to Stairns' place for dinner Thursday with her husband and the kids." He didn't wait a beat before he said, "You think Maizie will be okay with my brother-in-law?"

"We'll be there, so I think she'll be able to handle it," Kenna said. "Do you think they'll be okay with Ramon?"

Jax chuckled. "I don't know if *I'm* okay with Ramon."

Kenna pulled up to a stop light and watched a guy on the sidewalk eye her vehicle. She kept one eye on him the whole time, until the light went green and she could pull away. "Ramon just volunteered to protect a newborn baby from bad guys who would sell her to collect on a debt. In fact, he insisted."

"Fine," Jax said. "He'll grow on me, I guess."

Kenna pulled into the strip mall parking lot where the bail bondsman's storefront was. "Whoa."

All the parking spaces were taken, and at least two black-and-white cop cars and one unmarked filled the few there were. She even spotted a white forensic van.

"I should go," Kenna said. "Have a good day at the office, dear."

Jax chuckled. "You, too. Stay safe."

Kenna got out of the car, determined to find out how many lives had been lost last night.

Chapter Nine

Kenna slid her phone into her back pocket, then produced her ID. She'd left her gun in the glove box this time. Not that they'd pat her down or anything, but the cop on the tape was nervous enough. Or getting antsy from standing there so long.

It was barely morning, so she figured he'd been there all night and was expecting to be relieved soon so he could end his shift.

"Morning." She handed over her driver's license and a PI one for the closest state she had a license in.

"Kinda far from home, aren't you?" He had flat brown hair, and cautious eyes.

"I'm Kenna Banbury. I was here last night when all this went down."

He pretty much flinched. The five o'clock shadow on his jaw shifted, and he lifted the clipboard to write her name. Then he grabbed his radio. "Sarge, this is Alecks. There's a woman out here says she's a witness."

"Copy that."

Alecks let go of the radio, clipped to his shoulder. "Sarge will be out shortly."

"Thanks," she said. "About to get off shift?"

"Any minute now."

That meant she wouldn't see him when she left—if they let her inside. "Have a good one." Kenna ducked under the tape and went to meet the tall guy who approached her with sergeant's stripes on his sleeve.

She introduced herself.

"Sergeant Martinez." He didn't offer his hand for her to shake. "You saw something of what happened here?"

"Pretty sure I saw the whole thing." But she still didn't know if Reggie was dead or alive. "Since I was inside at the time."

"If you could tell me what happened here, it will help us put together a complete picture."

Kenna nodded. "I know." She paused. "I was an FBI agent for a while."

That could go either way, depending on his interaction with feds. There wasn't much interagency animosity these days. Not since 9/11 had cemented the need for departments and agencies to work together rather than in opposition. It wasn't perfect, but it was a whole lot better than when her father had been an FBI agent.

"Let's go inside." He glanced around, where a few passersby had gathered, and a news reporter did a live broadcast. Given his expression, he had a lot of animosity for the local news.

"Trouble with the press?" Kenna eyed him.

"Alina Cardenas. Dated one of my officers all so she could get him to talk about cases he was working. He caught her trying to log into his department-issue computer." He tugged the door open.

"Wow. Sounds like a piece of work." She stepped inside.

"And then some." The door shut behind him.

Reminded her of Momma Landry, just in a different industry. Enterprising. Willing to do whatever it took to get a result.

Kenna saw blood on the floor, interspersed with evidence markers. They stayed where they were and an evidence tech in white overalls came over, handing them each blue booties to put on over their shoes.

Martinez took both pairs of gloves. "Ms. Banbury won't be touching anything. She's only here to tell us what happened."

She was surprised he didn't say *her version*, but it didn't matter either way. The truth was the truth. She couldn't speak to what she hadn't seen.

"First, I have a question."

Martinez's eyebrows rose.

"Did you find the business owner Reginald Montego deceased?" Kenna asked.

"We have three victims. None with that name," Martinez said. "He's a friend of yours?"

She shook her head. "Acquaintances. But he was a good guy."

She explained about Nora telling her that she was in danger, which led her to backtracking and going over the whole Garth thing. How she'd met Reggie. The operation that took her into the bayou with Ramon, who she only referred to as her "associate."

"Reggie said he'd hold them off," she added. "And I escaped out the back with Nora. She's currently at Mercy Hospital. She had the baby a few hours ago."

"That's quite a tale," Martinez said. "But it fits with what we put together about the events that led to three deaths."

"Did you ID them? Because if Reggie isn't here, then

where is he?" The guy could be injured somewhere—hopefully getting medical treatment. Or he'd fled himself to avoid the consequences of killing three of Momma's guys. If that was who these dead guys were.

"Their names are Steven Landry, Elliot Morris—a Landry cousin—and Georgie Landry."

One of her boys. Kenna winced. "Did he have some preexisting injuries?"

"I'll have to check with the medical examiner about that."

Kenna walked through the main office, the waiting area where she'd spoken with Nora. One of the victims had fallen just inside the door. Another lay in the middle of the room.

A third had hit the ground in the hallway. At least according to evidence markers.

"Your techs do nice work." She glanced at him. "Do you have someone going through the security footage?"

"You wouldn't happen to know Reggie's password, would you?"

She headed for the office, which he'd take to mean she knew the answer to his question. The reality was she had no idea. Inside the office, a tech in a polo shirt and khakis sat at the computer, looking frustrated. He wore glasses with a string attached that trailed behind his neck. A frown drew his brows together.

The phone on the desk rang.

"That thing..." He glanced at the sergeant. "Any ideas on the password? Nothing I'm doing is working."

"Ms. Banbury?"

"Sorry. I know Reggie had surveillance cameras, and he recorded their entry. Presumably, it recorded the incidents that took place after Nora and I escaped. But I wouldn't know how to get into his system."

Martinez pressed his lips into a thin line. "I see."

She hadn't exactly gained entry to this office under false pretenses. "You have no idea where he is?"

"Worried about him?"

"There were more than three guys who made entry," Kenna said. "Reggie had that gun in his possession, the one on the floor in the hallway. Which means at some point he dropped it. So then what happened and where is he?"

The phone started to ring again.

She continued, "If we could look at the security footage, it would certainly help us figure out if he's safe, or alive even." The information was stored either on hard drives or offsite— like on a cloud-based server.

Could Maizie access the network here? She might be able to find what the police couldn't obtain by legal means. But Kenna wasn't going to offer up Maizie's services without it being a last resort—or something the police never discovered.

The phone stopped ringing for a second, then immediately started again.

Someone else who wanted to know if Reggie was dead or alive?

Kenna grabbed a glove out of Martinez's hand and used a finger to press what she hoped was the right button on the console. "Yes?"

"Who is this?"

"Who is this?" Kenna echoed.

The caller chuckled, an older woman with a smoky cough. Momma Landry. "Kenna Banbury. I thought that was you goin' inside."

Martinez patted Kenna's shoulder, then made a circle motion with one finger and mouthed, *Keep her talking.* This conversation would be over before the New Orleans PD could trace the call, but she admired him for trying.

Maizie had sent her some basic details, so she decided to throw the woman off. "What do you want, Francine?"

Momma laughed. "Guess you think you know all my secrets."

"What a scary idea." Kenna sighed. "I think I'd rather not know."

"This one you'll want to hear."

Kenna didn't like getting suckered into interactions against her will. But if this was about Reggie, she'd have no choice. "What is it?"

"You know what I want, or you wouldn't have taken that girl from me. I'll settle for a trade."

"I don't know what you're talking about." Kenna bit her lip, trying not to get so mad she just hung up.

"You want to see Reggie alive again? Bring me that baby."

There it was.

Kenna's abdomen burned with fire. "Nothing on God's green earth will induce me to abduct a newborn baby from the hospital and her mother, and hand her over to you."

The tech stiffened, making a sound in his throat. Even Martinez looked like he wanted to be sick.

Now they knew what this was about.

Momma said, "Then you've killed him."

In the background of the call, a man cried out. A sound of deep pain.

Kenna's stomach flipped over and she tried to recall what Jax had said. That Reggie knew what choice he was making.

"Reggie knew what he was doing," she said.

The line went dead.

Kenna lifted the handset, then replaced it.

The tone silenced.

Martinez blew out a breath. "Woman, you are stone-cold."

"You think I should hand a newborn over to Momma Landry to repay a debt the father owes?"

He shook his head. "No, ma'am. I do not. That woman is a piece of work."

"I wouldn't mind seeing her behind bars," Kenna said. She needed to get out of here. The smell of spilled blood and the fact she couldn't touch anything—or punch a hole through any of the walls—was making her antsy.

"You and every cop in this county."

Kenna handed over her business card. "Let me know if I can help."

Martinez gave a slight chuckle as she let herself out, using the back door she and Nora had escaped through. She tossed the booties in a trash can.

Even though she was pretty sure Reggie was captured, she did a circuit of the outside of the building. Just in case she spotted him.

Who knew how long it would be before Momma killed him. She would probably leave him somewhere he'd be found as a statement. A warning about what happens when you cross her.

Kenna tensed her abdomen, scanning the area around the bail bond storefront. She saw a couple of vehicles with occupants, but instinct didn't flag anything.

She wanted to go for a run, burn off the frustration. A man was about to die. Whether he had chosen it or not didn't make it right.

If she could've done something about it, she would have.

There was no way to find Reggie or where Momma had taken him. Not without getting into his security system.

Was she just trying to convince herself there was nothing she could do? Probably.

Would she have done something if she'd come up with a way to save them both?

Of course.

She climbed in her car and headed to her place at the RV park. Determined to get her head on straight.

Two hours later, she walked from her car to the lobby doors of the hospital. If she couldn't save Reggie, she could at least do everything she was able to do to save Nora and Ellie from being hurt and separated.

Maizie had promised to look into the security footage. That was the first thing they'd discussed. The longer the teen hadn't texted to say she was getting anywhere, Kenna had grown less and less hopeful she'd get into the system.

She had worked up a full profile on all the Landrys, though. Maizie had sent it over and Kenna ate a breakfast burrito for lunch while she read all about how the Landrys had terrorized this county for years but had never been convicted of more than misdemeanors. And thus far, Momma had remained clean. More likely, she had plenty of people to take the fall for her if the police got wind of something.

She passed a group of teens huddled by the door. Slender, hoodies and jackets. Two girls and at least four guys. One was a foot shorter than the others, but he had wide shoulders and a stocky build.

One of the girls said, "It's not like we meant for it to happen."

"As if the cops will care. We'll all go to jail for murder."

One of the boys gasped. "He's dead?"

"Why don't you go find out." The boy, a tall kid with a young face, shoved his friend, who stumbled back two steps. "Go with him. Find out what we're dealing with."

"Neil is gonna kill us." The other girl whimpered.

The alpha kid said, "Make it quick."

One boy and one girl darted in front of Kenna to the front doors of the hospital. She kept her steady pace and followed them through the lobby to the elevators. Evidently, they knew where they were going because one hit the button for the fourth floor without even looking at the directory.

She stood a few feet away and tugged out her phone, making her essentially invisible.

"Boyd is gonna tell Neil that it was my fault that guy hit his head," the boy said. "If he's dead, they're gonna turn me in to the cops. I'll go to adult prison, and you know what'll happen."

"Yeah, you'll cry the whole time because you're a baby," the girl said with the hardness of someone who had been served hard times and pain so much in her life already that she'd become numb to it.

Kenna didn't need to worry about these kids. She'd come here to protect a baby from dangerous criminals who would kill a man just because Kenna didn't give them what they wanted.

The elevator doors slid open, and the two kids stepped on. Kenna did the same. She gave them as much of an assessment as she could before they would have noticed. Still, the girl clocked Kenna. The teen had to be at least fifteen at most, but she had street smarts most adults would never develop.

"What floor do you need?"

Kenna tested a theory, answering the girl's question by saying, "Maternity."

She hit six. Familiar enough with the hospital that she knew where all the departments were.

"You know your way around this place?"

The girl shrugged. "I've done my time in here. And I got out."

Kenna said, "You ever miss it?"

The girl made it sound like prison, but something in her tone gave Kenna the impression she might have shadows under the thick shell she'd cultivated. That she'd been here for a reason—like a loved one who'd been ill.

The girl stared at Kenna with something a whole lot like grief in her eyes. Then she blinked, and it was gone. "Whatever, lady."

The doors slid open, and the two teens got off.

Kenna hit the button for one floor up, took the stairs back down, and emerged on the fourth floor, looking for them.

Where had they gone?

Chapter Ten

In the hallway, Kenna spotted the two kids hiding in an alcove between the bathroom and a storage closet. They were watching a white-coated doctor advise a slender woman with slacks and a bronze blouse who was clutching a tissue in one hand. The doctor said parting words and then walked away.

Kenna watched from a covered position. The kids ducked away, going the other direction, and disappeared out of sight.

"Can I help you?"

Kenna spun around to find a nurse staring at her over the top of her glasses. She had frizzy hair and looked like she'd have made an amazing, scary school librarian. Kenna had the urge to wrack her brain and try to remember if she'd ever failed to return a book.

The bronze shirt lady remained in the hall.

Kenna told the nurse, "I didn't want to disturb anyone, but I found my friend." Kenna pointed at her, then wandered over. "Hey, girl."

When the woman looked over, Kenna held out her hands.

The woman did the same on a reflex despite the fact they'd never met before. She had no idea who this woman was.

"I'm a private investigator. But my case isn't related to you." At least not so far. "Do you know the teens who were standing over there a moment ago?"

Kenna let go of the woman's hands and pointed to the corner where they'd been hiding.

The woman frowned over in the same direction. "I don't really know what you're talking about." She lifted her chin, her expression losing all its civility and taking on a hardness. "But I know that if you were sent here by Damien's wife to find out about our relationship, then you can just leave."

"This isn't about his wife. Or you, really. Not as far as I know." She motioned to a couple of chairs. "Can we sit?"

The woman frowned. "Fine, but only because a man in a coma is incredibly boring, and I've had enough of worrying when he'll wake up."

"I'd be happy to take your mind off things." Hopefully, that's what she would be doing.

They settled into two maroon-colored chairs against the wall, and Kenna introduced herself. "I'm working a case that involves a woman in maternity. She just had a baby, and my partner and I are keeping them both safe."

The woman's features softened, and Kenna knew she'd made the right call. "Why aren't they safe?"

"I'm afraid I don't disclose personal information when I'm working a case." Even if this one was pro bono. "But as I was entering the hospital just now, coming back from an errand, I encountered several teens. They came up here and listened to whatever the doctor told you. They seemed concerned about a patient outside, but the gist of the conversation was that they were perhaps responsible for what happened."

The woman gasped.

"Can I ask your name?"

"Oh, right." She smoothed her hands over the thighs of her pants. Brushing off nervousness? "I'm Camra Tenison."

"Nice to meet you." Kenna smiled. "What happened to Damien? He's the one who was hurt, right?"

Camra sighed. "I've been over it so many times with the police."

"Just the highlights are fine. If I can ID the people responsible, the police will be able to bring them to justice."

She wouldn't be working an official case with that one either, but two jobs for free was fine right now. They'd been paid for bringing Garth in, so Ramon was good for a while.

Until he got antsy from inactivity and insisted they go out and rustle up some work.

He was the reason they'd done some bounty hunting jobs. At least, that's what she'd told him. Kenna thought they were fun.

"It's been all over the news," Camra said. "Everyone I know has called me. I haven't answered. It's too tricky figuring out when Damien's wife will be here and making sure she doesn't see me."

Ah. An affair?

"What happened to him?" Kenna asked.

"There's been a rash of breaking and entering incidents lately. That's what the police told me. But Damien's was different. He was supposed to be out." She blushed. "With me, actually. But I wasn't feeling well. I had a migraine. His wife was out with some girl-friends. He stayed home. I guess he was going to do some work."

"They broke in?"

Camra nodded. "There was a fight. The police thought he surprised them. Damien was..." Her voice caught. "They hurt him. Shoved him, and he hit his head on the corner of the coffee table."

Kenna winced. "Will he recover?"

"He's in a medically induced coma until the swelling in his brain goes down."

He was the guy from the news. A local man. "Does he work for city hall? I think I saw that on the news."

She nodded. "That's where we met." She sniffed. "He said it's been over between them for a while."

"His wife?" Kenna asked.

"He was going to tell her this weekend that he's leaving her."

"I'm sorry this happened." Kenna waited a second. "Do the police have any idea who did it?"

Surely, someone had cameras. Or there was a witness in a neighborhood. If this wasn't the first instance, then with each crime they increased the chance someone would see them. Or be looking for them, made aware by the news reports.

"They think it's a crew of professionals, but I think they told Damien's wife more than they did me. After all, I'm 'just his mistress.'" She flushed. "Can you even believe they said that to me? Like it's some tawdry thing. We're in *love*."

"Who would know that neither Damien nor his wife would be home that night?"

Camra shrugged. "They have a housekeeper, but I don't know."

"No kids?"

"Damien and I are trying. They can't have kids, but it isn't because of him." The edge of a smirk entered her smile.

"Thank you for talking to me." Kenna shifted to the edge of the seat.

"More interesting than staring at the wall waiting for him to wake up."

Kenna figured a trip to security might be a good idea. Given the perpetrators might've been in here earlier, she could pass the tip to the police.

Camra got up when Kenna did. "Hey, you said you're a private investigator, right?"

"That's right." Kenna nodded.

"So I could, like, hire you?"

"Do you have a case you need help with?"

Camra nodded. "If Damien is going to divorce her, he'll need dirt on his wife, right? Something he can use to really nail her to the wall. That way she can't say anything when it comes out that he's with me now."

"Sorry, but I don't work those kinds of cases," Kenna said. "I'm sure there's a local PI you can hire for that. Someone who knows the area and won't stick out like I might."

"Right. Like an old white guy. It won't look suspicious that he's taking photos and acting all creepy."

"Right." Kenna was so done with this conversation. "Sorry. And thanks for your help, Ms. Tenison."

She hit the lobby first, and checked outside, but the kids were all gone. Next stop was the security guard's office. She knocked on the door and entered when the response was given.

"Clive?"

"Yes, ma'am." He sat behind a desk in front of a bank of monitors. "Problem upstairs?"

He had the feed for maternity up, and she could see Ramon standing at attention in front of the door.

"Not so far as I know. Looks like you're keeping a good eye on them."

"He went with the baby to the nursery and watched over her while she had a hearing test. Some other things. Now I believe they're working on feeding."

"You know all that?"

"Six grand babies."

"Is it okay if I sit?" Kenna pointed to a chair. When he nodded, she explained about the kids and their connection to the local news story.

"Let's take a look-see." He ran his finger over a roller ball on the side of the mouse, scrolling through digital recorded footage of the hall. Past where Kenna had spoken to Camra, back to the conversation with the doctor.

"There." Kenna pointed to the teens in the corner of the screen. "It's almost like they know that's practically a blind spot." But then, one of the kids had known the hospital well.

"We can't zoom or anything. This isn't like one of those TV shows. But we can look at the next camera down the hall." Clive clicked a few buttons, and four feeds in a square were replaced with one.

Kenna looked over at the image with Ramon, satisfied things were still good.

"Here we go." Clive clicked the mouse.

Two teens ducked down the hall into the stairwell.

"Not enough to get a good image for facial recognition." Kenna leaned forward. "But it might be worth a try."

She had him scroll back and pause the video. She took a terrible photo of the screen with her phone, so she didn't have to ask him to break hospital policy by sending an image to an outside account. The last thing she wanted was to get a good man in trouble.

Kenna's phone gallery would sync with Maizie's computer, and the teen would have the image in seconds. She texted Maizie to let her know what it was.

"Thanks, Clive." She sat back in her chair. "Think you could pass a tip to the police to look at these kids in connection to the breaking and entering case?"

If he did that, the cops would be one step closer to solving it. And stopping whatever was going to happen next. Which could be far worse than one man in a coma.

"On the basis of what? Kids in the halls?" Clive scratched his chin. "I'd need a reason I believe they're connected. Like say, your statement that you overheard them."

"I don't need to get involved with a police investigation. My focus is Nora." And Reggie.

She'd managed to distract herself from his fate for a while.

But it wouldn't be long before she learned what happened to him.

God, if it's possible...can You keep him safe?

She knew He didn't always answer prayers, even ones spoken to save a life. Things didn't always go the way people thought they should. It was just the reality of life where God wasn't a magic ticket, or some kind of drama-free card to play at will when someone didn't like what was happening.

Clive shook his head. "Unless I can give a reason I believe they're connected, it will just look like me being vindictive. Like I think these kids are roaming my halls and I just want to get rid of them."

Kenna huffed, folding her arms across her chest. "Fine."

Clive chuckled. "You sound like one of my girls."

At least she had the image. Maybe Maizie could work some magic.

Clive shifted quickly and leaned forward on his chair. On the screen, two vans pulled up outside the hospital. "What's this now?"

Multiple people exited the vehicles onto the sidewalk in front of the entrance. All of them carrying weapons.

"Active shooter protocols," Kenna said.

He snatched up the desk phone. "Already dialing. *Go.*"

Kenna headed for the door. It was three floors up to the

maternity ward, and she was going to have to get there faster than Momma and the guys with her.

As Clive issued lockdown orders, she ran out the door, racing for the stairs. Kenna hauled the heavy door open and hurried up as fast as she could without stumbling on concrete steps. At the sixth floor, she shoved the door open and raced out onto the maternity ward floor.

"Ramon!" She sprinted around the corner, already tugging her gun out of the holster.

A nurse turned to her, already huffing her displeasure. She saw Kenna's gun.

"Clive is on his way up!" Assuming the nurse knew the security guard's name. "They're locking down the hospital, but it will probably be too late."

Ramon didn't leave his post, his body tight. Gun already in his hand, anticipating the fight to come. "They're coming up here?"

"At least half a dozen." She told him about the call with Momma and what she'd said about Reggie.

He winced. "Not good. But you did the right thing. There was nothing you could do to help him."

She'd rather have a way to help him.

Sometimes the truth sucked.

"Nora and that baby are our priority." She grabbed the handle, knocking at the same time she entered. Nora held the baby in her arms. "You might hear some crazy stuff, and I might come in here and tell you to get down. But everything is going to be fine. Now one is going to touch you or Ellie."

Nora blanched. "She's here?"

Kenna wanted to reassure her, but she didn't want to lie. "She's here. Sit tight and wait for me. Got it?"

Nora gasped.

"And pray." Kenna shut the door.

A nurse raced over from their station, a long counter down the hall a bit. "What's going on?"

"We've got a situation here," Kenna said. "Security is aware, and they're taking steps to prevent armed intruders from gaining access to this floor."

"You're disturbing the patients with this...whatever it is." She waved at them, then gasped. "You can't have guns in a hospital!"

Ramon told her, "When armed gunmen show up on this floor, you'll be glad we do have guns, ma'am." He sounded exasperated, but Kenna actually thought he did pretty well keeping more pronounced irritation from his tone.

"It's not our intention to disturb anyone," Kenna said. "Just to keep our client safe."

"What about everyone else?" Another nurse by the station stood. "Are you going to keep us safe?"

"That's why the hospital has protocols, and I'm sure the police are on their way."

Kenna looked back at the nurse in front of them and saw a shift in her that didn't spell anything good.

"Shame they'll be too late to do anything about it." The nurse pulled a gun from the elastic at the waist of her scrubs and swung it up.

She was a Landry.

Ramon squeezed off a shot faster than Kenna could get her arm up. The round embedded in the nurse's forehead, and blood sprayed behind her, catching the other nurse in the face.

The bystander screamed.

The dead nurse hit the ground.

At the end of the hall, the elevator dinged.

Chapter Eleven

Two guys exited the elevator, both carrying weapons, and Kenna yelled, "Everyone get down!"

She and Ramon dragged over a couple of chairs and hunkered down, even though waiting area seats gave them no protection from armed men.

She knelt and held her weapon up with her forearms resting on the back of the chair. "Don't come any closer!"

The two men took cover behind the doorway, where the wider lobby area narrowed for a second where the doors had been wedged open. Just enough narrowing to hide behind— but only barely. Kenna still knew where they were, and if she had to take one out, she could get off a shot and hit her target.

"Give it up, Kenna!" one of the men yelled. "Is she worth all this?"

"The police are on their way!" she called back, ignoring the question. "Lay down your weapons, and no one gets hurt."

Their reply was a low chuckle. One of them called back, "Where's the fun in that?"

A nurse stepped out of a patient's room off to one side.

Ramon yelled, "Get back!"

But the curious staffer moved too far, and the gunman eased out from behind cover.

Ramon squeezed off a shot, wide so that it would only be a deterrent.

The guy grabbed the nurse's arm and dragged her back. He stepped out from behind cover, using her as a shield as he moved forward.

The woman screamed and fought him. "Let go of me!" She employed some choice language from her arsenal, giving some gusto to the way she expressed her displeasure.

The gunman seemed to find it amusing, even while he fought to keep her close to him.

She stomped on his foot.

Someone else started crying. A baby also cried, in tandem with the person. But the sound wasn't coming from Nora's room.

Ramon moved left around the side of the chairs they were using as a barricade.

Kenna kept her aim on the nurse and the gunman. "Let her go, or this will get worse." He had to understand. "You're digging a hole, and you're about to bury yourself in it! Is Momma really worth all this?"

These guys appeared to be more scared of her than they were of prison. Kind of like those kids she'd just seen, who knew what was going to happen to them if they were locked up.

That was why she believed it was a show of force meant to be a deterrent to anyone else who thought they could cross Momma. She might be able to handle losing five hundred thousand, but she couldn't afford to lose the respect of anyone who feared her—or should, but wavered.

The second man poked his head out from behind the wall. Claude Landry. The anger on his face gave her an indication how he felt about her questioning his mother to their associates.

Instead of engaging them further, Kenna simply squeezed off a shot. She hit his shoulder square on.

"Nice one," Ramon muttered.

She didn't respond. She'd said enough by taking that shot. "Give it up, Claude! You can stop this before you and your guys end up dead or in prison."

They couldn't possibly think they would get away with opening fire in a hospital. Or were these guys the sacrificial lambs in this situation?

Had Momma turned them over for a reason?

Kenna couldn't shake the feeling something else was going on.

Claude clutched his shoulder. "That baby is coming with us!"

The nurse being held at gunpoint whimpered, all her energy to fight gone now. She'd used it up in the initial attack.

"Let her go. Stand down!" Kenna shifted slightly, still covering Claude, who she considered the wildcard, while Ramon covered the nurse and the guy holding her. "Before this gets any worse."

She could see his face, and the change in him was visible. Determination suffused his features, and his mouth set in a hard line.

Don't even...

He turned, his gun arm coming around to point at her.

The other guy moved between Kenna and Claude, getting in the line of her shot. If she took it, she could hit the nurse.

"Ramon!"

He tensed, close enough she could feel it.

A door slammed open, and boots pounded the tile floor. "Drop your weapon! Hands on your head!"

Kenna turned and raced into Nora's room to make sure she was okay.

Two gunshots slammed against the door behind her.

It never closed.

She looked around but couldn't find Nora. The gunman with the nurse backed up from the cops, all the way into the room. Out in the hall, she could hear Ramon saying, "It's down! I'm not one of them. I'm private security!"

She had no idea where Nora had gone. The only option was a bathroom behind her.

The gunman spun. "Where is the baby?"

"Guess you're out of luck. She isn't here."

He shoved the nurse away from him and shot her.

Kenna started to yelp but swallowed it back. Before she could raise her gun and shoot him, he had his aim on her.

If she fired, they would both die.

"I've been shot enough for one lifetime. I don't really wanna get shot again." Plus, the more time she wasted, the more likely the cops would bust in here. Take this guy out for her.

"Guess you're out of luck," he said with a sneer. "Where is she?"

From behind her on the other side of the door, a baby started to cry. They had hunkered down in the bathroom.

The door from the hall crashed open so hard it bounced back and hit the wall. A cop in all black, helmet and vest, fired his weapon at the gunman. In the same second, Kenna rotated her gun in her hand, so it was pointed down, and then she opened her other palm. She didn't move.

He looked at the dead nurse, then at her. "Put it down."

She crouched slowly and set it on the floor. "I need to check on my friend and her baby."

The officer said, "Stay there."

He waved a couple more cops in, and they opened the bathroom door while Kenna remained where she was.

The guy in the front grabbed his radio. "Get Martinez up here."

Kenna frowned. "Is there something I need to know?"

"When your boss meets a famous investigator, word gets around. Now you're at two scenes in one day."

Nora whimpered. "Don't touch me!" The baby started to cry louder.

"May I?" Kenna pointed at the door.

The guy nodded.

She said, "Excuse me," at the door and eased around the two cops.

There wasn't much room in the bathroom with four people and a baby, but with Nora curled up at the base of the shower, holding her baby to her chest, they made it work.

Kenna crouched. "Good idea, hiding in here. You did good. You protected Ellie."

Nora held her baby, probably in too much shock to speak.

"Now it's time to go," Kenna said. "This place isn't safe anymore."

"It doesn't matter. They'll find me." Nora sniffed. The baby let out some breathy coughs, but the crying had waned.

"Even if they do, didn't I say nothing would happen to you?"

Kenna needed a safehouse, stat. But in a city where she had little resources, that was going to prove difficult to find and set up in time. What she needed was a team she trusted, and a location that was defensible. But could they keep protecting Nora while Ellie grew up? Exactly how long would Momma Landry keep coming after her before she gave up?

If this lasted years, they would end up feeling as if they lived in captivity. But what was the alternative?

Unless Landry was taken down.

Even then, could Kenna get Nora and her baby some kind of witness protection deal?

"Ready to get out of here and find somewhere safe?" Kenna asked. The girl did look exhausted, and a bathroom floor was no place for a new mother.

"I don't think I can get up." Nora winced. "Can you help me?"

Kenna could take Ellie, but Nora might not want to be separated from her newborn right now.

"Fellas." Kenna turned to the cops. "Can one of you lift her and the baby?"

One of them stowed his weapon right away, swinging it to his back on the strap. "I've got her." He looked like he wanted to do it, which was good because Kenna doubted her arms could handle even helping Nora to her feet.

Kenna stuck her hands in her pockets, just to take the pressure off her forearms.

It wasn't worse today than normal, but tension made it worse for sure. Time under tension on occasion got to the point where she could barely lift her arms for days. But it didn't happen often. She could keep it from happening soon by resting her arms now.

One cop went out first. The second carried Nora and the baby.

"On the bed?" he asked over his shoulder.

"For now," Kenna said. "But she won't be here long. It's not safe."

"Care to explain that?" Sergeant Martinez stepped into the room, and the lead SWAT guy shook his hand.

"You!" Nora gasped. "I told you not to come around me anymore."

Kenna looked at her.

"He was in here earlier, bothering me." Nora paled. "Your friend kicked him out."

And Ramon hadn't told her that. Though, she'd come running in because the gunmen were here. Maybe he just didn't get the chance.

Martinez didn't seem bothered by Nora's opinion. "Looks like you might need my help after all."

Kenna moved to Nora's side, which put her between the girl and the cop with the added bonus that it meant Nora couldn't see the dead nurse.

"Care to explain that?" Kenna paused. "After all, it seems like you responded pretty quickly. You were busy at a crime scene not long ago."

"And you were also at both scenes." Martinez shrugged. "So I guess that question goes both ways."

"We can talk when she's safe."

Martinez paused while the SWAT guys left, except for their team leader.

"I didn't catch your name." Kenna held her hand out.

"Parson." He shook.

"Ramon!"

Both men flinched, which was satisfying. When her partner didn't come in, she said, "What happened to my associate?"

"We'll get to him," Martinez said.

"Nope. Bring him in. I need him to help me guard Nora and her baby. Clearly, the threat level is so high it's practically out of control."

"Seems like we did okay. The threat is neutralized."

And more than one nurse was dead.

"The nurse out there, on the ground, was a Landry." Kenna glanced at the door. "Ramon!"

Finally, she heard back, "Kenna, they're arresting me!"

She zeroed her attention on Martinez. "Let him go and bring him in."

Martinez stared at her for a second, then turned and headed out the door. Parsons had an almost-smirk on his face.

Ramon came back in, followed by the police sergeant. "Thanks."

"You're welcome." She gave both cops her most unimpressed look.

Ramon swiped her gun off the floor and handed it to her, holding it with two fingers. Probably the only reason the cops didn't shoot him.

She holstered it back on her belt.

The baby let out a mew.

Kenna glanced at her. "We should have a doctor check you both out."

Nora said, "Are we leaving?"

"Do you feel safe here? Even if it's only for now, while we figure out how to keep you safe from the Landrys."

"Maybe in another room." Nora bit her lip. "Are they going to try again?"

"You tell me." Kenna wanted the girl's impression. The cops weren't interrupting their conversation, probably because they were giving these guys a bunch of intel just talking in front of them.

"She won't stop." Nora swallowed, shifting her baby closer to her chest. "She'll kill anyone to get Ellie."

"Just to collect on Garth's debt?"

"Mm-hmm. She's determined."

"Enough she'll sacrifice her sons to get you both?"

Nora nodded.

Martinez let out a grunt. "What did you get yourself into, girl?"

"Doesn't matter," Kenna said. "What matters is that Nora here can help you take down Momma Landry."

Nora flinched. "I'm not a rat!"

Kenna turned to her. "You wanna run forever, always looking over your shoulder expecting her to snatch you? You'll have to work from home and homeschool Ellie because just going outside will be too risky. She'll never be able to go to school, play at the park, or even be outside like a regular kid. It'll be dangerous."

Nora's eyes filled with tears.

"Unless you have unlimited funds for personal protection," Ramon said. "And even that isn't foolproof. Eventually, one day, Momma will get to you. Then what will you have?"

"I can keep you safe right now." Kenna was willing to promise that. "But neither of us wants to do that forever."

Martinez said, "For your baby's sake, this needs to be over. So she can have a life."

Nora stared at Kenna. "You're gonna leave me high and dry."

"You asked for my help. Unless you have the money to pay for me to protect you full-time the rest of your lives, this is how it works."

For a second, betrayal flashed on Nora's face. But the young woman knew they were all speaking the truth.

The SWAT guy, Parsons, said, "Ramon, isn't it?"

When he nodded, the two of them stepped to the side for a quiet conversation Kenna wasn't going to worry about right now.

"We have another problem."

She looked at Martinez. Given his expression, it was serious. "I'll have the doctor come in and check them both out. Is that okay, Nora?" When she nodded, Kenna said, "Let's step out."

It would give the girl time to think about what they'd said at least.

Martinez and Kenna went out into the hallway. It was a mass of people, mostly cops and some hospital staff. She spotted Clive, who lifted two fingers in a greeting.

Martinez said, "Friend of yours?"

"I'm just glad he's okay." She flagged down a doctor and explained that Nora needed to get checked out. She also needed to move rooms because there was a dead nurse in the room, but she wasn't to go far.

The doctor said, "If it's not high risk, then take a number. We'll get to everyone."

After she'd wandered off, Martinez said, "The whole hospital is in chaos. It's going to take hours to sort through what we're dealing with."

Kenna looked around. "It wasn't just this floor that got hit?" She'd wondered why only two of Momma's guys had come onto this floor. She'd been expecting them to come at her and Ramon from another side, more than just those. But it never happened. Instead, the cops had shown up first.

"One of the gunmen got out on the fourth floor and took out a patient and another person. Two people killed in cold blood. We aren't sure why, and we may never know if it was a hit or they were random victims. We took out the shooter."

Her stomach sank. "Was the patient Damien...something? Darn, I don't know his last name."

Martinez frowned. "Want to tell me how you can immediately tell me the victim's name?"

"He's dead? And the woman with him?" Assuming it was Camra Tenison that was dead. "When I spoke with her, she was wearing a bronze blouse."

He sighed. "The two of them were killed in a targeted hit, weren't they?"

Kenna nodded. "What on earth is going on here?"

Chapter Twelve

Kenna's phone rang, waking her from a frustrating dream where she'd been trying to stop Ramon from arm wrestling that cop.

She rolled over and looked at the clock. Two in the afternoon.

Between the police and reporters gathered outside, Kenna had passed through a gauntlet of people wanting answers to their questions. After a night in the Neonatal Intensive Care Unit—because they had buzzer entry, and it could be more easily secured—Ramon had relieved her.

Four hours of sleep, and she was still tired.

The screen of her phone said "MZ," so she swiped and managed to tap the speaker button.

She flopped back on the bed with the phone on her stomach, the speaker pointed toward her. "Yeah."

"I woke you. Sorry."

"Don't worry about it, Maze. There will be time to sleep later when we figure out where to stash Nora."

Maizie said, "Is she going to cooperate with the police?"

"I hope so. She might be our only shot at getting Landry

put away." Kenna rubbed her eyes. "Anything on the police band about Reggie?"

"You mean did they find his body yet?" Maizie sounded mad. "That's what we're talking about, right?"

"If I'd gone looking for him, I wouldn't have been at the hospital when those guys showed up to get Nora and Ellie."

"You didn't know that."

"I can only do what I can do." Kenna sat up in bed and leaned back against the wall. This was a conversation that needed coffee, but she'd have to get up and press the button to start the brew first.

Jax might have the right idea about a bedside single-serve setup.

Kenna sighed, looking around at her empty room. "Going head-to-head with her when I had so little intel would've been suicide. Look at what she's capable of."

Which, of course, sounded like fear.

She continued, "It's a lifetime of instinct. Years of training. More time working cases, taking jobs. I don't like that Reggie is suffering, or has, and now it's over in a horrible way, but sometimes life is horrible."

"I'll find out if he has any family. No one has come forward yet."

"Thanks, Maze." Kenna got up then, moving to the coffeemaker. She hit the button since she'd preloaded it with water and coffee grounds. While the coffee trickled down, she set the phone on the floor and did some warmup stretches.

"If you groan any louder, I'll assume you have food poisoning."

Kenna chuckled. "Anything on that surveillance video?"

"Right," Maizie said. "I was looking at that. And I did find something. But then I was just worried about Reggie and listening to the police band during the hospital incident, and I got distracted."

"Tell me what you've got."

Negotiating life with a teen wasn't easy at the best of times. Considering all Maizie had been through, she was amazing. But one of these days if she decided to "act out" or rebel a little against the advice that Kenna, or Stairns and his wife, gave her, then Kenna wasn't going to be surprised.

It was an entirely normal thing to do for any kid. Let alone someone like Maizie, who needed as much normal as she could get. She couldn't possibly be this reasonable and accommodating all the time.

"Two kids you saw," Maizie said, "plus the others I got from the surveillance outside, and the car they were driving. Although, it didn't have plates that I could read—so nothing on that."

"It had plates, though?"

"They must have covered the license plate number, or sprayed it with something that obscured it on the camera. So no-go on that. And it's nondescript, so there are thousands like it in the area."

"Okay, what about the kids?"

"My program scans their faces, and then scours the entire internet for matches. Unlike the police who are looking at local DMV and arrest records in order to find out who someone is."

Lying on her back, Kenna started doing leg raises, because the coffee was taking forever.

Maizie continued, "The group matched an account I found on social media. A platform mainly used to share video. They're talking about a recent score. Hanging out at a mausoleum and drinking."

"Underage?"

"Maybe one isn't. But the rest look too young for alcohol."

Kenna sat up, breathing hard. "So they're a crew."

"Probably the ones who have been breaking and entering all over New Orleans."

She climbed to her feet and stretched her arms, then grabbed a mug and poured her coffee. "Do you have names?"

"The account is under a fake name, like a famous person spoof account used to scam people. I'm watching all their posts to see if they mention specific names, or a school."

"Got it, thanks." When Maizie didn't respond, Kenna set her mug down. "What is it?"

"Don't they have families? It seems like they just hang out with each other, drinking and complaining about life. Why don't they go home?"

Kenna said carefully, "Maybe home isn't a good place to be."

"Do you think they're like me?"

"Not a lot of kids in the world like you, Maze. But they could be runaways, or kids in the system. They could have trash parents. Or they could be from nice families, and they aren't interested in the cookies and milk at home. They wanna express themselves by making dumb choices and learning the hard way."

She finished off her coffee and got dressed with Maizie still on the line, but silent.

Kenna was on the edge of her bed, tugging on her Converse, when the teen said, "Do you have anywhere Nora can go so the baby is safe?"

Kenna checked the rest of the notifications on her phone. "I'm still working it out. I'd like to get Nora and Ellie in the RV and drive them over to Pensacola. Maybe stick them in a nice hotel to rest up while we figure this out. She doesn't want to leave the area, though. She wants to be close to Garth."

Today, at least, they would have a clearer idea of whether Nora could go into witness protection. Kenna figured she wouldn't want to leave the father of her baby either. Unless the feds could also guarantee Garth a new name in another prison, and she'd be able to regularly visit him.

In that case, it had to be federal. Kenna didn't think the cops here would want to give it all up for the FBI or those ATF agents who were here to take down Landry. The local guys would want to take care of this local problem themselves.

"Families should be together," Maizie said, pretty emphatically.

"Find out who these kids are, then. So I can make sure they're safe." Kenna's phone rang. "I have to take this call."

"Bye." Maizie hung up.

Kenna checked her screen. A local number, and not one she had saved in her contacts. "Yes?"

"This is a collect call from Gauchet County Correctional Facility, from inmate—" The voice changed, noise in the background. A woman said, "Answer the phone." The voice changed again, and the electronic one said, "Do you accept the charges?"

Kenna shifted to the edge of the bed. "Yes."

A second later, it clicked through. "I figured it was fifty-fifty whether or not you'd pick up." Even though the voice had matured, there was no one else local who'd call her like this or start a conversation like that.

Kenna rolled her eyes. "It's you."

"Of course, it's me. Who else would it be?"

Kenna winced. "Can I help you with something, Lottie?"

"I figure you owe me. So it ain't help. It's repaying a debt." She paused. "I don't have much time, so here it is. My kid is mixed up in this B and E thing."

"You have a child?"

Lottie huffed out a breath. "Try to keep up. He's thirteen, and he don't need to be part of this business."

"How do you know he is?"

"Mothers know. And I ain't been all that maternal. I might've got my rights taken away from me a couple times, but that ain't the point. My boy is in trouble, and I figure since you owe me, you can go save him. Isn't that what you do?"

"How do you figure I owe you?"

"You know."

Kenna sighed. "Where can I find him?"

"There's a pawn shop on Hammersmith and Rye, just down from the liquor store. Start there."

The line went dead.

Kenna wanted to flop back on the bed and flip the covers over her head. She wanted to bury herself in blankets and forget this case ever happened. Tracking Garth had turned into a run-in with the Landrys. When Nora asked her for help, it turned into another run-in with the Landrys—one where people had died.

Given she had no proof the teens were responsible for the break-ins, the police had to do their own investigation into the youths and hopefully produce enough probable cause for a warrant. She wanted to help figure out how to hit back at Landry for murdering people in cold blood at the hospital.

Given the girlfriend had been killed while she was at the hospital with Damien, the wife might be inclined to offer more information. But how much did she know?

Kenna could get out and try to find Reggie. Maybe do surveillance on the Landry's places of business, or where they lived. See if she could spot him. Or follow someone and see if they led her to where Reggie was being held.

Or she could do what Lottie had asked and find her son.

You owe me.

Kenna got up, gathered her things and filled a hot cup. "There's nothing you can do about Reggie."

Still, his face filled her mind. Followed by an image of him broken and lifeless, the way Kenna had seen so many others.

She tugged out her phone and texted Maizie for a list of numbers that had called the bail bondsman's storefront. She gave her the approximate time Momma Landry had called to threaten Kenna with his life.

As if she would trade a baby for a man who had opted to risk his life to save the mother.

She stepped outside. The RV door snapped closed behind her, the sound loud enough she flinched. "I have issues. But what else is new?"

Outside, the sun beat down, even though it was fall. A trace of ocean breeze blew off the gulf, barely rustling the trees. The RV park had gained a lot more residents over the last day or so.

Where it had been almost deserted before, now it bustled with couples milling around fifth wheels. Tiny dogs being walked on their leashes. A family with little kids—at least four of them, though Kenna spotted one set of twins—raced by her on their bikes.

She was struck by the dissonance between this scene of sunlight and recreation and the world she so often lived in…

One filled with gunfights, newborn babies in peril, and murder.

Kenna could hardly process the difference. Light and darkness couldn't be more opposite. But the reason she did what she did was to keep people like the ones around her now safe from that world—the one criminals would rather not inhabit. Being reminded of good, law-abiding citizens and the lives they lived only made their actions clearer.

They destroyed.

Others chose to live.

No matter what, Kenna would do the work she did. Otherwise, a life was taken, a person was broken, and she would know she might have been able to stop it.

She always knew.

Kenna needed a way to protect Nora.

She tapped her finger on the steering wheel as she eased slowly down the lane through the RV park to the entrance. Before she pulled out, she dialed Preston's number. She didn't have Bear's direct line, but she had the boss's info.

"Lightwood."

"It's Kenna. Is Bear nearby? I need to ask him a question."

Silence greeted her. Then, "I saw you on the news."

"What did they say about me?"

"Surprisingly little," he said. "But it's clear you're onto something. Do I want to know?"

"Any idea who Momma Landry is?"

"No."

"Then you don't want to know, no."

He chuckled. "If you want to speak to Bear, I'll text you the address. You sound like you didn't eat breakfast, and I have something to show you."

Kenna sighed. "I don't have time to—"

"I'll see you soon."

The line went dead.

"Of course, you hung up." She rolled her eyes and pulled into the next store parking lot. She pasted Bear's address into her maps app and hit Directions. "As if I have time for this."

But she wanted Bear to tell her if he had anyone who could help them protect Nora, or even a local safe house. Assuming that wasn't where they had Preston.

The address was fifteen minutes away. She finished her coffee in the first five. Maizie texted her the number that had called the bail bondsman's store, but Kenna had already decided the police would've run the number. She doubted Momma Landry was dumb enough to use a number that led the police right to her.

Probably an unregistered phone she'd ditched right after.

Kenna pulled onto the street and got a look at the huge houses, three stories like something out of a picture book of the perfect residence. Whitewashed stucco and black shutters. Window boxes spilling out with flowers. Pumpkins on the front steps. Leaves that looked decorative, not like yard debris someone needed to clean up.

"I bet dogs don't even dare poop on this street," Kenna muttered.

Someone knocked on the passenger window.

She twisted around, startled. Already reaching for her gun.

Bear?

He mouthed something.

She hit the button to roll the window down. "What?"

"I was gonna ask the same thing." He shifted. "If you're done talking to yourself, park around back." Two taps on the roof of her car, and he walked away.

Kenna found an alley at the end of the street and pulled behind the residence. Back here were stone walled gardens and a row of parking spaces allocated by number. A blonde wearing a suit exited a gate and directed her with a wave to an empty spot. She had her hair tied back behind her head and couldn't be more than five two. Still, she could probably toss Kenna up in the air from the look of her. Which was probably the point.

In the second-floor window, a sheer white curtain shifted.

Kenna parked her car, grabbed her empty coffee cup, and went to the gate.

Bear appeared behind her, his movements completely silent.

"You know, I really just had a question for you," Kenna said. "I didn't need to come over."

"Right." He nodded. "But he still wants to give you his sales pitch for London again. Apparently, he really needs you."

"I've got a protectee with a newborn. Now isn't the time to worry about the next job."

Preston appeared at the back door. "We can talk about that, too."

Chapter Thirteen

Four hours after her discussion with Preston and Bear, Kenna walked beside the woman in the wheelchair, Ramon on her other side. They made their way along the edge of the hospital lobby toward the exit doors, headed toward a curb used for picking up patients.

"Let's wait right here," Kenna said, just inside the door.

The guy in scrubs pushing the wheelchair gave her a look but stopped.

Ramon went outside, where an SUV had pulled up. He stuck his head back in a moment later. "It's clear."

"Let's go." Kenna held the door and protected their backs as the new mom and her baby were wheeled to the rear door of the car. They were loaded in the back seat and Ramon got in the front passenger side. Kenna slid in behind the woman they were guarding.

As soon as the doors shut, the patient said, "I sure hope they bought it. This wig is itchy."

Kenna grinned. "I guess we'll find out somewhere between here and wherever we're going."

Allie, as she'd introduced herself, was the blonde who

worked for Bear. In the three years they'd supposedly worked together, they'd grown close enough the guy teased her like his little sister half the time and the other half treated her like the Marine she was—or had been for years. In turn, Allie stared at him like she couldn't believe he hadn't realized that she had feelings for him.

Maybe Miami Security International had rules against dating coworkers.

"Where are we going?" Ramon asked.

Bear held the wheel in a tight grip, his forearms flexed. "Nowhere near the safe house. We have a backup house that we're gonna burn. Unless Landry makes her move before then. But we're pretty sure it got leaked what route we're taking."

"Plenty of places to hit along the way." Allie tugged off the wig and pulled the bobby pins from her hair.

The baby lay on the seat beside her, a plastic doll.

Kenna stared at the boss. Team leader. Whatever he was. "It's weird seeing you out of a suit." She tipped her head to the side, studying Bear. "Also, at some point, you should tell me your real name, so I can quit calling you Bear."

Allie chuckled. "He likes it. But I doubt he'll admit that. Right, boss?"

That was what the rest of the team called him. None of them had let slip a last name, or first, or even a call sign. Apparently, they were going to keep her in the dark. Because he'd ordered it?

"I'll figure it out." Kenna pressed her lips together, trying to work out how she was going to get a fingerprint from something he touched. Or a sample of his DNA. "You know I have a tech specialist who could just look you up. Tell me everything to know."

"I thought you could do that on our website." Bear chuckled.

"Stephen Morris?" Kenna huffed. "As if that's your real name."

Allie snorted. "Maybe it is."

"Yeah, right." None of them had ever called him "Morris."

Okay, sure, it could actually be his real name. But it was more fun to pretend he had some secret past that meant he had to live under a false identity.

Ramon twisted around in his seat. "If we're choosing our names now, can I be 'Q'?"

"You wanna go by one letter?" Kenna asked.

"I'll sound like a gadget genius. Plus, it's faster to say in the heat of a firefight. Which you discovered."

"And it has nothing to do with the fact that anytime a cop or fed hears your name, they immediately distrust you."

Ramon just shot Kenna a look—which meant she was right.

"Change your name to whatever you want." Kenna shrugged. "But I'm not yelling out something dumb in the heat of a firefight."

Ramon settled facing forward. Probably figuring out how to drive her crazy by choosing something she'd have to learn how to say automatically under stressful circumstances.

"Look alive." Bear spoke into the mic on his collar. "All positions, we have contact."

Kenna desperately wanted to look behind the car at who was following them. Instead of giving the Landrys a clue that they were onto what was about to happen, she stayed sitting straight.

"Heads up," Ramon said. "There's a stoplight coming up."

"We have to turn," Bear told him. "Fifty bucks says they'll block us in the alley and try to take her by force."

"I'll take that bet." The two guys in front shook hands.

Kenna glanced at Allie, who rolled her eyes.

Seconds after they turned onto the side street, they found out Bear was right.

A freight truck pulled in at the far end and blocked their exit, except for the sidewalk on either side. One corner had a fire hydrant, so that side was out. Would Bear try to squeeze them between the building and the truck?

She turned to look back.

Through the rear windshield, she saw two full-size trucks pull in, each one up on a curb so that they blocked the sidewalks and street more effectively than the truck at the other end.

"We're boxed in," Kenna said. "Looks like they're getting out."

Momma Landry stepped out of the rear door on one of the trucks. She had no visible weapons, but the two men who climbed out and flanked her had pistols.

Bear turned to Kenna. "She might be luring you out, making you think she wants to negotiate, and then she's gonna kill you."

Kenna grabbed the door handle. "Let's find out."

"Wait for me." Ramon touched her arm.

Knowing what that meant, she held off for him to climb out.

He opened her door for her so she could straighten out of the car like a famous person or a dignitary. Was this what Preston felt every time Bear's team did it for him? No one was immune to the rush of power they got when someone else deferred to them, and all it did was corrupt.

Kenna was opening her own doors from now on.

Ramon followed behind her, watching her back as they approached the Landrys.

"You've paid a high price so far." Kenna stopped several feet from Momma Landry. "Is all this really worth sacrificing your sons? Your men?"

The older woman wore a denim shirt over a mustard-green T-shirt, a denim skirt, and tennis shoes. A cross hung from her neck. Given the lines on her face and the whisps of hair out of place, she'd had a long day. "I decide what price I'm willing to pay."

Kenna waited.

"Give me the girl and the baby."

"And in exchange, I get...what?" Kenna shrugged. "You're going to have to make it worth my while if you want to trade."

Better that this woman think Kenna considered herself one of those folks who had all their doors opened for them. That she didn't get out of bed unless someone made sure it was worth her while.

Kenna said, "You give me Reggie, and I'll think about it."

Momma laughed. "Too late for that."

"Where is he?"

"Nah," Momma said. "It'll be more fun watching you figure it out."

"Nora and her baby aren't going anywhere with you." Kenna lifted her chin.

Police sirens split the night air. Flashing blue lights hit the brick walls on both sides as cop cars surrounded the Landry vehicles at each end of the street. On the rooftops, armed officers held their aim on the Landrys.

Someone called out over a bullhorn, "New Orleans Police Department. Put your weapons down and your hands up. You are under arrest."

One of Landry's guys spun around, waving his gun.

A sniper took the shot. The guy fell to the ground. Momma didn't move after that, and neither did the rest.

Ramon smirked under his breath. "I can see the appeal of being a cop."

Kenna figured the power wasn't too far removed from the whole door-opening thing.

Cops swarmed the alley and an officer—one of the higher-ups—put Momma Landry in cuffs.

Kenna and Ramon watched while each one was arrested for their part in shooting up the hospital and the murder of four people. Two of the dead were innocent bystanders, and two had been specifically targeted.

But neither were connected to her case. Except for Nora and her baby being the subject of the same incident.

Was it really a case of two birds with one stone?

Kenna wanted to get in the interview room with Momma Landry and see if she'd answer some questions. Then she could find out if this woman had been paid by someone else to kill those two people—the guy in the coma and the girlfriend—or if she was the one who wanted them dead.

Instead, she stood there while the cops took away Landry.

Finally, the officer in charge came over. "As soon as we get that truck moved, y'all can head out. So long as I get a statement from you."

"Thank you, Captain." Kenna nodded. "We need to get back to our protectee and make sure she's safe."

"Understood."

Ramon said, "I'll move the truck."

Even though Landry was in police custody, Bear still took a roundabout way back to the house.

As they climbed out, Allie said, "Shame I didn't get to use my disguise. I was looking forward to wailing about my baby... before they realized she's plastic."

Kenna grinned.

Bear eyed Allied. "Let's focus on the job, shall we?"

"Of course, boss. Let me just change out of the new mom padding and toss this baby in a dumpster."

Kenna pressed her lips together to keep from laughing. Allie managed to hold it in while Bear stomped up to the house.

Even Ramon laughed. "He sure gets his undies in a knot."

Bear stood by the door. "You owe me fifty bucks, Ramon."

"Yeah, right." He stepped past Bear into the house. "She didn't take the baby by force. She wanted to negotiate. That means you didn't win the bet."

Kenna patted Bear's arm. "Sorry you didn't get to fight your way out."

"Yeah, it's a shame," Bear said the words with such a flat tone she had no idea how to interpret them.

Kenna just stepped inside Preston's house.

One of Bear's guys said, "Preston is in his study. The mom and baby are settled in the yellow guest room. Second door on the right upstairs."

"Thanks."

He continued, "Preston is ordering a crib, and a bunch of other stuff. I have no idea what it is. Ms. Thibodeau had a snack and some tea but requested soda. Allie, you're on dinner, right?"

The other woman paused, kicking off her shoes. "Right. It's in the fridge. Heat up the oven, okay?"

"On it." He spun and followed Ramon into the kitchen.

And just like that, Kenna and Ramon were rolled into the detail watching Preston—and now Nora and Ellie as well.

Kenna went to the study door and knocked, even though it was open.

Preston looked over. "Everything go okay?"

"It would've been hard to make it go better than it did."

"Good."

"Thank you for letting her stay here," Kenna said. "We'll try to make it as undisruptive as we can."

Preston waved a hand. "It'll be nice to have someone in the house other than me."

"Did she recognize you?"

The guy had done twenty years for murdering his wife, but maintained his innocence the entire time, and had found God in prison. He was famous enough that the team had to deal with people recognizing him when they were out.

Preston shook his head. "I showed her so she doesn't find out later and get scared. I explained my side of the story, but she was so exhausted from coming here that I kept it brief and let her get settled."

"Thanks."

"Don't worry," he said. "I'll collect on your goodwill."

Kenna chuckled.

Bear tapped her shoulder and eased by her. Given his size, that meant she had to get entirely out of the way so he could enter the room.

Kenna said, "I'll leave you guys to it." Then headed upstairs and gently knocked on the second door.

She heard a quiet, "Come in."

The walls had been painted a bright summery yellow. Floor to ceiling drapes had been drawn. The bed was wide, and Nora had laid her baby on a U-shaped pillow, so her head was supported. Tiny pink lips pursed in her sleep.

"She just fell asleep." Nora smiled adoringly at her child. "So we're good for at least thirty seconds, until she needs something."

Kenna smiled. She moved around to the opposite side of the bed, so they didn't talk over the baby and wake her. "Can I sit?"

Nora nodded, settling back against a stack of pillows beside the one nestling her child.

Kenna perched on the end corner of the bed. "How are things?"

Nora smiled slightly. "I have no idea. I'm okay right now, but exhausted. I'm too nervous to sleep. But I also want to lay here and watch her because I can hardly believe she's real. But I'm so tired."

"You're safe. Momma is in jail."

Nora absorbed that, but she didn't look convinced Kenna was right.

"It might take some time to sink in. But right now, all you need to worry about is Ellie."

"Thank you, Kenna."

She nodded. "We can talk more later, but if you're up to it, I'd like to ask you about something that happened at the hospital while those men were trying to reach you."

Nora frowned. "What happened?"

Kenna explained about Damien, who'd been in a coma, and the recent rash of local breaking-and-entering incidents.

"I've heard about those."

"Any idea who was behind them, or if they have to do with the Landrys?"

Nora hedged.

"Even a theory would be welcome at this point," Kenna said. "I haven't even started looking into the case. I just want to make sure I know if it connects to you or not. In case there's an element of your protection I'm not aware of." No one trying to guard a life wanted to be blindsided with something they hadn't known.

Nora shifted on the bed, her eyelids drooping. She fought it long enough to say, "I had a friend who was in a crew. Petty theft, but they would break into houses when people were out. They did it for years before they got caught."

"How long ago was that?"

Nora shrugged one shoulder. "Few years. We were in school together. He was in a foster home, like a group home. They were all kids who lived there." She let out a long breath, her eyes closing.

"Get some rest." Kenna patted her arm. "Don't worry."

As soon as that baby cried, someone in the house would be around to help out an overwhelmed young mother.

Kenna eased the door closed.

"Getting your baby fix?"

She glanced at Ramon, sitting on the floor in the hall. "She *is* pretty cute. You taking the first shift?"

He nodded, lifting a mug of coffee from the floor beside him. "Get some sleep yourself."

"Sure. After I go check out a mausoleum."

"Huh?"

"The kids' social media accounts," she said. "Bear will probably go with me. So don't worry about staying here. Someone needs to protect Nora and Ellie."

He shifted, then settled back. "Right."

Kenna smiled to herself. At the top of the staircase, she turned. "I won't be long. Keep an eye on them."

He nodded. "Keep telling yourself you don't want one."

Kenna trailed down the stairs. "I never said I didn't."

"I'll draft a press release."

"I'll tell them you lost a bet but won't admit it." She got to the bottom of the stairs, where Bear stood.

His brows rose. "Everything okay?"

"Sure. I need to run an errand. Wanna go with me to a mausoleum?"

"Instead of being on hand to accept a rush delivery of baby stuff? Yeah, I'll go with you to a graveyard."

Kenna grinned. "I'll even let you drive."

Chapter Fourteen

Kenna sat in the passenger seat finishing her drive-through fries. Stopping for something to eat had been a good idea. While she had only ordered fries and a small milkshake, Bear had eaten two cheeseburgers and a large fries on his own.

He glanced over at her. "So Momma runs some kind of B and E ring?"

"Nora told me someone she knew was part of it. Could be Landry is responsible for all the break-ins, or someone else took the idea and ran with it." She scrunched up the trash and stuffed it all in the bag, rolling over the top. Squeezing out the air. "Nora was pretty tired, and hopefully when she's more awake at some point—probably in about six months—I'm hoping she'll be able to tell us more. Maybe give us someone we can go talk to."

"Which is why you want to go check out this mausoleum, wherever it is? Because that's easier than waiting?"

Kenna wasn't going to argue with his assessment. "I won't be able to sleep anyway, wondering over everything going on right now. If we can't ID these teenagers, we need another way to figure out who they are." She reached over and dialed Maizie on the dash screen.

The phone rang a couple of times, and the teen said, "Banbury Investigations?"

"If you know it's me calling, why do you give me the business line answer?"

"How many times do you call me and I'm on speaker and you're with someone else? It makes us sound more legit this way. Not like you wear sneakers to work, and I live in a trailer."

Bear barked a laugh.

Through the open phone connection, Maizie said, "See! That's what I'm talking about. Someone is on the phone with you."

"It's just Bear," Kenna said.

Not that she thought the man in the car beside her was "just" anything. In fact, he was so broad that he had the driver's seat of her vehicle pushed all the way back. No one would be able to sit in the rear seat. His shoulders were so wide he filled the space on the other side of the car and made her want to scoot closer to the window. If the guy had never played football, the world had lost out.

"You sound like you're doing okay there, kid," Bear said, affection in his tone. "And for the record, very professional sounding."

"That's what I mean," Maizie said. "It's better than sounding like we have no idea what we're doing. Especially when the ATF is calling trying to find out where you are so they can connect with you about the Landrys."

"They called?" Kenna asked. "What did you tell them?"

Maizie let out a low sound. "Well, I actually pretended like I was the secretary. I put them through to Stairns, and he did the whole federal-agent-to-federal-agent thing. It sounded very impressive, but I have no idea what he was talking about. He said he told them you'd be in touch."

Kenna frowned. "He never said anything to me about it."

Bear glanced over. "Probably just giving them the runaround, and he has no intention of you talking to them."

Kenna wasn't entirely sure how she felt about Stairns making that kind of decision, but Maizie had likely filled him in on how busy she was right now. "Let him know I want to get filled in, please?"

"Okay," Maizie paused a second. "Are you going to the mausoleum?"

Kenna opened the maps app on her phone. "Only if you tell me where I'm going, so we don't end up walking around for hours looking for the right one."

Maizie had used the last name on the wall of the mausoleum that had been in the kids' video to ascertain which family it belonged to. From there, she had given them the name of the cemetery they were going to.

Now Kenna just needed the plot number.

All because she felt the need to walk around where the video had been taken, just in case she might find something that would tell her who the kids really were.

Bear said, "Just send us a screenshot of your map with an X to tell us where to find it."

That wasn't how Kenna and Maizie usually did things, but she supposed it was one way to convey the information.

"I can do that," Maizie said.

"Thanks." Kenna's phone buzzed. "Got it. Hanging up now."

Maizie sighed. "Do I need to remind you to be careful?"

"Call you later." Kenna hung up.

"Sounds like she's doing well," Bear said.

"Only way to go from when you last saw her was up."

Considering they had met in the aftermath of when Maizie had been abducted in Mexico. "Although it is pretty cute that she's all worried about us coming across as professional."

"Because you're looking to expand the business?"

"No," Kenna said. "That's why it's cute."

Bear chuckled. "What about Ramon? Seems to me like you've taken on a partner."

"I agreed to train Ramon for old time's sake, and because it's safer to know where he is and what he's doing at any given time. Otherwise, I'd be lying awake wondering what he's up to rather than wondering how I'm going to solve a case."

"So he's not necessarily joining your team?"

"Why, are you hiring?" she asked.

"If I was, Ramon wouldn't be the one I was considering inviting to join the company." He pulled up to the curb and parked.

Kenna waved off his last comment. "Working together would ruin our friendship."

She climbed out of the car and looked around at the dark cemetery.

Bear got out on his side. "And you know that because we're working together now, or because you put such high value on our friendship that so far has lasted almost three days?"

"When you tell me your real name, Steven, then I'll know we've reached a new milestone in our relationship." She pulled up the map on her phone, listening to him chuckle as he came around the car.

"It's a good thing I don't want to wreck our friendship."

She studied the map. "Is that what happened between you and Allie? You work together, so there's a line you can't cross personally?"

A look of pained distress flashed on his face. "We aren't talking about Allie."

"Got it." She'd been hoping to get him to open up about his colleague, but it seemed as if that topic of conversation wasn't on the table. "Let's go find this mausoleum."

He walked beside her, scanning the graveyard around them for threats. Constantly alert in the way only those who had been trained by missions—probably as part of the military—conducted themselves. That kind of situational awareness didn't even happen with police officers, who spent hours off duty. Rather, it was honed through deployment in other countries, with barely any downtime and the constant worry of impending threat.

Not that Kenna knew what it was like to serve in the military.

She turned to Bear. "Thanks for coming with me, by the way."

Kenna knew he didn't have much choice when Preston was the one who had decided they were also going to protect Nora. It wasn't part of their original contract that the company had signed with Preston, but she figured they were adding it to the job description now. Later, she was going to find out if Preston was personally footing the bill for this team to add Nora and her baby to the list of people they were protecting.

If he was, she would absolutely be offering to contribute. Preston didn't need to fund the entire thing, even if he wanted her to go to London in exchange.

Kenna didn't like being backed against a wall and paying fifty percent of what the company was charging for this protection job would give him less leverage to get her to take another job with him.

"I see it over there." She motioned to a limestone structure over in the northeast corner—one squat stone building in a grouping of mausoleums that protected the deceased from the soft ground of this area, where a lot of the graves had been buried above sea level.

No one wanted to see their loved one's casket floating down a river during a flood, but sadly it had happened.

"The groundskeeper is out by the look of it." Bear motioned with his head to the left. "I hear a golf cart."

"I see lights on inside."

Dim, flickering almost like candles. They were too far for her to figure out what was going on, but it seemed as if someone was inside the mausoleum they were visiting.

Kenna picked up her pace, determined to get answers from whoever was in there.

As she closed in on the gated entrance, she saw it had been swung open wide. The padlock and a set of bolt cutters lay beside the gate. The gaping maw of an opening that led to a place of death invited her inside.

With such strength that Kenna's steps faltered.

Bear touched her arm. "I can go first," he whispered quietly.

Kenna didn't want to seem like a chicken, but she nodded. They both drew their weapons, and he ducked to go inside.

"Hey!" Bear practically barked the word, loud and fast.

Kenna heard the scramble of footsteps, and then someone slammed into him, knocking him to the side. She braced, but whoever it was barreled into her as well. The tackle sent her back onto the ground, where she landed with a thud that shook the wind from her.

She gasped for breath, staring up at the ceiling.

A second later, she rolled over and looked at the person's retreating feet. She pointed her weapon at the person, but they were now too far away for her to shoot them. She would no longer be trying to defend her own life. She would be shooting someone in the back.

She rolled again and came up to sit, then scrambled to her feet. Putting her gun back in its holster on her hip. "Bear, you okay?"

He groaned. "That guy hit like a full-size truck." He shifted, slumped against the wall. Turning so she could see his front.

Kenna knew then how far she'd come when she didn't say a word she might have said several years ago. Instead, she swallowed what would have been a surprised expletive and rushed over. "He stabbed you?"

"Huh." Bear reached for the five-inch knife handle sticking out of his chest, high on his shoulder.

"Nope." She stayed his hands. "You aren't going to pull it out. That's like pulling out a plug."

Right now, they needed as much of his blood to stay in his body as they could possibly achieve.

"I'll call an ambulance" Kenna dug her pocket and pulled out her phone.

Bear shook his head. "No paperwork. Use my phone." He gasped, pain in his expression. "Call my people."

At least he wasn't pretending that he was fine, trying to be all macho.

She accepted the phone from him, finding Allie's name in his contacts.

"Just call the first speed dial, it's the on-call point person."

"I already found her." Kenna put the phone to her ear, listening to it ring. Regardless of their protocol, she knew the other woman would want to know what happened here. She glanced around, looking at the interior of the mausoleum, and nearly choked. "Holy—"

"Yeah, boss?"

"It's Kenna. Your boss needs a pickup because we've been here two minutes, and he's already been stabbed. He needs a hospital."

Bear said, "No hospitals."

Allie said the same thing, almost at the same time.

"Whatever you guys need to do, do it fast," Kenna said. "Because there's a dead guy on an altar in this mausoleum and I need to call the police. Bear doesn't need to leave any of his DNA at this murder scene. Both of you got that?"

"Is the assailant alive?" Allie asked.

"He tackled us and ran off."

"Get him outside and wait for me. I'm already on my way. I know you aren't going to leave a murder scene unguarded."

The call ended.

"Smart woman," Kenna said. "She didn't tell me to get you all the way to the road, because she knew I wasn't going to leave the mausoleum." She made sure Bear could stand on his own and left him against the wall. "I just need to check something."

She moved quickly but not rushing over to the altar, reached out with two fingers, and checked the victim's neck for a pulse.

Dead.

"We got here too late." And she knew already the victim's name. "It's Reggie."

Her heart sank, realizing that what she had feared had happened. But in one of the most horrific ways possible.

Reggie might have been determined to safeguard their way out by offering his life as a sacrifice for theirs. But he likely never imagined that the end of his days would come like this. Laid out on an altar surrounded by all kinds of bizarre objects and candles.

This almost looked like something ritualistic. Not like a man who had taken up a gun to protect an unborn baby.

Kenna rushed back to Bear, helping him walk as much as she could. They made their way up the steps, where she looked around for whoever had run off. "He was wearing some kind of robe, right? Or was I just imagining that?"

"And a pair of white sneakers."

"I guess it could have been a woman. But if it was, she needs to be on a rugby team."

She knew she had successfully distracted Bear when he chuckled. The sound quickly dissipated into a groan.

She said, "Sorry."

"Don't worry about it. Just let me pull this thing out. It's annoying me."

"It stays in, and it only gets pulled out by whoever you guys use for medical treatment. Hopefully not some back-alley quack."

"We'll take care of it." He winced.

"That's what I'm afraid of." She watched the street that ran through the cemetery, more like just a single-lane black-top. Probably more for the golf cart than any larger vehicle.

"You worry about other people too much."

"I'm not sure that's actually a fault," Kenna said. "But I have to say, it's a lot more inconvenient actually having friends than it was when I went months without speaking to anyone at all. Except whoever was involved with the case I was working."

"Welcome to the dark side."

"Don't tell me there's cookies. I don't even really like cookies." Except under certain circumstances. And given the choice between that and a brownie, Kenna would never choose the cookie.

"Now I know you're crazy. I should make you my mom's double chocolate chip. Those will change your mind."

Kenna watched a car speed into the graveyard and down the lane, stopping close to where they stood. "My mind doesn't need to be changed."

Allie raced over. "What is he being stubborn about now?" She pulled up short. "Whoa, that's a big knife. Let's get you somewhere we can stick you with a needle and make you feel all warm and fuzzy."

Allie got under his shoulder. "Thanks, Kenna."

She watched them hustle toward the car and dialed 9-1-1 on her phone. It took a while to explain what she needed once she used the words *dead body* and *murder scene*, but the dispatcher honored her request—at least to an extent.

She knew they had, because seconds after a black-and-white police car with flashing lights pulled into the graveyard, another car pulled in behind it.

An unmarked.

Martinez was here.

Chapter Fifteen

Kenna walked around the altar, observing the scene element by element. As useful as it was to take in the whole, it also proved worthwhile to study each piece of the puzzle on its own.

The air in the mausoleum chilled, as if all the warmth left with the life that had been in Reggie's body. Gone, now.

The protective booties over her Converse crackled on the stone floor. The only other sound in the room was the relentless click of the camera as the technician took scores of photos to be entered into evidence later.

Sergeant Martinez glanced around. "We'll lose the scene as soon as two detectives are assigned the case. So tell me what you see while we're still here."

"The bottom of his feet are clean, and his shoes are missing. So either they were removed when he was placed on the altar, or someone cleaned the body." Kenna shrugged. "Or he floated in here."

"They didn't bother to clean up the blood."

"Maybe that's the point," Kenna said. "There are some knuckle bones over here, but they don't look real to me. The candles are brand-new, and there is no way that knife is anything special. I'm pretty sure you can get that at Walmart."

"You're the one who saw the killer leave. You think this guy is legit, or some kind of pretender who staged the death to look suspicious?"

"I would have said ritualistic. But that's never been something I had a lot of experience with." She looked at Martinez. "How about you?"

"This is New Orleans," he said.

"So that means every murder has to be tied to some kind of black magic, at least depending on what month of the year it is."

"And, of course, I have a creepy blind medicine man as a confidential informant who I go to on matters of dark spirituality."

"Of course." Kenna might have rolled her eyes, but this wasn't really the place to do it. "So you aren't a believer?"

"Depends on whether it's my mother asking, or my priest, or what month of the year it is. Because if you mess with my observance of Jesus' birthday, we're gonna have words. But if you're talking about some kind of thing like when King Saul used witchcraft to raise Samuel's ghost from the dead, then that's another thing entirely."

"Okay." Kenna folded her arms. "So what do you think this is?"

"It could be an observance of ritualistic sacrifice. But then again, that's kind of cliché, don't you think?"

She smiled but let him continue.

"There are elements of voodoo observance that are a blend of Roman Catholicism and African traditions. So you have practitioners who might be almost indistinguishable from your average Catholic. Then you have others who utilize their beliefs to contact the spirit world."

"Doesn't voodoo have a bunch of different names?" Kenna asked. "Like hoodoo. Or Obeah."

"More like they are all different things in their own right. TV likes to get a lot of stuff wrong, or lump it all under hexes and dolls, potions and superstitious nonsense that gets good ratings because it sounds exciting. Mostly because it's all about some other culture, and what they are doing. We like to pretend that it's scary, when in reality the people that practice it would say it has nothing to do with anyone else."

Kenna said, "It's easier to control something if we can put fear of it in a little box. Fear can be exciting if it can also be controlled." That was what made murder shows so popular, true crime or anything to do with the bizarre. "Fear of something foreign we can't understand means we can pretend we're safe in our bubble, or more enlightened. More civilized."

There was a disconnect with fear when the subject matter was purely for entertainment value. It kept the viewer separate from the actual events and the impact they had on real people.

Even those predisposed to higher levels of empathy were only getting a facsimile of that emotion. A safe way to exercise feelings without ever having to meet the person whose life had been destroyed.

There was a sense of control and freedom in containing the fear of things a person didn't understand to situations that actually didn't directly affect them. Like a TV show or podcast. Once it was over, the consumer went back to their normal life.

Martinez shifted out of the way of the technician, motioning Kenna toward the wall. "Hoodoo is more about contacting your ancestors. Voodoo is about contacting the spirit world. But it's the same as with any religion. There are those who devote their entire lives to it, and there are others who are more just passive participants. Or casual observers."

"People can practice the same thing in different ways. Or they twist something for their own gain, in order to give them power over other people." Kenna had seen it. Usually in situations where she worked to rescue the victim.

But it was too late for Reggie.

She continued, "So it's not just all creepy ritualistic sacrifice. Surprise, surprise, reality has complexity and nuance."

He gave her a small smile. "And the investigation all depends on if you think you can bend the spirit realm to your will or not?"

"Because we're going to go contacting it to try and get a lead?" She lifted one eyebrow.

Martinez laughed. "I'd like to see that. But I also wouldn't, because I do believe it's very real."

Without a spiritual realm, Kenna's entire faith fell apart. So she had to believe there were both good and evil forces as part of the world. Things that were kept from people's physical sight by a veil that obscured the reality beyond it from regular everyday life.

Martinez continued, "I think people believe they can have power over it because that's what the dark forces want you to believe. It's just manipulation, and we're the victims. Like a great cosmic joke, but we're the punchline and it's not funny at all. But that's also what I was taught—drilled into me by my granny." He lifted a hand and crossed himself. "God rest her soul. She would have something to say about this. You don't mess around with dark forces."

Kenna had to say she agreed with that, but given how little she understood about the spiritual world, it felt too much like the thing she put in a box so that she could control her fear of it. What was it the Bible said? *Perfect love casts out fear*. Maybe she didn't need to be afraid of it, but it was still very much something worth being concerned by.

Especially when it cost someone their life.

A gasp erupted from Reggie's body.

Kenna spun around in time to see Reggie launch up into a sitting position. "Reggie?!"

Martinez yelped. The technician stumbled back and fell to the ground, landing hard on the stone floor.

Kenna raced over to the formerly dead man, reaching him just as he slumped back onto the altar. "What on earth?"

"I thought you said he was dead!" Martinez dragged her back and reached in, pressing two fingers to Reggie's neck. "He has a pulse!"

"Your EMTs came in here and said he was dead as well!"

Kenna wasn't the only one who had declared this man deceased. Now he was alive? This made no sense.

"Tell them to come back," she said, trying to catch her breath. "Maybe his heart rate was too low for me to detect with my fingers, but the EMTs checked his heartbeat and heard nothing. They had the doctor declare him dead."

"The medical examiner will be here in a minute. But we should probably get an ambulance to take Reggie to the hospital."

Kenna said, "You think?"

Martinez just shot her a look and radioed for an ambulance. After an excruciatingly long couple of minutes, the EMTs showed up to load Reggie on a stretcher and took him away.

Kenna followed the crew out of the mausoleum into the open air, dark but thick with humidity. Clouds obscured the stars, at least the ones visible despite the light from the nearby city filling the sky.

"Here come the detectives." Martinez motioned.

The man was abnormally skinny, and at least six two. The woman had a round figure and wore her suit in a way that flattered her fullness. Both of them had dark hair, but that was where the similarities ended.

The male detective said, "He isn't dead? I thought this was a murder."

Martinez sighed. "I guess it just got amended to an attempted murder. This is Kenna Banbury, she's a private investigator."

The woman's dark eyebrows lifted. "You have a private investigator consulting on this case?"

Another sigh. "More like she's a material witness."

Kenna shook both their hands, figuring the only reason why the New Orleans Police Department hadn't signed her on as a consultant by now on this mess of cases they had on their hands was a simple matter of finances. Most local departments would say they didn't want assistance from anyone, but it was also because they didn't want to spend the money even if it meant taking work off staff members' plates. Kind of like any job with a corporation where staff members routinely did more than one person's worth of tasks.

"Detective Byrd," the female officer said. "This is Detective Fisher."

"Nice to meet you both." Kenna nodded. The two cops from the Broadway Hotel, the ones interviewing that hooker... about Damien.

"You were the first on scene?" Fisher asked.

Well, that was where things would get sticky.

Kenna didn't want to get caught in a lie, so she said, "I was the first on scene, but I wasn't by myself. I had an associate of mine with me, but he had to leave. We encountered someone I presume to be the killer when they tackled us and ran out of the mausoleum. That was when we found Reggie."

Byrd's eyebrows rose. "Can you give us a description of the killer?"

Kenna shook her head. "Not other than that they were wearing a dark robe and white sneakers."

It might not help at all, but she figured they would have her look at sneakers to ascertain a brand and style at some point. At least, she hoped they would do their due diligence on every part of this case. Who knew what might prove useful?

She wasn't sure if she could actually help.

"Kind of coincidental, don't you think?" Fisher said. "You just happening to come out here tonight, right when the killer is working on someone you know?"

"Is that your way of asking me what brought me out here tonight?"

Kenna was pretty sure she heard Martinez snort, but she ignored it. There wasn't much funny about this, or even slightly amusing. She couldn't believe she'd thought Reggie was dead.

Because she had been thrown off by their getting tackled, and Bear being stabbed?

Now there were two men she needed to check on. Hopefully, neither of them had taken a turn for the worse as a result of their injuries. Only time would tell how Bear and Reggie recovered.

Even the EMT hadn't been able to find any signs of life from Reggie.

Did that mean the killer had given him some kind of substance, a drug or a medication, that slowed the victim's heart rate to such a degree that they appeared lifeless? There were substances like that which existed in the world.

"Very well," Fisher said. "I'll ask. What brought you out here tonight?"

"Despite my being connected to the recent arrest of Momma Landry, and bringing in Garth Sanders, I was actually here because of the breaking-and-entering crew that's been hitting houses all over."

Martinez turned to her. "What does this mausoleum have to do with the B and Es that have been happening lately?"

"We found a connection between the teens I saw at the hospital and this mausoleum."

"And the fact the latest victim was shot in the hospital during an incident involving you?"

Kenna shrugged. "I don't yet know how it's all connected. That's what I was here trying to figure out."

"You get that it's epically convenient, right?" Martinez pointed out what the rest of them already knew. Most of all her. "You seem to be in the middle of everything going on around here for the last week or so."

"As far as I can see, you wouldn't know that Landry connects to the breaking and entering crew without me. And a mother with a newborn baby would probably be dead."

"Reggie nearly was," the sergeant said. "And the guy isn't exactly a national treasure, but murders are generally considered bad."

"But without them," Fisher said, "Byrd and I would be out of a job."

His partner smacked him on the outside of the arm, but it didn't have much power to it.

Fisher lifted his chin. "Let's go look at the scene."

Byrd glanced at Martinez. "Sarge, you aren't letting her go, right?"

"Correct," he said.

Great. Another night where she wasn't going to be able to get any sleep, and Ramon would have to pull a double shift watching out for Nora.

"As long as you aren't arresting me," Kenna said. "Because that would be ridiculous."

Martinez eyed her. "The last thing I want to be accused of is being ridiculous."

Kenna glanced around, spotting that golf cart again. "We should talk to the groundskeeper before we do anything else. See if he saw the killer running away."

Martinez called over to the mausoleum, where Fisher and Byrd were almost out of sight. "Interview the groundskeeper before you leave. We'll see you at the police station."

The two detectives disappeared into the mausoleum.

Kenna turned to Martinez. "What makes you think I'm going with you to the police station?" He'd said *we*.

"If you'd like to give me the name of the person who arrived here with you, so I can corroborate what you say happened before I arrived, then maybe we can avoid you being questioned at the police station."

Kenna crossed her arms. "You can't possibly think I'm a suspect."

"The alternative is that you have been in the wrong place at the wrong time on more than one occasion this week. Enough that it's actually starting to look suspicious that these cases are unrelated to what you're working on...and yet happen to be repeatedly colliding with whatever it is you're doing at the time." He lifted his chin. "Besides, the ATF has been looking for you and you can talk to them there."

"Fine," Kenna said. "Give me the address of the precinct, and I'll meet you there."

Martinez chuckled. "It *is* fine. Because you're going to ride with me."

She glared at him. "The last time a cop wanted to give me a lift somewhere, it was so he could pull into a deserted area and murder me."

"I guess you'll have to take your chances. But given what happened tonight, the odds are on your survival. Even if for a while it was gonna look like you're dead."

"Too soon." Kenna walked ahead of him in the direction of his unmarked car. "In fact, forever will probably be too soon to joke about that."

Martinez opened the passenger door for her. "Good to know."

She lowered onto the seat.

A second later, shots rang out across the graveyard.

Martinez flinched. Kenna launched herself out of the car and tackled him, shoving him down to the ground, where she covered him while the gunfire continued.

Chapter Sixteen

"Is this what you wanted?" Martinez held out a dry erase marker.

Kenna was still jittery an hour later, and the fact he was as well made her feel better.

"Yes." She took the marker from him and went back into the conference room, where they had parked her and Martinez, along with a couple more detectives. A lieutenant, a chief, and two ATF agents who had shown up.

So far they'd had been updating each other on the shooting at the graveyard, as if it wasn't Kenna and Martinez who were the ones who had been shot at.

No one had seen the vehicle license plate, but the spent shell casings had been collected by Byrd and Fisher. Those two were only overseeing evidence collection. Which meant they were here, out of the way of the techs actually doing the job.

Kenna walked over to the whiteboard on the wall and started with Garth's name, since that was where she entered this picture.

Under that she wrote *Nora*.

Landry and her sons, and the gunmen she had encountered, came next. She drew an arrow from Garth to Landry and then from Nora to Landry. Next, she wrote down, *breaking and entering crew,* and underneath put the word *teens* and a question mark. Beside that she wrote Damien's name, and then Camra Tenison.

Martinez came over to stand beside her. "Who is that last person?"

Kenna pointed to Camra's name. "Her?"

He nodded. "Who is that?"

"I'm assuming she's the second person who got shot when Damien was killed at the hospital."

The room had quieted down, the noise of conversation dulling to almost silence.

Kenna looked around. "Who was the second shooting victim at the hospital?"

Martinez glanced at one of the other detectives. The guy looked at a paper in front of him on the table. "The medical examiner identified her as Mrs. Stafford, the patient's wife."

Kenna pointed at the name on the board. "Then we need to talk to Camra. Because she's Tenison's girlfriend, the woman from work he was seeing on the side. If the wife is dead and he's dead, she could have more information about what's going on."

The chief in the room pointed at the detectives. "Go find her. Bring her in to be interviewed."

"Yes, sir." They both left.

Martinez turned to Kenna. "Any more to add to this?"

"You tell me." She didn't want to explain that she'd eavesdropped at the Broadway Hotel when the police had been interviewing that hooker. "Did you find any other connections Damien had when you looked into his life?"

"Nothing about a girlfriend. We can follow up with any colleagues or other...associates...as well."

"You're the ones with Garth in custody, and with Landry and her guys in custody." Kenna eyed him. "You can't find out whatever from them?"

Martinez shrugged one shoulder. "Seems like you're doing pretty well investigating this all by yourself. Putting the pieces together and making connections we wouldn't have otherwise made."

One of the ATF agents, a guy with silver hair and the bearing of a former college football player, came over. "He's right. In just a few days, you've got a better grasp on Landry's operation than we've had in a long time. It took us months to piece this together."

"Have you at least tried talking to Garth?" Kenna asked. "He's in the county jail right now."

Martinez motioned to the boss. "So far we've been ordered to keep him in protective custody. Just to make sure none of Landry's guys get anywhere near him. It was decided that we would give him a few days to sweat, and then lean on him and get him to start talking."

The commanding officer nodded. "Not my call, but it's a solid one."

Kenna stared at her notes on the whiteboard. "It was a good idea making sure he's safe. My guess is that Landry will be coming for him now that Nora and her baby have slipped out of her grasp."

"Landry is headed for a date with a federal judge." The ATF agent folded his arms. "We are meeting with the US Attorney in the morning to figure out precisely what the charges are going to be."

Kenna wanted to make sure they had no plans to give that woman any kind of deal—or heaven forbid, witness protection

—in order for them to find out what she knew. It happened, thought. Criminals were often valuable enough that they could earn their way to a new life in a new city under a new name. But as far as she was concerned, a woman who came after a new mother in order to the profit off her baby didn't deserve any kind of concessions.

But all that mattered was Nora and her baby were safe.

Kenna turned to Martinez. "Any update on Reggie's condition?"

Martinez glanced at the ATF agent. "Montego. The bail bondsman." He looked back at her. "The hospital said he's still not conscious. They have no idea when he'll wake up. Or if. They're running tests to find out what he was given."

Kenna capped the marker. "Does that scene, and what should have been his death, match any other murders that you have had in this area over the last months or even years?"

The agent said, "I appreciate a serial killer as much as the next guy, but you don't need to go reaching for something spectacular when this is just your average dirt bag case."

"So you'd rather I didn't ask the question, and we potentially risk missing a lead we could have followed that meant someone else didn't fall victim to whoever this guy is?" Someone who would stab Bear on the way out, not even hesitating to plunge a knife into her associate. "Because you don't think spectacular happens all that much."

There were still innocent lives at stake.

Martinez crossed his arms. "I'll have admin pull up related cases, and we can see if there's something to your theory."

Kenna nodded. "That's all I ask."

The agent pointed at Nora's name. "Does Ms. Thibodeaux have any intel for us?"

"I've spoken with her a little," Kenna said. "She seemed to

believe that breaking and entering crew was something that has happened before. Possibly with someone she knows. As soon as I can get out of here, I'm going to follow up with her. If she's up for it."

Martinez studied her. "Aren't you worried that whoever shot at us is going to come back and try again?"

"We have no idea who it was, so what's the point in worrying?" Kenna shrugged. "They'll either try again and risk us getting a lead on who they are. Or they'll give up, and I'll be fine."

The agent shifted. "It really doesn't bother you that you have no idea who it was?"

"I'm going to wonder, but it's not going to keep me awake at night. I need my sleep if I'm going to track them down and bring them in the way that I did with Garth."

Someone chuckled. The chief?

"In the meantime," Kenna continued, "maybe you guys could interview Landry and her men and find out why she's been doing all this."

"What does it matter if we already put a stop to it?" the agent asked.

"Did we?" She wasn't so sure. "I don't think we did stop it."

"Either way," Martinez said, "there's a killer still out there. And someone took a shot at the police."

"Best-case scenario, Landry works for someone up the food chain and you get the recognition for taking them down. Worst case, you've already done all the work and she's in custody." Kenna stared at her scribble on the white board for a minute. "If she's behind all of it, then Landry is a fantastic strategist. After all, she used the attack on the hospital to try and get at Nora while at the same time taking care of an entirely different problem."

"The Landry's are known for being pretty isolated," Martinez said. "I would be surprised if they're working for someone else, but it's not out of the question."

The chief said, "We can talk to the prison where she's being held. See who she talks to and if there's any indication she's reporting to someone. Not just the visitor logs. But whoever she associates with in the prison could prove useful."

"Where is she being held?" Kenna asked.

The ATF agent chuckled. "Why? You wanna go in undercover?"

"That would be problematic, considering she's seen my face." But if they were going to do that, Allie might fit the bill. If Bear's colleague wanted to take the risk of doing a job for law enforcement.

As far as Kenna was concerned, the cops or ATF should have someone who could go into the prison and try to make friends with Landry—find out who she was working for, or what her end game was. But that would take time. Undercover operations relied on someone getting into the target's good graces first, building that relationship, and then reaching the point where trust had been established and information began to flow.

Martinez said, "She's in Gauchet County Correctional." Kenna must have reacted in a way that was noticeable, because he said, "What?"

"Nothing," she replied.

Other than the fact she knew someone in that facility. Someone who might be able to get close to Landry faster than an undercover agent could. But that would mean Kenna owed her even more than she already did.

She still needed to find her friend's son. Make sure he wasn't involved with all this.

Pull his butt out of the fire if he was.

"If it was me," Kenna ventured, "I'd go through Momma's lawyer. See what she wants and if she'll talk. But I'd start with Garth and Landry's guys first, see who breaks. Then I'd hit her up as a last resort."

The chief nodded. "Let's make that happen. And Kenna?"—she turned to him—"I'd like to hear more of what this Nora person has to say about Landry and the breaking and entering crew. Before they hit the next house."

"Any idea when that might be?"

If there had been a series of these incidents, then the police must have an idea how long the crew went between jobs. At least, she would have figured that out if it was her case.

"They seem to be going at least a week between jobs. Sometimes more." The commander glanced at the ATF. "I also want the girlfriend interviewed." Then he headed out of the room, leaving the door open behind him.

Martinez turned to her. "You'll keep me updated with what this Nora person says?"

Kenna nodded. "Let me know if Reggie wakes up. I want to speak to him if I can."

"That's a good idea," the special agent said. "We will take point on working out who Landry's associates are."

Kenna said her goodbyes and headed for her car, hoping that she didn't betray the fact she knew someone in the same jail as Landry—today or in the future. Though today, those guys might just write off her reaction to the facility name as being related to the shooting. So maybe she didn't need to worry that much.

It was her business that she planned to keep to herself, along with how she and Lottie had met in the first place.

As soon as she slid in the front seat of her car and turned the engine on, Kenna called Maizie.

"Are you okay?" the teen asked.

Kenna frowned at the dash screen. "Do you have my heart rate connected to some kind of tracker?"

"If I did, I'd be even more freaked out than I usually am that something happened to you. Right?"

Kenna pulled out of the parking lot, smiling to herself. "I'm not going to say nothing happened, but I am okay."

"I've been digging a little more into these kids and their social media accounts."

"Would you conclude they are the crew that is committing all these robberies?" Kenna changed lanes, heading for Preston's house. She decided to go a roundabout way in case she was being followed by whoever had taken that cheap shot at her and Martinez.

"I have enough for you to pass to the police," Maizie said. "There's a video of them in which you can clearly see an item that was reported stolen from one of the first robberies. So they have, at least at one point, been in possession of something taken, even if they aren't specifically the ones who broke in and stole it."

"I'll give you an e-mail address for Sergeant Martinez, and you can pass it along."

"Do you want me to do it anonymously, or would you rather establish some additional goodwill with the department?"

If the e-mail with the evidence came from Kenna's business account, it certainly would make strides for them in earning more trust from the department.

"Send it from me," Kenna said. "Since we aren't saying it's for sure these kids, but it at least gives them intel they can move on."

"Okay," Maizie said. "Someone at the police department might be able to ID them where I haven't figured out who they are because none of their personal information is on social media. It's just a bunch of fake accounts and videos of them goofing off."

"There is someone whose name I want you to run." Kenna wasn't sure how much she even wanted to explain to Maizie. She gave the teen only the boy's name, and nothing else.

"Got it," Maizie said. "Who is this?"

"It might be the name of one of them. But I'm hoping it isn't, and either way I just need a wellness check on this kid."

Would Maizie accept that it was simply a favor for an old friend?

"Okay, I'll see what I can do to find him."

"Thanks," Kenna said. "I just need to know where to look."

"Because you're locked in to solving this breaking and entering case?"

"Not officially. At least for now, Ramon and I are protecting Nora and Ellie. As part of that, it's worth finding out what else Landry is up to. Then we'll know for sure that no one else is going to come after them in the future."

"Have you thought about talking to Garth?" Maizie suggested. "He might be able to shed some light on all of it."

"That's what I told the police. He will at least be able to corroborate what Nora says."

"You think she might not be telling the truth?" Maizie said. "Or hiding something?"

"I'm not sure yet. I want to talk to Ramon and see if he has a read on the situation."

"What about whoever stabbed Bear?"

Kenna smiled. "The list of open items is getting long. That's my other reason for going back to the house. I want to check if he's okay, but I also want to find out if they're all in on finding this guy."

"Because they're gonna be upset that their boss got hurt?"

"I am, and I don't even work for the guy."

Maizie sighed. "I almost feel sorry for whoever it is when you catch up to them. I don't think they realize who they messed with."

Chapter Seventeen

As soon as Kenna got out of the car, she spotted Allie. She clicked the locks on her vehicle and pocketed the keys, then made her way to the back gate, where Allie met her on the sidewalk.

"How is he?" Kenna asked.

"Tell me again how he got five inches of a blade inside his shoulder?"

Uh-oh, she wasn't happy. And aside from that, Kenna hadn't told any of these guys anything about what happened. "He was in front of me, and the killer ran at us, too fast for him to react."

"Of course, there was time." Allie huffed. "Otherwise, he wouldn't have taken that blade for you. And he managed to get it in his shoulder rather than somewhere vital."

"Good point." Kenna wasn't sure what else to say. "Did he get stitched up?"

Allie nodded. "Fifteen stitches, some of them inside and some of them outside. Did you get what you needed from the scene?"

"We did. And the police are still processing it. After the drive-by, we had a meeting at the police station."

Allie flinched. "Did anyone get hit?"

Kenna shook her head. "It's all good."

"I'll let you go inside." The other woman wandered off, disappearing into the shadows between the trees.

Kenna let herself in the back door. A yellow glow came from the living room, and soft music played somewhere in the kitchen. The air inside had a faint hint of something spicy, and she hoped there were leftovers in the fridge.

She found Ramon reclining on the sofa, wearing a pair of shorts but no shirt, with his eyes closed and the baby asleep on his chest. A pistol lay on the coffee table in front of him. He cracked one eye open, evidently not completely asleep and aware she was in the room. He lifted two fingers and waved at her.

"Are you good?"

"As long as the baby doesn't wake up again," he whispered.

"Need anything?"

He shifted slightly on the chair and adjusted his hold on the tiny baby. "I'm good."

Kenna stared at them a second longer. She never would've expected him to be like this around a child. And yet, at the same time, she wasn't surprised at all.

She walked over to Bear, who was perched on a stool at the breakfast bar. Laptop open in front of him, trying to type one-handed.

"Need some help with that?" Kenna asked.

"Nah, I just need to go to bed soon. But if I do that, I'll end up taking a pain pill."

She checked the fridge and found a container of leftovers, which she stuck in the microwave to reheat. "Let me guess, you put off taking pain pills because they make you groggy and you don't like feeling out of it."

"You too?"

Kenna shrugged. "Did you get a look at his face?"

He shook his head and didn't comment on the fact they'd had this conversation.

"Yeah, me neither," she said. "How have things been here?"

"The baby cried for like two hours, and Nora asked for us to get some formula and bottles. She has an appointment tomorrow with a pediatrician, but I also have someone who can come here for that if it's decided that she shouldn't leave the house."

"Where is she now?"

"She took a bath, and Allie made sure she didn't stay in there so long she fell asleep." He smiled a little. "Allie said she was falling asleep brushing her hair, so we got her settled and Ramon took over watching the baby."

She glanced toward the living room.

Bear lifted his chin. "I guess your friend doesn't mind being on babysitting duty."

"After everything we've done together since we met last year, this probably seems like a vacation."

"I know what you mean." Bear smiled full-out.

Kenna pulled her dinner out of the microwave and stirred the spicy rice dish with a fork. "How have things been going with Preston's protection? Any sign of the brother-in-law?"

"We found indications online that someone might have been hired to come after him. We sent the information to a particular friend of yours at the FBI, so he can pass the tip to whoever needs to know."

"Huh, good idea." Kenna dug into the food. Two bites later, she said, "Who made this? It's amazing."

Bear smirked. "I guess you will have to come to London with us and find out."

She shook her head. "Nice try."

He laughed aloud. "You're really writing off the whole thing?"

"Not so much. I could, and it depends if the timing works, but it's not something I can think about right now when someone could hit this house at any moment. Or we're walking around a graveyard, and you get stabbed."

"Good point," he said. "If anyone does hit this house, you don't need to worry. We've got it covered."

Kenna wasn't sure she would be so certain if she was the one in charge of the protection detail over this house, but she also didn't know all the ins and outs of the work Bear had done over his lifetime. Who knew what missions or operations the guy had been on. Then again, maybe he had zero military training. Maybe he'd been a fed the way she had, or a cop.

Either way, however it shook out, she was grateful they had the skills. "I appreciate knowing you've got it covered."

"You're headed out again tomorrow?"

"I have no idea," Kenna said, "but I need to talk to Nora whenever she wakes up."

"She's been pretty closemouthed. Don't get me wrong, she's polite enough. But she's keeping to herself, and so far Ramon is the only one who's been allowed to hold the baby." Bear shrugged. "Not that I know what that means."

"All the more reason to talk to her. Maybe she's just wary." Kenna shoved another bite of rice in her mouth, finishing it off. "I can make breakfast sometime. Unless you've got some kind of rotation going."

"You wanna pitch in? We'll take it."

"Take that pain pill and go to bed. You look awful." She turned and headed to her room.

As she threaded through the house, she heard him laugh and say, "Yes, ma'am." Hopefully not so loud it woke the baby, or anyone else.

When she woke up the next morning, Kenna rolled over and spotted her phone beside her on the bed.

She must've fallen asleep in the middle of a conversation with Jax. He'd been at home for the evening, working out in the fitness center at the townhouse complex where he lived.

She was still wearing her clothes from the day before. She sat up in the bed, her senses reaching out for the unmistakable earthy smell of coffee drifting through the house.

She sent Jax a text and took a quick shower before changing into fresh clothes.

What she wanted was a picture of Ramon holding the baby that she could send to Maizie and Jax, but she hadn't thought of that last night.

On her way down the hall, her phone rang. Sergeant Martinez was calling.

"Kenna Banbury." She stepped into the kitchen, and one of Bear's guys pointed at the coffee pot, leaving the room with his own full mug. She lifted her chin and mouthed, *Thank you.*

"Hey, I spoke with the girlfriend, Camra Tenison," Martinez began, "and she's willing to talk to me this morning. She mentioned you spoke with her at the hospital, and I think you should come along. I think she'll open up more if there's a familiar face there."

"I can meet you soon. I still want to touch base with Nora this morning as well, but it depends if she's awake yet." Kenna grabbed a coffee mug.

"You're staying in the same place that she is?"

"That tends to happen on a protection detail." Kenna

looked for some milk but gave up before she found it and sipped it black.

"I'm supposed to meet Camra in an hour. I can pick you up."

Kenna didn't have enough coffee in her to figure out a neutral place where he could swing by and get her so that he didn't find out where the house was. It put too many people in danger if others knew where the safe house was.

She simply said, "I'll meet you there. Tell me when and where."

"I'll text it."

At least he didn't argue with her suggestion.

"Got it." She ended the call and drank her coffee, watching out the window at the backyard area. A strip of grass with the walkway cutting down the middle of it, which led to a brick wall with an arch over the gate. Beyond that were the parking spaces.

She kept drinking coffee and stared out the window, waiting for her brain to kick in.

Only a trash truck disturbed the quiet morning air, the rattle and thump of each can being dumped into the opening overhead. Then the engine revved, and it headed for the next can.

Ramon wasn't in the living room. She knocked on his bedroom door and eased it open, finding two twins, which were both occupied. One had a very sleepy Ramon laying there with a pillow over his head, the tattoo on the back of his shoulder visible. Bear slept hard on the other twin, neither of them even stirring as she took them in and then left them to their rest.

She knocked quietly on Nora's door and heard, "Come in."

The baby lay on a blanket on the floor, close to where

Nora sat with her back against the bed—looking completely exhausted, as if she could burst into tears at any moment.

Kenna wanted to sit beside her shoulder to shoulder, but she also wanted to see the young woman's face while they talked. "I can get you some coffee if you'd like?"

Nora shook her head. "I've never liked the smell of coffee. And I already had a soda, thanks."

"How are things going?" Kenna settled on the other side of the blanket, crossing her legs in front of her. She had opted for black stretchy pants that looked like nice slacks with poor excuses for pockets, and a T-shirt which meant the scars on her forearms were on full display.

"I have no idea." Nora let out a breath and rolled her eyes. "I think that might be normal, but I have no idea about that either. I've been watching a lot of videos online about new moms. Most of it's gross, half of it is terrifying, and the rest just tells you to take a nap every time the baby does."

"That's more than I know about childbirth." Kenna took a sip of her coffee. "But as far as I can see, you've been doing great."

"I get the idea other things have happened since I showed up, but no one has filled me in."

Kenna nodded, starting with what Nora already knew. "Momma Landry is in jail, and won't be getting out anytime soon. Most of her guys also got arrested. There's a chance some stragglers are still out there, but as far as we can tell, the bulk of her operation has been shut down."

Unless, of course, Nora had any intel to offer about Landry's operation. But the first indication of that would come from her reaction to what Kenna had just said.

Nora visibly shuddered. "I hope she just tells everybody to leave me alone. Hopefully, she'll be too busy dealing with lawyers and attorneys to worry about coming after us." She touched her baby's head, smoothing the dark hair back.

Were babies usually born with hair?

Kenna didn't think it was common, but it was cute.

"Would you be able to give me any information on the reach of her operation? I just want to make sure there won't be any surprises if there are more of her guys than we knew. I wouldn't want to leave anyone still out there." She could tell Nora about the gunman last night, and about Reggie almost being murdered. But those weren't things this scared young mother needed to worry about if she didn't have to.

"I mean, if you have photos of people involved, then I can tell you if I know whether they're connected to her or not. But I thought after the hospital that you arrested them all."

"The police definitely got a lot of them," Kenna said. "Maybe even just some known hangouts would be helpful. I only know about that bar in the bayou."

"She has a chop shop on the west side of New Orleans. I'll find it and send you the address. Other than that, there's maybe another bar on the edge of the city. But I think maybe that got taken over by another gang, because I heard Garth talking about it on the phone."

"I'll take both addresses if you're willing to give them to me. Thanks."

"You saved our lives, Kenna. I don't think we're ever going to be able to repay that." Nora's eyes glistened with tears.

"You take care of that baby, and we're even."

Nora sniffed. "Okay."

"And tell Ramon or me if you need anything, okay?" She gathered her coffee cup and gave the baby a kiss on her forehead.

"I will."

Kenna ate a banana while she refilled her hot cup with

fresh coffee and a splash of milk. She gathered some snacks for just in case and left a Ramon a note. Then took a detour via a drive-through and grabbed a breakfast sandwich before heading to Camra's house.

On the way, she connected her Bible app to the speakers in the car, listening to the daily reading. At least trying to attempt to start off today with some kind of anchor. Giving her thoughts the rest and reassurance that she didn't have to handle all this on her own.

After all, in the middle of total chaos and confusion—and more cases than she knew what to do with—she didn't have much else to keep her grounded. For years, she had relied on her strength and skills to keep her alive. Lately, she had a much deeper and wider source to draw from, and the contentment that gave her was something she had needed to get accustomed to.

Somewhere deep inside, she knew she was avoiding the issue of the phone call she had received from Gauchet County Correctional Facility. That part of her past wasn't something she wanted to revisit, kind of like a lot of the rest of it. But before this was over, she may very well have to dig all the way back into one of the darkest parts of her childhood.

Right back to where this particular nightmare began.

Kenna turned off the main road onto a side street in the residential area where Camra lived.

Her engine sputtered and then died, clicking as she coasted along with no power. She stared the car off to the side of the street and managed to park it before she lost all momentum.

She turned the key, but nothing happened.

Chapter Eighteen

Kenna shut the passenger door of Martinez's car and waited on the sidewalk as he rounded the hood. "Thanks for picking me up." She looked at the time on her phone. "Hopefully, the mechanic won't take too long diagnosing the problem."

Waiting for a tow truck to arrive was always the longest part of breaking down.

Thankfully, Camra hadn't planned to go to work today, so she could wait for them to arrive. Now it was almost three hours past the time they were supposed to have shown up, and they were only just getting here.

"You wanna take the lead here?" Martinez said.

Kenna shrugged, approaching the front door. "Sure, but you're the only one with a badge in this scenario."

"Funny," he said, "I thought you were the only one who forgot that."

Yeah, real funny.

Kenna rolled her eyes and knocked on the front door. The young woman who opened the door wasn't the same person she had met in the hospital. Now she wore yoga pants and a tank top, her face free of makeup. Her eyes red rimmed.

Camra led them into a modern townhome that she had decorated with bright-colored fabrics, dark wood, and vibrant artwork with a Latino style to it. "We can sit in here." She gestured to a sitting area with a slimline sofa and single chair with wood arms.

"Thanks." Kenna chose the end of the couch near the chair, which Camra took. Martinez came and sat on Kenna's other side, so she was between the other two. When she'd settled, Kenna said, "How are you doing?"

Given all this woman had lost in the last few days, Kenna didn't want to express her gratitude that the lady she had spoken to at the hospital was alive.

Initially, she had assumed Camra to be the second victim of the shooting. The fact it had actually been Damien's wife who was shot along with him wasn't necessarily something to be grateful for, considering those two had at one point worked to build a life together. Then again, Kenna could be grateful for the fact the two of them didn't have children.

None of it softened the blow that Camra had lost someone dear to her.

The young woman shrugged.

"I can say from experience that grief can be a surprising thing," Kenna said. "At some point, you'll feel like you're doing better. But then it'll hit you all over again and feel as fresh as when you found out."

She spotted an empty wine bottle and dirty glass on the end table, beside the lamp and Camra's phone. Behind all that was a framed photo that looked like Camra and an older couple who had to be her parents.

She leaned toward Camra. "Is it okay if we ask you some questions about Damien?"

Camra reached for a tissue, tugging it from a box on the coffee table. A couple of tissues lay next to the box, bundled up on the table. "It'll be a nice change from all the texts, emails, and DMs I'm getting from people who knew Damien's wife."

Martinez said, "Are you being harassed, Miss Tenison?"

"Apparently, I'm a homewrecker who should be grateful that they're dead so I can change my ways and live right next time." Camra winced. "I don't think that one was from one of his wife's friends. They have been a little more strategic about how they're coming at me."

"If you allow the police department access to your messages," he said, "we can work to put a stop to it."

To his credit, Martinez seemed genuinely concerned that she was being bothered in a time of grief. In that way, he earned a little more of Kenna's trust and respect. And, the world needed as many cops like him as it could get.

She dabbed an eye with the tissue. "Right now, I'm just ignoring it. My parents are coming over later, and I figure it will die down eventually."

Martinez shifted on the other end of the couch. "Even so, please let me know if you'd like assistance."

After Camra nodded, Kenna said, "We talked a little bit at the hospital, but I was just wondering if you've had any time to think about how Damien was in the few weeks before the break-in."

"I've been trying not to think about what you said. It's easier to I believe it was a random horrible tragedy, rather than some kind of malicious targeted attack. But I also don't need to bury my head in the sand."

"It's smart for you to at least be aware of what's going on." Kenna needed her to understand the issue here could be more complicated than ignoring her phone. "Given the manner of their deaths, it's more than likely that the break-in was a targeted attack and someone came back to complete the task."

Kenna didn't want to say *finish them off* because she was trying to be at least somewhat diplomatic about this. "While I don't believe you're in danger, it's possible you might be able to aid the police in their investigation."

"How would I do that?" Camra asked.

"Was Damien under any kind of stress at work, or in another part of his life?"

"Only the usual. A few months ago, there were some budget cuts, and the city combined a couple of departments into one, and Damien is over all of it." Camra leaned back in the chair and sniffed.

While she was talking, Kenna looked around the room. Books and DVDs had been lined up on a shelf beside a Bluetooth speaker. The TV hung on the wall. A rolled-up yoga mat rested beside the white TV unit, which had a couple of candles on it. The fact they looked similar to the ones on Reggie's altar wasn't a connection Kenna needed to make.

She turned back to Camra. "So he had a shift in his responsibilities at work?"

"Now he oversees the entire floor. Or he *did*." Camra sounded proud of him. "Not the department I work in, but I still saw him all the time at work. And I heard what other people said behind his back. I guess now I'm hearing what they said behind both of ours."

Kenna shifted on the couch. "So there were disgruntled city employees where you worked. Did any of them have a grudge against Damien because he was their new boss? Maybe someone who was passed over for promotion...or lost their job?"

Camra frowned. "The manager over buildings and

permits was let go when Damien took over that department and social services. But I had heard it wasn't because of the budget cuts, it was because he'd been inappropriate with one of the other men in the office."

"Can you tell me his name?" Martinez asked. When she did, he wrote it down in the notes app on his phone.

Kenna said, "Did Damien leave any of his belongings here?"

Camra nodded. "I don't know who to give his clothes to. Or if anyone will even want them. But he had a couple of things here from when he stayed over, when his wife went away with her girlfriends a month ago."

"Anything else? Electronics...or otherwise?"

"I think he had a tablet that was here, in his duffel bag. He mentioned it after I told him I had that migraine. I was going to give it to him at work."

"The police department would like to have the tablet, Miss Tenison. It could be important for our investigation." Martinez was about to jump out of the seat at the prospect of new leads to explore. "Along with anything else that belonged to Damien, whether or not you consider it relevant."

Camra looked a little shocked. "You want to take everything, even his toothbrush?"

Kenna wasn't sure this woman necessarily wanted to keep that for posterity. It was simply that the toothbrush was the first thing that came to mind.

"It's hard to say what's relevant." Martinez paused. "It's much better that we have everything than risk something being missed which could lead to finding Damien's killer."

"I'll go get everything I have." Camra rose out of the chair as if she was significantly older and less active. She disappeared into a back room.

As soon as she was out of sight, Martinez leaned over. "She opened up to you."

Kenna shrugged her shoulder. "I don't know about that. It might not even produce anything relevant."

If she'd come on her own, she would have that tablet and be able to get Maizie to access it. As it was, the police department would likely have to figure out a way past whatever security features Damien had placed on it. No one had a device these days that they didn't lock with some kind of pin code, or even facial recognition.

When Camra came back with the belongings all in a duffel bag, Martinez thanked her.

Kenna said, "Can you give us the name of the coworker who was fired?"

"Ravi Hall. I don't know him all that well, he just seemed like a crusty old man at work. He used to stomp up and down the halls and grunt like everything was wrong."

"Thank you for your time." Kenna smiled. "You have my number if you need anything, but if you believe at any time that your life is in danger, you should call 911. They'll be able to help you a lot faster and more effectively than I can."

Camra nodded. "Thanks."

They headed for Martinez's car, and he opened his department computer on the dash. "Let's see where we can find this guy."

"You don't want to take that tablet in and get your technicians to look at it?" He could drop her at the mechanic, and she'd be able to find out what was going on with her car.

"I can do that when I head back to the department today."

While he typed in Ravi Hall and ran a search, Kenna said, "Have you heard anything from the others about their interviews with Garth and Landry?"

"The two detectives are talking to Garth this morning.

Who knows when the ATF is going to figure out their approach to get Landry to talk."

Kenna didn't want to get herself more in debt to an old... Lottie wasn't exactly a friend. Neither was she especially an associate. She checked her phone and saw that Maizie had updated her about finding the kid.

If Kenna had no idea where he was, she couldn't approach his mother about anything. In fact, she shouldn't even show her face at the prison.

Not just because Landry might see her talking to the other woman. Someone they might use later to make an approach.

Maizie had found his name on the registry for a local public middle school. But she had also accessed his criminal record and discovered a couple of arrests for petty theft, charges for fighting and resisting arrest.

Kenna eyed Martinez. "What do you know about Mitchell Sutton Middle School?"

"Looking into local schools?" He plugged the address for Ravi Hall's last known residence into his GPS.

"Not because I'm moving here."

Martinez chuckled. "Heaven forbid. Terrible idea. But actually, that school is one of the roughest in the city. Why are you asking about it?"

"A friend of mine, her son attends school there. I might need to hit them up and check on how he's doing."

"Because the mom isn't getting information from the school about her kid?" Martinez glanced over, then pulled out into the street.

"I just want to see what I can find out."

He made a *huh* sound but didn't say anything else.

"After we check on this Ravi Hall guy and find out what

he knows about Damien, you can drop me off at the garage. I want to find out about my car."

"That's a shame. I was thinking about lunch, and I was going to treat you to the buffet over at Fiesta Puerto Rico."

Kenna glanced over. "Is it any good, or are you paying me back for something?"

"You did save my life last night. Whether I want to admit it or not, I probably owe you more than all-you-can-eat chimichangas."

"Keep that in mind when this thing starts kicking off and I need some goodwill with the police department."

Martinez chuckled. "Noted."

She noticed he had a nice laugh, and he was a decent guy. Maybe Camra needed a rebound in a few months. "Are you married, Martinez?"

"Divorced," he said. "We have a six-year-old, and she will not be going to Mitchell Sutton Middle School despite the fact my ex lives in that area."

"Are you close with your daughter?"

"I try to be, as much as I can with my schedule. When I have her but I'm working a case, she spends a lot of time with my mom. Which they both love. Before the divorce, I was a detective in homicide, and the hours were pretty brutal. I never even expected her mom to stick it out as long as she did. I took the sergeant's exam and transferred to working alongside detectives, instead of as one of them, but she still wanted the divorce." He glanced over. "How about you? Ever been married?"

"I figured the police department would have already run a full background on me."

He shrugged one shoulder as he drove. "We did, but it doesn't always have everything in it. Especially when someone has such a low profile on social media as you. But I read an article all about how you and some FBI agent have a star-crossed true love thing going." He frowned. "But then I read another that said you're in a tawdry relationship with some other guy from Mexico."

Kenna laughed. "That would be Ramon, who you met at the hospital, I guess." She shook her head, hardly able to understand what some people believed. Or what they chose to do with their free time. It wasn't like her life was actually that interesting. "But the part about the FBI agent is pretty much correct."

"So there's no room in your life for an over-the-hill police sergeant with a failed marriage who plays on a bowling league occasionally and pretty much does laundry for fun?"

"In situations like we find ourselves in, you can never have too many people you trust to watch your back when things get crazy."

He nodded. "That's certainly true."

When Martinez pulled onto the street where Ravi Hall lived, he almost immediately hit the brakes. More than one cop car, and an ambulance, were parked blocking the street outside the residence.

"This doesn't look good." Martinez pulled up behind one of the cop cars and then backed into an open spot on the curb. "Let's go check it out."

Kenna could probably surmise that Ravi Hall had been found dead this morning, but she didn't want to speak something out loud with no proof. Not when words had power. And as with Reggie, the guy could still be alive.

She prayed as they walked over to the closest police officer. Mostly for the next of kin who might be suffering the way Camra currently was, but also for the wisdom for her to find the answers to what was going on.

"Sergeant." The officer at the edge of the scene nodded at his boss, then glanced at Kenna.

Martinez tilted his head in her direction. "She's with me."

"Even still," the officer said. "This one's pretty bad. Might not be a place to take a civilian."

Kenna lifted an eyebrow. "What do you mean *pretty bad*?"

Chapter Nineteen

"Okay, so that was pretty bad." Kenna walked back to the car, having spent twenty minutes walking around the scene. Looking at every angle of what had happened to Ravi Hall.

"Does it get worse than that?" Martinez asked her across the roof of the car. "Because that's about the worst thing I've ever seen in my life."

Kenna slid into the passenger seat. "I don't envy the techs that have to catalogue every piece of that evidence and all the DNA."

Martinez started the car, looking a little paler than he had before. He grabbed a water bottle out of the cup holder and took some slow sips. "Did you notice how it looked a lot like the mausoleum where we had found Reggie?"

Kenna opened the notes app on her phone. "Small bones, candles just like the last scene. But this one seems like they had more time. They were certain no one was going to show up, the way I did at the mausoleum."

"You and your associate."

Right. "Or it was done before Reggie, and this Ravi Hall guy has been dead for several days."

"You think so?" Martinez asked. "The medical examiner didn't think he'd been dead for more than a day."

"Liver temp isn't always a good indicator. There are too many variables with environmental temperature. And forget narrowing it down to a small timeframe like within an hour or two. That only happens on TV."

"Okay, so how do we find the killer?"

Kenna hoped that question was facetious. Unless New Orleans PD wanted to put her on retainer and pay her consultancy fees. "Are you sure you don't have one of those confidential informants who's an expert in this stuff?"

"Unfortunately, no. Though, not for lack of trying." Martinez shrugged one shoulder. "The closest we can get is asking my mother's priest what he thinks. He'll probably get the vapors and collapse just hearing about it."

"So now we have a murder and one attempt, both with a similar MO." Kenna chewed her lip. "Anything from police department records about other similar deaths, either recently or not?"

Martinez said nothing at first, and a muscle in his jaw flexed.

"Spit it out. Whatever it is."

"It was a few years ago. Not any of my cases, but I heard about it through office chatter. The brass didn't want it going public, because everyone would demand we call the FBI and turn it over to one of their bizarre crimes units, you know?"

"Do I?"

"Fine," he said. "But the killings stopped, and we ran down every lead we had. That's the story that was going around, and nobody could ignore murders. But the truth is, no one was ever convicted for the crimes."

"How many?" Kenna was about to ask for all the files but didn't want to jump all over this if she was going to end up in a minefield of police department bureaucracy. Still, this was exactly the kind of thing she investigated.

"Three." He sighed.

"So we could have another victim still to go? If it's a trio of victims compulsion." She shifted in her seat so she could look straight at him. "Someone out there is living on borrowed time, completely unaware that their entire world is about to be upended, and it will result in them dying a horrific death. Sacrificed to some dark spirit, or whatever on earth that was back there."

It would take months, if not longer, for Kenna to get those crime scene images out of her head. Ravi Hall splayed across his bed, blood everywhere. Half the comforter burned by one of the candles, which had fallen over. And yet, the flames hadn't reached his body. Because there had been so much fluid from the blood?

She figured her mind would wrestle with the question in her dreams. If there was an answer to be found, she would get there—not in her waking life.

Martinez gripped the steering wheel.

"Get me all the case files," Kenna told him. "We need to know if this person is back."

"Whoever they are, the third victim might be dead already. Maybe Reggie was the last one and we already saved him."

"Great. Then we'll stop it from ever happening again to anyone else."

Martinez lifted one hand off the steering wheel. "Okay, geez."

"I'm about to tell you to pull over so I can get out of this car and walk away from you right now."

"I guess you're not so much different than my ex-wife after all."

Kenna shifted in her seat and grabbed the handle. "All right, that's—"

"Okay, I'll get you the files." He blew out a breath, exasperated.

She stared at him, not completely convinced she wanted to stay in this car. But she also didn't have a ride without inconveniencing someone else. "You can drop me off at that middle school."

"How do I know if you go off on your own that you're not going to end up the third victim?"

"Go speak to your mother's priest about that. I've survived this long without your help, and I can carry on doing it after I walk away from you." She paused. "But you *are* going to send me those files."

"It doesn't have anything to do with this case. These cases." He sighed again. "With whatever is going on here."

"You don't know that," Kenna said. "You have no idea what's going on, or the first clue who this person is."

Part of her realized they were picking at each other like this because of what they had just seen. Trying to process the insanity of that murder. The powerlessness of not having been able to stop something like that. Getting there too late. All of it bubbled up inside them both in a way that erupted, causing them to take out their frustration on each other.

Then again, there were a whole lot more unhealthy ways to get the feeling out than bickering.

"Okay," Martinez said. "So you're going to help us find out. Right?"

She knew the moment had blown over because he pulled into the drive-through of a fast-food place that specialized in salad bowls, soups, and sandwiches. She usually didn't frequent this chain because it was overpriced, but if he wanted to buy her lunch, that was his problem.

He pulled up behind a silver Lexus and turned to her. "Well?"

Kenna crossed her arms. "I haven't decided yet."

Martinez ordered his lunch and recommended the BBQ chicken sandwich.

"I'll have the Thai salad," she said.

He smirked. "Of course, you will."

She got on her phone to text Jax. She needed to ask him if the local FBI office had a bizarre crimes unit or some other department that specialized in religious murders. Assuming those covered whatever on earth that had been back there.

He texted back,

Bad?

Kenna replied,

I don't think I've ever seen worse.

The horror that one person could perpetrate on another was bad enough even in the simplest of ways. Like the knife wound that could have killed Bear if it had been even slightly to one side of where it landed.

The state Ravi Hall had been in was on another level. One she could barely even comprehend, let alone describe.

He replied,

I'll find out about the locals and call you on my way home.

Kenna replied with an absurd emoji simply because she

needed something so completely opposite of that scene. A kissy face was about the furthest thing you could get from death. Aside from a newborn baby.

So sweet and innocent. So unaware of what horrors existed in the world. Untouched by evil. Ellie never needed to know any of this.

When she got back to Preston's house later, she needed to have a long cuddle with that tiny being. Assuming Nora was okay with it.

Martinez pulled into a parking space, and they ate in silence. As soon as they were both done, he drove to the middle school, only a couple of minutes away. Which told her he'd been headed there all along, regardless of what she decided. But he wouldn't have known who to speak to if she hadn't been in the car. He had no idea how she was connected to this child.

They stood at the school entrance, waiting to get buzzed in. Martinez flashed his badge, explaining through the intercom who they were. When they were admitted, they approached an entryway with another set of doors. The front office staff sat behind a glass window, which the receptionist slid open.

She had a dark-blue polo shirt on, and her hair pulled back into a ponytail. "What can I do for the two of you?"

Kenna stepped closer to the window. "I need to know if Anthony Alvarez showed up for school today."

Martinez shifted, but he couldn't know who she was talking about. However, the receptionist clearly did.

"I've seen him this morning." She made a face. "I'll call him out of class if you want to speak to him." She sounded as if she thought they were here because Anthony had committed a crime and was now under arrest.

"And the school resource officer," Martinez added. "We'd like to speak to both of them."

She picked up the phone. "I'll track down the SRO, but it's going to take me a couple of minutes. I'll have Jenny here show you to the resource alcove."

The woman beside her stood, letting them in the interior door where she led them to a sitting area beside the nurse's office. "You can wait right here."

They settled into chairs side by side. After a few seconds of complete silence, Martinez said, "Thanks for not getting out of the car even though I was being a jerk."

Kenna eyed him. "Thanks for lunch."

They didn't get the chance to say anything else, because a uniformed police officer strode around the corner at the end of the hall.

In front of him walked a gangly dark-skinned youth, who had clearly seen plenty of rough things in his life so far. The kid wore oversize basketball shorts and a tank top, a double set of chains around his neck, and an earring in one ear. His dark hair was shaved close. He looked seventeen despite the fact this was a middle school, and he was barely thirteen.

He stopped in front of them, shrugging but not saying anything.

"Nice to see you, Martinez." The SRO looked at Kenna. "I'm Officer Jarrett."

"Kenna Banbury." She noticed a flinch from Anthony and glanced at him. "You know who I am?"

He lifted his chin. "She told me about you when she saw you on the news. Said ya'll used to know each other or somethin'."

"Or something," Kenna said.

She felt his attention on her but didn't look at him. Did Martinez know who Anthony's mother was?

The kid shrugged. "Whaddya want?"

She studied his face, trying to place him outside the hospital in that group of kids, but couldn't be certain he'd been there. One of the youths had his hood pulled up, so she hadn't been able to see his face.

"You aren't in trouble. At least not so far as I know," she added. "I'm here because Lottie asked me to check on you. She's worried about you."

He huffed. "Must be bad if she sent *you*."

Martinez eyed him. "Maybe your mother doesn't want you to turn out like her."

Kenna jumped on the opportunity and turned to him. "You're talking about someone I consider a friend. So watch yourself when you talk about her like that." It was an untrue statement, but it served a purpose. Now that she'd come to his mother's defense, Anthony might open up a little more.

Martinez closed his mouth, pressing his lips together in a thin line.

"She asked me to make sure you are all right," she continued. "But she also knows who I am, and that means if there's something to figure out then I'm going to investigate what it is."

Anthony sniffed. "I don't need you sticking your nose in my business, woman."

The school resource officer looked like he wanted to slap Anthony up the backside of the head, but of course that would be something that would get him fired. Restraint was a quality skill set anyone needed. Not just cops.

Kenna said, "I met a woman the other day, and I talked to her in the hospital. She thought the same thing. A day later, two people got shot five feet from where I was standing talking to her. For all I know, she could be next."

Officer Jarrett glared at Anthony. "If you know something

about a crime, you should tell them. No sense getting in over your head and having no one to go to when you don't know what to do next."

Kenna shifted her stance, shoving her thumbs in her pockets. She still had the image of Ravi Hall lying on that bed in her mind. The last thing she wanted was for this young man to end up the same way—or any of those other teens.

"Have you ever had any business with Momma Landry?" she asked, studying his face.

The kid remained completely impassive. With his street smarts, he'd learned—probably the hard way—to keep his feelings and reactions to himself. So no one knew what was going on inside his head.

Finally, he shrugged. "I dunno who that is."

"Sure you don't," Officer Jarrett said. "Except that you go to school with one of the cousins' kids. Means you know all about Momma."

Another shrug. "I heard she was in jail."

"She is." Kenna nodded. "Because I worked with the police to put her there."

His brows lifted. "You did that?"

She could hardly believe she was talking to a middle schooler. For someone with a knack of getting in trouble, this whole demeanor likely didn't help him stay out of it.

Kenna nodded. "I did."

His gaze narrowed. "What do you want from me?"

"All your mom wants me to do is make sure you're safe." Kenna shrugged. "But if you tell me who is on this breaking and entering crew, then I can make sure that happens for real."

His face shut down. "And if I don't rat on them, you leave me hanging out to dry. Right?"

"The cops here might operate like that, but I don't. When I say I'm going to do something, I do it."

The two cops in question, standing beside her and Anthony, probably didn't appreciate her drawing that line of distinction. But a kid like this needed to understand that she wasn't a cop. Not anymore, and not ever again.

"What do you say, Anthony?" Kenna paused. "Are you gonna let me help you?"

Chapter Twenty

Kenna parked Allie's car in the visitor lot at Gauchet County Correctional Facility. As soon as she turned off the ignition, her phone rang.

Of course.

But it wasn't Maizie, Ramon, or even Jax—who was overseeing a multiagency surveillance operation for the next few days.

"Hey, Martinez." She sat back in the seat, leaving the engine running so cool air could blow in her face.

"Update on Garth and Landry—"

"That was quick." Which probably meant what she thought it did—that neither had talked. "Are they still alive at least?"

She didn't want to have to tell Nora that Ellie's father was gone. The young woman seemed attached to him. If either one had a hit out on them, it wouldn't be long before they could no longer fight the inevitable.

At least with Garth in protective custody, they had a shot at keeping him alive.

But it wouldn't last forever if he didn't give the cops something.

"Mm-hmm," Martinez said. "Garth is alive, I just spoke with him. He isn't interested in talking about anything with us, not even with a sweet deal from the district attorney's office signed and in writing. Not until he sees Nora and the baby."

"That's what he wants?"

"More than anything. Then he'll 'think' about talking. Can you believe that?"

A man who cared about his family? Of course, she could believe it.

Even if it was only about stringing along the cops with the only leverage he had. But Kenna didn't think Garth was that kind of guy.

"He wants what he wants." She figured that with most people making a deal was about finding out where the leverage was. This seemed more like a negotiation.

Thankfully with no hostages.

Nora and Ellie were safe.

"You know anything about where the baby mama and the kid are?" Martinez asked.

"Tell Garth it'll take time to organize a detail to get her safely to the jail to visit him. And it's risky. But if what he really wants is for her to be safe from Landry, it's in his interest to talk to us."

Martinez muttered something she didn't hear.

Kenna said, "What about Landry?"

"Clammed up. Won't talk. Her lawyer won't even entertain the topic of a deal." Martinez sighed. "She's not gonna give up anything, but we have her under surveillance."

Kenna stared through the windshield of her car at the

industrial-looking building with slim frosted windows and wire fences. "I'm working something on my end."

"Gonna clue me into what that is?"

"If it amounts to something, sure. No point wasting your time when it's nothing yet."

"Right." He waited a beat. "You could be working on getting the baby mama to the jail."

"Sure, but I'm not nearby the team protecting her. Because I'm working *something else*."

She'd swung by the house but, given everything going on, she could lead a dangerous person there anytime she did. So she had to keep trips there to a minimum for their safety. Whenever she visited, she put them at risk.

Kenna could just as easily check in by phone and go sleep in her RV. That way, she didn't run the risk of someone tailing her there.

Besides, her skills were better put to use working the case and figuring out how all these things fit together rather than sitting around on protection detail. Something Preston should've taken into account when he considered her for his trip to London.

"I sure hope whatever you're doing gets a result," Martinez said.

"Me, too." Kenna wasn't going to explain what it was, even though it sounded like he wanted her to. "I'll keep you posted. Anything from the murder investigations, or the ATF case?"

"I'll keep you posted," he echoed. "Later."

Martinez hung up right after he threw those words back in her face. But she figured it was mostly just the frustration of this case.

"I guess that's that," Kenna said to the quiet car.

Now she just had to convince the warden of this prison that she should be able to see a convicted killer outside visiting hours, and in a spot where no one would know they'd met. Which, in a place like this, was going to be a hard secret to keep.

Kenna handed over her ID and checked in. Just as she was about to ask to see the warden, the officer behind the desk said, "This way."

He let her through the buzzer door into a stark hallway with white linoleum and dingy white walls. Signs posted on the walls and closed doors.

He led her to the warden's office and eased it open. "Ms. Banbury is here."

Kenna kept her face impassive, even though she had no idea what was going on. They were expecting her?

She spotted three men inside the office. A dingy space with a metal desk and a couple of waist-high bookshelves that looked dusty from being ignored.

The warden stood behind his desk, and the two ATF agents who'd been at the police department were over to Kenna's left.

No one spoke.

She lifted her chin. "Good to see you guys."

The warden wore brown slacks and a shirt that was off-white at best. He had some hair on his head, mostly around the back like a monk. "Ms. Banbury, is that right?"

"It is."

"I'm Nester Cartwright."

She eyed him. "You were waiting on me?"

It seemed unlikely, since they hadn't summoned her here. Though, she also got the impression they were expecting her.

One of the ATF agents said, "Figured you'd want to be part of getting information from Landry."

Kenna glanced between the agents and the warden. "I doubt she'll talk to me if her lawyer won't even talk deal."

The other agent stared her down. "How about the fact you're lying to us about your connection to this prison?"

Kenna said, "Excuse me?"

Warden Cartwright ruffled a paper. "We're referring to this." He held up the page. "Where you're listed as the next of kin for Leticia Alvarez."

"The convicted murderer," the first agent clarified.

The other one shifted. "Care to explain?"

Geez, they were so pleased with themselves.

"Apart from the fact it's none of your business?" Kenna wasn't going to be bullied into believing she'd done something wrong. "I had no idea I was listed as her next of kin. We haven't spoken in twenty years."

They both smirked. One said, "Likely story."

"She'll be here momentarily." The warden closed the folder on his desk. "Then I'm sure your personal connection will assist in convincing her to get close to Landry in order to get her to provide the ATF with valuable intelligence."

Kenna couldn't believe this. She sucked in a lungful, about to argue, when the door behind her opened.

She spun around as a pair of officers walked Lottie into the room. Kenna hadn't seen her in decades, so contemplating how much she'd changed was redundant. Who didn't change from the time they were twelve to being in their thirties?

Lottie looked around. "Is this an intervention?" She chuckled, the sound brittle as if at any moment it would shatter.

She had a few tiny braids that hung down on one side of her face. The other side had been shaved close to the side of her head. A tattoo snaked out of her collar up the side of her neck, and tattoos covered the back of each hand. Two teardrops beside her left eye.

She was barely five six, which meant Kenna stood at least three inches taller than her.

Kenna turned to Warden Cartwright. "You want me to talk to her? That isn't happening with an audience."

Cartwright lifted his chin at the ATF guys. Neither of them appreciated being dismissed, but they didn't comment as they left the room. One officer remained.

"Warden?" Kenna stood her ground.

"I'm afraid I can't be liable for—"

"I'll be fine. And I'll sign whatever you want." She didn't believe Lottie would hurt her. At least, not before she heard what Kenna had to say. "This conversation happens in private."

Cartwright had her sign her initials on a paper, then he left. "The officer will be outside."

And no doubt the rest of them would somehow be listening in. Probably using the phone on the warden's desk, or some other device. She wasn't going to presume this would be a private conversation—or waste time looking for a bug.

The door closed. Kenna settled on the edge of the desk. "Next of kin?"

Lottie smirked. "Not like there's anyone else. Besides, if I'm dead, you probably need to investigate because it won't be natural causes."

"Noted." Even if the idea was incredibly sad. "What about Anthony?"

"He'll need 'support' or whatever. Just make sure he doesn't end up like me."

As far as Kenna had seen, he might be well on his way to exactly that. "He's tall. Taller than me, nearly six foot already."

"His daddy was tall." Lottie's expression betrayed zero emotion. She shifted, jingling her shackles, and slumped into one of the two chairs facing the desk. She kicked the other around and put her feet on it. "Guess you'd better make it worth my while."

"Because you're in?" As if it would be that easy.

"No, for whatever's gonna happen to me when everyone finds out I had a meeting in the warden's office."

Kenna winced. "Sorry."

Lottie just shrugged. "My boy is good?"

"You've heard about the crew breaking and entering."

"Rich people's houses." She snorted.

"Sounds like it got out of hand. Someone got hurt." Now Damien and his wife were dead, because Landry didn't like loose ends. "Anthony told us Momma Landry isn't the one calling the shots. She's only a middleman, as it were."

"Did you look at whoever runs that home where he's at?"

"I'm sure the police will look into everyone that connects the kids on the crew, including teachers and caregivers."

"You think they actually 'give care'?" Lottie made air quotes.

"I can check on that as well," Kenna said.

"But you're here to offer me a deal. Lemme guess. More yard time, so I can feel the sun on my face or whatever. And in return I've gotta...what?"

"The feds wanna know who Landry works for."

Lottie snorted and shook her head.

"Anthony is in the middle of this. If you find out this information and we take them down, he's safer."

"So that's why they want you in here asking." Lottie leaned back. "'Cause you're the only way they can turn up the heat."

Kenna figured that was probably true. They'd used the

personal connection between Lottie and Kenna against them both.

"So don't." She shrugged. "I'll get Anthony safe. The feds can find another way to take down whoever Landry works for. Doesn't bother me. Because like you said, I already owe you."

No doubt that wasn't what the warden or those feds told her to say. But her loyalty wasn't to them. It was barely to Lottie, except for the fact Kenna really did owe her. But she could also argue she'd done what Lottie asked already. She'd checked on Anthony, and if he needed help, he knew to contact her.

She spotted the edge of a smile on Lottie's mouth. Was she contemplating what the repercussions of saying no might be? The warden, or the feds, could make life hard for her if they wanted.

"They need someone to get close to Landry," Kenna said. "She's seen my face, so I can't go undercover in the prison and get the intel."

"Plus, it'll take too long." Lottie shifted far enough in her chair that she made a motion Kenna comprehended. Easier to cut someone and bleed some words out of them along with the red stuff.

"How would you..." Kenna frowned. "Never mind, I don't wanna know." Better to let whoever might be listening believe Lottie hadn't said anything. Otherwise, her expressing intention could be used against her.

Lottie looked Kenna up and down. "You always were a scrawny thing."

"Don't worry, I can hold my own," Kenna said. "As long as it doesn't require the use of my arms." She pushed her sleeves up, aware she was giving away her vulnerability. Not to Lottie —that wasn't the problem. But if the feds were currently listening, she'd clued them in on her Samson-level weakness.

In the Bible story, he'd given up his secret out of pride, and in his brokenness decided to do the right thing in the end. Kenna's journey was different, but also the same in a lot of ways. She didn't see her injuries as some kind of Kryptonite. Just a way for Lottie to know that Kenna understood maybe at least *some* of what had driven this woman to the place she was.

Lottie lifted her feet off the other chair and sat up, leaning forward in her seat. "I saw it on the news." She whistled, shaking her head. "Some guys are sick, you know?"

"I do know," Kenna said. "And sometimes a person gets in over their head and can't see a way out."

Did she know Kenna was referring to this woman's crimes?

Lottie shrugged. "Sure, he beat me. Whatever. The court told me to see a prison shrink. She thinks I need to 'let go' of my trauma or whatever, like I don't have every reason to be angry. You think I didn't do that letting-go-of-it-all thing when I stabbed him eight times?"

Kenna bit the inside of her lip. "And the second guy?"

"You need to convince yourself you're not like me, fine. I'll tell you. But at least admit why you're asking."

"I've killed more people than you have," Kenna admitted.

Lottie's eyebrows rose in two peaks.

Kenna shrugged. "I just do it legally."

Lottie tipped her head back and laughed. "I should've figured out how to do that." She kept laughing, and when it had wound down, she sighed. "The other guy." She shook her head. "His brother came in. Saw what I'd done and decided to take vengeance the way he would if Tanner was pissed. But he wasn't there, and his brother was."

So they'd both abused her.

"I knew he'd start in on Anthony when he was done if I

let him put me on the floor." Lottie sniffed. "So I put him in the ground."

Kenna wasn't going to ask why she hadn't called the police, or simply taken Anthony and left way before this happened. People in situations like the one Lottie had been in didn't have to justify their actions as far as Kenna was concerned—they just had to live with the consequences.

All Lottie had known was that it would take one thing to survive. Now she was paying for that freedom, and in a way so was Anthony.

In the heat of the moment, Lottie got free of her abusers.

Kenna wasn't there, so she didn't know enough about the whole situation to pass judgment. She would never understand what it had been like to be Lottie in that moment.

"That's the kind of person Momma Landry is," Kenna said. "The kind who kicks someone when they're down, who uses others for her own gain. Forcing kids to commit crimes, and for what?" She hadn't managed to get Anthony to tell her. "And he's right in the middle of it. So it might be time to save him again."

"That was a good speech." Lottie clapped, her shackles jangling. "I'll think about it." She got up and yelled, "Guard!" Then turned back at Kenna. "Good to see you, yeah?"

Kenna nodded and watched her leave.

The two ATF agents came in.

"Thought you were supposed to be persuading her to help us?" The guy crossed his arms.

"I don't know you," Kenna said. "And I probably wouldn't trust you if I did. So here's the thing. Leticia gets to decide if she wants to take the risk. We aren't going to strong-arm her into helping us. She has nothing to gain and everything to lose if she does this. But you don't understand that, because all you're concerned with is closing this case."

"And you don't care if the case is closed?" he asked.

But it wasn't her case.

Kenna just stared at him. "What I care about is when people get hurt and it could've been prevented."

"So you're a do-gooder now?" the other agent said.

"Who I am is none of your business." Kenna hopped off the desk and headed for the door. "Ask her what she wants. Make it worth her while to help you instead of making everyone miserable because you need to hit your quota."

Chapter Twenty-One

"So the ATF are your enemies now?" Jax chuckled.

Kenna smirked at his amused tone. "I needed more excitement in my life." She shifted the phone between her shoulder and her ear, so she could grab a dish with both hands. These dishes had been in her RV dishwasher way too long. She hadn't stepped foot in her rig in days.

"Did the mechanic get back to you about your car?"

She tucked the dish in its spot in the cupboard, where it wouldn't clank into anything else while she was driving and wind up breaking. "The mechanic said they jimmied it back together, whatever was loose, and I'm good to go now."

"That's great."

"The last thing I need in the middle of a chase is car trouble." Kenna sighed.

"You get into a lot of those?"

"More than you'd think." She grinned, surveying the empty RV. "But not lately." It reminded her of the comment she'd made to Lottie, though she wasn't going to tell Jax what she'd said.

Maybe she should...

No one in her life knew about that stint in New Orleans. Or how she felt as if she owed Leticia a debt.

He would agree with her that she'd done the right thing at least. She knew that.

Nah, that would just be chatter. He didn't need to know about Lottie when Kenna would only have to explain the whole story about how they knew each other. He was tired, and his work was crazy right now.

Whatever was in her that made her stay closed-mouthed about that part of her history didn't want to air it like dirty laundry when Jax needed to rest.

"Everything else okay?"

"Yeah," Kenna said. "I stopped by the house. Ramon said he didn't need help protecting Nora and Ellie. He's 'got this' apparently, and he seemed kind of mad about it. But Preston has an event in two days, an evening benefit party or something. So I should be available to help Ramon then, since he and Nora will be alone in the house. With Preston and the team all out for the evening."

"Any sign of the threat there?"

"All quiet so far." Except that presented its own kind of problem. "Which means when something does kick off, it'll be well thought out and big enough we'll have trouble trying to fight them off. Either Preston's brother-in-law, or Landry's people coming for Nora."

"Be careful," Jax said.

"I told them I could park my RV in front of the house. But apparently, if I do that I'll get towed." Kenna stretched out on the bed, holding the warm phone to her ear. Then let out a long sigh. She'd recapped the case, and now she was talked out and feeling wrung out. "In the morning, maybe I'll have some better ideas."

"Sleep is a good idea."

"How's your case?"

"When things start moving, I'll catch you up." Jax's voice softened against her ear. "Goodnight, Kenna."

Love you.

She should just say it. He was probably waiting for her to say it. Holding out until she admitted aloud how she felt. "Bye."

He chuckled, and the call ended.

Kenna let the phone slip onto the covers and closed her eyes. It wasn't that big of a deal. People said I love you every day. Three little words and all that.

Not like it wasn't true. But if she admitted her true feelings, then it was only a matter of time before they had to have the conversation of where this was going. Their *relationship.*

What the next step would be.

Neither of them would be content with this status quo they had right now if it carried on for years. When the trade-off for not being a big chicken was closeness, comfort...having to live in one place.

Kenna let out another long breath.

Not ready.

The alternative was to get married and live like the kind of couple where one or both was in the military and deployed. People made that work every day. It would be tough to maintain, but when the alternative was trying to figure out how to live in a house when she'd never stayed in one place for long...

Her phone ringing cut through her thoughts.

The RV was fully dark. Night had fallen while she drifted off and had slept for a while.

Kenna rolled over and looked at the screen of her phone. A local number. She slid her thumb across it, sitting up, and hit the button for speaker. "Kenna Banbury."

"It's Anthony." He sounded out of breath, either from

exertion or fear. "One of my friends...he's freaked. He's gonna jump off a bridge or something."

"A kid on the crew?" She shifted, setting her feet on the carpet and trying to figure out where she'd put her shoes. Pants would be good—not the athletic shorts she was wearing.

"He was freaking out at school," Anthony said. "We tracked him down, but this guy at his work said he was saying he was gonna kill himself tonight."

"That's not what someone who's planning to die says." Kenna slid on fresh clothes and headed for the door. "It's someone who wants help. Which is what we're gonna give him."

"But he said he'll kill himself!"

Her stomach clenched, but she remembered to lock the door before she got in her car. "If *you* were planning on suicide, would you announce it?"

"If I wanted someone to stop me."

"Exactly." Kenna turned on the engine.

His voice came through the speakers, "...guess that makes sense."

"So there's a chance we can talk him out of it." Kenna opened her maps app. "Now tell me where to go. Or where to pick you up."

"I'm on my bike. I think he'll go to the Woodland Bridge." The kid sounded terrified. "It's where his mom jumped."

Kenna's stomach twisted into a knot. "I'll be there."

The drive took Kenna longer than she wanted, but she made it to the bridge. A concrete structure with little in terms of a barrier. She drove onto the bridge, because it would take too long to park and traverse up it on foot. Even at a run, she might be too late to stop this kid from going through with his plan and ending his pain.

She spotted a bike on the side of the bridge, coming up

ahead of her. Anthony had leaned it against a low concrete wall. Nothing that would stop anyone—or any vehicle—from going over. There wasn't even a barricade, just that low concrete wall.

But she didn't see him—or the other boy.

Kenna checked her rearview and saw there was no one close behind her. She flipped on her hazards and pulled over by the bike. Close to the barricades as she could get, she had to climb out the passenger side.

A passing car honked at her.

Kenna shifted her jacket so her holstered gun was visible. Someone driving by might believe she was on official business.

The boys were by the barrier on the far side, the oncoming lane.

Kenna crossed the two lanes on her side, then hopped the center concrete divide, which was barely as high as her knee.

A truck passed, and the driver laid on the horn. Wind whipped warm air, and the smell of the ocean mixed with exhaust against her face.

Kenna jogged across the other lanes, between two cars, to where Anthony stood with another boy.

The kid spotted her and climbed up on the sidewall. "Don't come any closer!" He faced the horizon, the water a dark mass below them.

If he jumped, he wouldn't survive. But then, if this was how his mother had ended her life then the kid knew that.

She shifted Anthony behind her. "What's his name?" She practically had to shout over the sound of traffic.

"Jacob," Anthony said.

"Stay back." She said the words over her shoulder, praying none of them got hit by a car. Traffic was starting to slow, the few cars on the road this time of night rubbernecking her as she walked toward this kid. "Jacob! I'm Kenna."

"Leave me alone!" he shouted, not turning to look at her.

"Jacob, Anthony is worried about you. He doesn't want you to get hurt." She took another small step toward him. If she could get close enough, she could grab him and pull him back onto the asphalt of the street.

"I don't need help!"

"Everyone needs help with something, Jacob. That's just life." She inched forward. "Whatever is wrong, we can talk about it. Figure it out." She got a little closer. "If you get down from there, we can figure it out."

The kid wasn't as tall as Anthony. He looked barely old enough for high school, but beside the taller boy, he probably got mistaken for the younger of the two. He stood straight, wearing beat-up tennis shoes on his small feet. His arms shaking. Basketball shorts and T-shirt too big for his frame.

None of that mattered when he could end up little more than a footnote in some report. A victim of the suicide rate, rather than a success story.

Kenna wanted him to live.

"Jacob, listen to me!"

Traffic had started to back up on the far side, where she'd left her car mostly blocking one lane. On this side, a pickup truck pulled over, and some guy got out.

She held up a hand for the man, whoever he was, to hang back. "Jacob, let's talk!"

The boy hadn't jumped yet. As far as she was concerned, every second she had was a chance to convince him.

"Come down. Let's talk about it. I can help you. You don't know this, but it's what I do. I find people, and I help them. No matter what. I don't give up when someone is in trouble."

His determination faltered. She saw it in the tiny shift. He still hadn't jumped, which meant he hadn't decided yet.

She took another step closer. If she reached out, she would be able to grab him.

"Get down, kid." The man inched closer to Jacob. "This isn't the way out."

The teen flinched, evidently unaware someone was on his other side.

Kenna grasped his wrist then. She pulled hard to get him back on the ground. The guy on Jacob's other side slammed into him. Which meant he slammed into her.

Jacob's shoes slipped off the concrete side wall, and he started to fall, his upper body coming toward her. Kenna's legs crumpled, and Jacob's waist hit the concrete.

He screamed, sliding backward off the side of the bridge.

Kenna's upper body launched forward with him, dragged toward the edge. She tightened her one-handed grip on his wrist.

Jacob scrambled to grab her, screaming in her face.

Too close. She was going to go over after him, and there was nothing to gain purchase.

The guy who'd slammed into them grabbed for Jacob's shirt but just ended up sliding it up to his armpits. His elbow glanced off the side of her head.

Her grip loosened.

"Jacob!" Anthony muscled in beside her, grabbing his buddy.

Someone honked their horn, as if that would help.

Kenna grabbed the kid with both hands. She heard a rush of feet and didn't let go of whatever she was holding. She realized she was bent to look down over the side of the bridge.

It was so far down.

Jacob screamed. His running shoes battered the concrete side of the bridge, trying to gain purchase on the smooth side.

"Hold on. Hold on." She said it more to herself than to

him, or anyone else. Her forearms screamed, the pain so blinding it was as if the nerve endings had been burned off. Hot pain locked her where she was.

Burning.

Someone grabbed Jacob's shorts, or his hips. He was lifted sideways, so his body turned toward her. Kenna's balance shifted back with the momentum, and they landed in a heap on the asphalt. Anthony partially under her hip, and Jacob on her legs.

Kenna had no strength left in her. It all seemed to bleed from her muscles onto the sun-heated bridge under her.

Why was it still so hot at night?

She slumped back, unable to hold herself up by her arms. Her back hit the asphalt, and Anthony yelled, "Whoa! Kenna." He caught her head.

She stared up at the sky, breathing hard. Adrenaline had blocked everything out so that she had no idea what the real problem was. But she'd been grabbing Jacob hard. She'd been holding his weight over the water below, at least to an extent with help from others.

But still far more than her arms could withstand.

"Kenna?" Anthony's face swam into view.

She felt the tears slide out the corners of her eyes.

Around her, people yelled. Someone calling the police, and she heard, "Ambulance."

Kenna tried to lift her hands.

Nothing happened.

She moved her legs, kicking out because it was all she could do. Jacob lay on the ground, crying. The old guy looked mad.

Anthony's face appeared over hers. "What's wrong? What's happening?"

She managed to say, "Phone."

"Where?" He looked her over.

Kenna planted her foot and rolled her body left, so he'd see her back pocket.

"Sorry." Anthony pulled the phone out. "It's your thumbprint."

"You have to do it." She fought to get the words out but managed it.

He moved her arm barely an inch.

Kenna screamed.

"What?!" Anthony yelped. He dropped her hand.

"Just do it." Kenna gasped. Each breath was a sharp, desperate inhale. "Just do it."

"Who am I calling? There's an ambulance coming."

Jax. Maizie. Ramon wasn't going to leave the baby. Preston. "Bear."

Anthony ducked his head over the phone. "I see a Bear in your call list. It's ringing." He put the phone to her ear.

The call connected. "This is Hunter Jones."

She wanted to say something about his name. All that came out was, "Bear." A single, broken word.

"Kenna." She heard rustling. "It's Kenna." Then, "What's happening?"

She couldn't get the words out. "Bear."

"Don't go anywhere. Do not move. Ramon can track your phone. We're on our way."

No, that was a bad idea. They couldn't both leave Nora, the baby, and Preston.

She gasped.

"We're coming to you."

She panted for breath.

"Done?" Anthony said. When she nodded, he ended the call. Then he leaned close to her face. "What's wrong with your arms?"

Jacob had shifted back, sniffling. The older guy still looked angry. She wanted to say something—anything.

What was there to say?

"Cops are here." The old man looked over behind Kenna, down the bridge. "And an ambulance."

"Don't let them take me." Jacob shifted, moving back. Putting distance between them. "They'll put me in jail."

"You should be in jail," the old man said. "Causing all this trouble." He frowned, shaking his head.

Anthony had stiffened.

"Don't say anything," Kenna cautioned him. "Just tell the truth." She shot the older man a look, then looked at Anthony. "If they put you in a squad car, don't say anything unless it's you asking for a lawyer. Got it?"

"What about you?"

More tears leaked from the corners of her eyes. "Help me sit."

Anthony got his hand under her shoulders and helped her sit. Her hands lay useless in her lap. So much pain.

She couldn't even flip her shirt over her gun, holstered on her belt, and she didn't care. All she could do was breathe and not think about the pain, or how bad it might be that she couldn't even lift her hands right now.

What had she done?

She gritted her teeth and pushed all thoughts from her mind. She hadn't considered the consequences when she grabbed him. All she'd done was try to save the life of a teenager. He was alive, so she'd done that.

Now it was only about not moving her arms.

Kenna blinked, sniffed.

"The cops are coming," Anthony whispered.

"You didn't do anything wrong." She glanced at Jacob. "Neither of you did."

She tried to turn to look behind her. Pain roiled through her arms, whipping like lightning, sticking around like the thunderclap that came right after it.

She bit back a cry.

Her gun holster moved, pressing into her hip for a second. Then the gun slid free. "Jacob—"

He scrambled back and stood up, holding her gun. Tears rolling down his face. "I'm not going to jail! I won't go there!"

The police closed in, yelling. So much yelling that the sound swirled in her ears. Anthony got up, and she swayed, not aware how much he'd been supporting her.

"Anthony!" Calling out his name jarred her arms, but he stepped out of view. Away from her. "Anthony, stay back!"

Her voice disappeared in the wash of sound.

And then gunshots.

Kenna's body jerked in surprise, and she screamed. Anthony stood by the side of the bridge, too close to the edge. He had his hands raised, and armed police officers grabbed him. They spun him and put on cuffs while she tried to fight through the pain to find a coherent sentence to speak.

She couldn't do anything.

They muscled Anthony away from the edge.

One of the cops spun to her, holding his weapon. "Put your hands up, or I will shoot!"

She stared at Jacob, his body on the ground. His lifeless eyes staring at her.

Anthony screamed. "She can't lift her hands! She can't do it!"

The cop's aim wavered, shaking just a little. "I said get your hands up!"

Kenna came in and out of awareness as the world spun around her. Pain washed into heat. Sweat and blood dampened every part of her.

Bradley's face swam in front of her, his lifeless eyes staring at her.

Then the killer.

Someone bumped her.

She cried out, and the world seemed to come back into focus.

Ramon touched her cheek. His mouth moved, but she couldn't hear what he said.

Beyond him, someone stood between her and the cop.

"Kenna."

She blinked.

"Kenna, look at me." Ramon turned her face to him. "Did you get hit? I don't see any blood."

She whispered, "Anthony." No, that wasn't the right word. "Arms."

He turned and spoke to someone. A second later, he slid his arms around her and lifted her, one arm under her knees. The movement jostled her arms.

She was pretty sure she screamed, but the night swallowed her up, and everything went black.

Chapter Twenty-Two

Kenna didn't know what time it was when she came to. Lying in a bed in an unfamiliar room. Warmth surrounded her, seeping into her bones. Her arms rested on the covers, and she expected to see bandages, but there was nothing but those old scars.

A tube ran from her left elbow to an IV bag hanging beside the bed.

In the distance, a baby was crying. The sound abruptly stopped, as if the baby had been pacified with something, replaced by footsteps in the hall. The door handle rotated, and Ramon stuck his head in.

"Hey." The word was croaky, but he heard it.

"I was just checking on you."

"I'm awake." She lifted her head, realizing where she must be. "Preston?"

"He insisted on giving up his room because it was the only one free. Bear's doctor came by and saw you." Ramon stood at the end of the bed. "Maizie sent the doctor your medical file, and she took a look at you."

"It doesn't hurt, but it should."

"Because they're pumping you full of the good stuff."

She frowned. The fact she felt lucid even hopped up on something wasn't a good sign. "I don't like narcotics."

He shrugged. "Who does? But they work, and you need them." He stared at her. "You passed out. Freaked out Bear, until I called Jax, and he heard it from him. Finally, he put it together."

"What?" She didn't understand what he was talking about.

"The fact you had no business up there on that bridge, trying to save that kid. The one who ended his life anyway. What do they call it? Suicide by cop."

"As long as that's what it was," she bit out. "I talked him down."

And then that officer had been about to shoot her.

"They didn't ask." She winced. "No one did." Her thoughts swirled around, making her forget the point she was trying to make. "Where is Anthony?"

"I've been here with a baby whose life is in danger. How do I know who that is?"

She frowned. "You said everything was good."

"Because you didn't have anything for me to do. You only had things for you to do." He folded his arms. "We shouldn't be doing this now. You're barely awake."

Kenna shifted her legs under the lightweight covers, trying to sit up.

"No running."

"I'm not trying to run!"

"You're always trying to run. You just haven't figured it out yet."

She clenched her abs and sat up, fighting to stay awake.

The meds had to be good for something. Her hair fell forward, but she got to a sitting position. The needle sticking in the inside of her elbow pulled—or the tape holding it down.

"Ramon, you—"

"We can talk about it later. Don't hurt yourself."

"—need to find out what happened to Anthony."

"Are you even part of this conversation?" He stared at her in disbelief.

"They arrested him, didn't they?"

Ramon took a step to the window, then two. Then he paced back and forth, looking out. "The doctor said when you're awake enough, she'll do a video call with you. Talk to you about your situation."

"I already know my situation." And it was the most frustrating thing she could imagine— not even being able to scratch her nose, which itched like crazy right now.

Anthony was in jail, and there was nothing she could do about that either.

She could only lie here completely helpless.

If someone came in now, or raided the house, she wouldn't even be able to defend herself.

Someone was running a crew in this city, pocketing the loot and making money off kids who should be protected. Nora and Ellie were in danger. People were dying. Active shooters. Bizarre murders.

None of it made sense.

"I'm going to need your help with this, Ramon." Considering she couldn't even get her hair off her face, let alone anything else right now, he had to believe that was true.

He turned to face her. "What do you think I've been doing this whole time?"

"It's been great that you've been protecting Nora and Ellie. Not having to worry about them allowed me to work this case."

"See?" His eyes widened. "I don't even know what the case is."

"Neither do I, really." Kenna shrugged, her arms no better than deadweight. *See?* They were talking. "There are so many things going on, and they seem like they're connected. I'm trying to work out what it even means."

"I guess you don't have to now. Considering you can't do anything." He motioned to her. "So you'll have to loop me in and let me take care of it."

"I can't protect Nora."

"Bear and his people are here. And Nora can find somewhere to go. Put her on a bus out of town. What does it matter?"

Kenna couldn't believe she had to explain it to him. "That baby deserves to feel safe."

"And so you take all the risk while everyone else is protected."

"Of course."

"We're supposed to be partners, Kenna. Or did you work alone so long you forgot what that means?"

"Of course, I didn't forget. What are you talking about?"

"Maybe the fact you haven't been here except to stop by so you feel better about staying away while you work the case. I haven't heard anything from you but a few texts asking how I'm doing. Like all I'm capable of is babysitting."

She stared at him.

"You don't fill me in on what you're doing," he continued. "Or ask for my help when you go out. You take Bear to the mausoleum. Then tonight you don't call anyone at all to go with you."

"Anthony asked for help with his friend." She shook her head. "There was no time to call, and I honestly didn't even think of it. You're here with Nora. Keeping her safe."

"And who is supposed to keep *you* safe?"

Kenna wanted to shrug again.

Outside, a siren grew in volume. Ramon said nothing. The police vehicle passed their street and continued on. She couldn't help the flinch or that she looked away.

So many things to do, and yet all she wanted to do was lie here and fall back asleep. Try not to think about what had happened. Definitely not think about the prognosis the doctor was going to tell her—the one she already knew.

She would far rather be out there working a case.

"I don't need anyone to keep me safe," she said.

She had plenty of people around her she could call for help. The cops were only three numbers away. Though, she would think twice about calling them for a while since one had held a gun pointed at her.

She couldn't imagine what people went through who had faced that type of trauma. She'd been given a tiny glimpse, and it terrified her.

"And when something happens to you, where does that leave me?"

She was about to ask why that was such a big deal when he said, "What about Jax? You think he wants to lose whatever you guys have? Or Maizie? You think Maizie wants to navigate the world without you there to help her figure it out?"

She stared over Ramon's shoulder, feeling the burn of tears in her eyes.

"You're not alone anymore," he muttered. "Maybe you could start acting like it."

Chapter Twenty-Three

Two days later, Kenna was still thinking about the words Ramon had said to her. And now, she would finally get to speak with the doctor over a video chat. She'd had to have Allie help her get dressed because she couldn't do it herself.

She shifted her legs on the bed, dressed in her comfiest cargo pants and a short-sleeved T-shirt. Ignoring Bear, who'd brought the laptop and barely said anything to her. Preston had come by to talk, but Kenna didn't have it in her to do anything but start crying over her current situation, so she'd turned him away. And Nora, with Ellie in her arms.

Two days of inactivity was enough to drive a person crazy. Even if she'd spent a lot of it reading the battered Bible they'd retrieved from her RV.

Kenna pushed aside all the thoughts swirling in her head and focused on the laptop screen beside her knee. "I was hoping you'd tell me it's not as bad as I thought."

The doctor was blonde, and probably midfifties. Trim in a way that indicated she prioritized strength and nutrition. She smiled. "I'm in the business of truth, not lies."

"Me, too." Kenna valued honesty, but that didn't mean she never wanted anyone to say something just to make her feel better.

"How bad did you think it was?" the doctor asked.

Bear stood in much the same spot from which Ramon had delivered his speech. All about how she was risking the rest of them—her family—being heartbroken if something happened to her. All he did was stare out the window. Maybe because he was waiting until the doctor was done to start in on everything she was doing wrong.

Kenna moved her fingers, her arms limp on her lap. "I figured I'd torn everything all over again. That I'd be looking at another surgery, and years of recovery. But I can move my fingers."

"The damage is substantial," the doctor said. "But as you said, you have movement. We will need an MRI once the swelling goes down, but in my estimation it's the worst kind of sprain you can imagine."

"Oh, I can imagine it." Kenna tried to keep her composure.

If she couldn't hold it together, what hope was there? She would wind up falling apart over anything.

After everything she'd been through and the strength she had from God that would hold her up, she knew she would always have something to cling to. A well of resource that gave her hope even when she had nothing.

These days she had such a full life she couldn't even believe it.

"I'm sure you can." The doctor studied her for a second. "How is everything else? This kind of reoccurring injury had to have brought up some dark parts of the past you'd probably rather not remember."

"People are calling to find out if I'm okay, but I can't answer the phone. Let alone type out a text."

The doctor's expression shifted. Yeah, Kenna hadn't answered the question. "Connecting with people who care about you is going to do you good."

Sure, just as soon as she got the image of that dead teen out of her head. She'd asked Ramon to check on Anthony, but the kid didn't know him. Martinez was her next point of contact.

She also needed to find out what was going on with Lottie, and her attempt to get close to Momma in prison.

The doctor continued, "Lean on your people for support and get plenty of rest. Keep taking the prescription meds I left. They're anti-inflammatory."

Kenna nodded.

"Do I have to tell you not to even grip anything, let alone lift something that weighs more than a piece of paper?"

"I doubt I could if I even wanted to." Which made brushing her teeth interesting, to say the least. Allie had managed to get her laughing about it. Much better than crying in the sink. Thankfully, the woman knew how to braid hair.

"I want daily updates. Physical, emotional, mental. Spiritual."

"Economical," Kenna said, trying to lighten the mood.

The doctor chuckled. "I already sent my invoice."

Kenna looked at Bear. He didn't turn around. Who'd paid for her care?

"Take care."

"Thanks, Doc." Kenna watched her end their connection, and Bear walked over.

He slammed the lid of the laptop closed and didn't look at her.

"Are you giving me the silent treatment?"

He sat on the end of the bed, facing her with an impassive expression on his face. "Ready to get out of this bed?"

So he only wanted to answer her question with a question of his own?

Two could play that game.

"Why, is Preston kicking me out?" She'd been wondering when she would outstay her welcome. Between her and the newborn, Kenna's business had to have seriously hampered whatever the guy was doing here in New Orleans.

"The opposite, actually. He said you can stay as long as you want. He's more determined than ever to have you go with him to London."

She frowned. "Because I'll be so helpful with useless arms."

"You'll heal," Bear said. "You think your life is over?"

"It wasn't over before, when I woke up and my arms felt like this, and I had nothing. Why would it be over now when I have way more than that?"

The skin around his eyes flexed. "Then why won't you talk to your friend, or your boyfriend? I'm sure they'd like to hear you're all right."

Maizie and Jax had been updated by Ramon. She knew they were worried, but when her arms screamed just to read their texts, it kind of put a damper on things. Not that she wanted them to show up and see her like this.

"There's nothing wrong with retreating when you're in pain," he added. "No need to talk to everyone who wants to talk to you. But they care."

"I know they care." That was why she *didn't* want to talk to them.

Maybe some people would think it was little better than

licking her wounds. But keeping her own counsel had been her only option for much of her life, and it would probably be her default forever. No matter how much her life changed.

"I don't even know what Ramon's problem is," she continued. "I've been doing my job. He just doesn't like how. And it isn't like he said anything to me about it. Not until after I got injured."

Bear frowned. "Yeah, he shouldn't have dumped on you like that. But in his defense, he had Maizie and Jax calling to get him to find out how you were."

She winced.

"For the record," he said, "both said they'd like you to call them when you're up to it."

So now Bear was in the middle of it as well, running interference in her personal life.

"I don't like being helpless." She pressed her lips together.

"Does anyone?"

She shrugged. "I've never really had to worry about anyone else. Unless it was a case."

"We all have to change." Bear paused. "We grow, and life moves on. People come into our lives, and others leave it."

"Who knew you were so emotionally astute."

He studied her for a few moments.

Kenna figured he was going to comment on her deflecting. But honestly, given how she normally did it, this was diminished-capacity Kenna. She was hardly at fighting strength.

Instead, he asked, "What do you need?"

"To not have to lay here for another day. My arms aren't going to magically repair themselves, and my legs work just fine."

"Let's go, then." Bear slid off the bed, surprisingly agile for someone built like a redneck version of the Rock.

Kenna set her feet on the floor, then slipped them into a pair of shoes she didn't need to lace. Her arms hung by her sides and didn't feel great, but she was done with the IV, and the prescription meds gave her enough relief she wasn't writhing in agony.

She followed him to the kitchen, where Nora sat at the breakfast bar, holding her baby.

Kenna said, "Hey."

Nora looked her up and down and smiled. "You look about how I feel."

"Great." Kenna slipped into the stool beside her. "I need Allie to braid my hair, I think."

Nora scanned Kenna's head and wrinkled her nose. "If you're planning on going out, that might be a good idea."

"Out?" Ramon turned from the stove, holding a spatula. He glanced at her and managed not to wince.

Kenna shrugged. Bear had disappeared, and she could hear him talking to someone in the living room.

Ramon set the spatula down and grabbed a cup from the fridge. A full glass of something that looked like a smoothie and smelled like peanut butter. He stuck a metal straw in it. "Breakfast. At least to start with."

"Thanks." She took a sip, wishing she could feed herself. A liquid diet didn't sound all that fun. Still. "Tastes good."

He nodded, then went back to stirring whatever he had going on in that skillet. "Wanna hit the PD and check on the case after you eat?" He was acting like he hadn't said all those things to her right when she'd woken up. Like this was any other day, and she was coming off having the flu or something.

"Sure." Kenna took another sip. "Any news from Anthony?"

"He's back at the group home. No charges filed."

"That's good, since he didn't do anything wrong and neither did his friend." Kenna's stomach clenched.

"As if that ever stopped the police from doing whatever they want," Nora said.

The baby fussed, and she patted her back.

Kenna figured it was never as simple as that but didn't want to get into a lengthy discussion. "How are you doing?"

The girl shrugged. "It's been amazing being here. Feeling safe and letting you guys take care of me. But it's also like a vacation. You know, like soon enough you'll be back in your real life, and nothing has changed."

Kenna couldn't recall the last time she'd been on vacation, though every few months she made the trek back to Colorado and spent a couple of days with Maizie.

That was more like checking back in at home base.

Maybe she should go to Hawaii. Or on a cruise.

"Do you know where you'll go next?" she asked.

"I've been talking to Preston about it," Nora replied. "I would rather be near Garth, but for now it might be better to lay low. Preston has a house on the coast in Washington. He said if I want to, I can stay there as long as I want, and I'll only have to earn enough to cover our incidentals since the house is already paid for."

"Wow." Kenna took another sip of her smoothie.

"I know. I wasn't sure what to think about him at first, since he killed his wife and everything. But he told me the story, and it makes sense."

"That someone else was in the house?"

Nora nodded. "And he said prison was the best thing that ever happened to him. That he got clean, and he found Jesus. He told me about that, too."

Ramon grunted but said nothing.

"I can answer any questions about that stuff as well,"

Kenna said, "if you want to ask anything. About the Bible, or Jesus."

"Thanks," Nora said. "I've never been to church. But now that I have Ellie, it's like... why not try to be the best person I can be for her?"

Kenna knew how that felt. Her situation with Maizie was so different, and yet she could understand what made Nora want to be someone Ellie looked up to.

A steady source of peace and the kind of affection everyone should have in their lives, and yet so many kids didn't get. Children like Anthony and Jacob. Left to flounder in the world with no anchor.

"You guys have been amazing." Nora shook her head. "But Preston told me about grace, and I guess it makes sense to want to give a gift. But it's still not normal to just give someone a house to live in."

Kenna smiled around the straw and took another long sip. She liked the thought that she'd done the same thing with Maizie, in her own way. Giving the girl what she'd never had.

Maybe she and Preston were more alike than she'd thought.

Ramon set a plate in front of Nora. He served his own into a bowl, which he ate standing up in front of the sink.

"I didn't know you knew how to cook." She took another sip. "And now you make meals and smoothies?"

He swallowed a bite, holding the fork above his bowl. "I can make a few things."

"This is really good," Nora said.

Ramon didn't look at her. He just ate some more.

From what she knew about having a newborn—which, admittedly, wasn't much—the first few days or weeks of a baby's life involved a whole lot of...she wanted to say trauma bonding between the parents.

There was probably a better expression for it.

And she at least *hoped* parents bonded over shared responsibility for a child. But still, was that what had happened with Ramon, watching over Nora and Ellie the past week or so?

Kenna's phone rang. She knew it was hers because of the ringtone. She turned on the stool, trying to locate the source of the sound.

Bear strode in, holding her cell. "It's Martinez," he said between rings. "Wanna take it?"

She shrugged. "I guess."

Bear answered the call and put it on speaker, holding it out in front of her, which meant she was stuck here where everyone would hear the conversation.

"Hello?"

"You finally pick up." Martinez sounded exasperated. "Camra Tenison is here at the PD, and she's flipping out. Tossing files and knocking mugs over. Says she wants to talk to you, and only you."

"That's what you mean by flipping out?" Kenna asked.

"Knocking over pamphlet racks and screaming at the desk sergeant."

Hmm. "Did you lock her down?"

"Of course," Martinez huffed. "She's in a cell, but she won't quit until she talks to you."

"And you have no idea what it's about?"

"You tell me. She didn't know how to reach you, I guess. Or couldn't. Kind of like when I had updates about the case to share with you."

Kenna's cheeks heated. Of course, there was yet *another* person mad at her.

The baby started to fuss, probably because of the noise.

Kenna slid off the stool and moved to the other side of the

island. Bear went with her, holding the phone in front of her face. "Updates like what?"

Bear's lips curled up, but only slightly.

"Damien's iPad, the one Camra gave us from her house along with all his stuff," Martinez said. "It's got zero pictures of them on it. There's no evidence from his phone that they were in a relationship."

"She's the 'other woman' in Damien's life," Kenna said. "So maybe cut her some slack, because she's grieving and apparently not handling it well. Maybe we don't tell her he didn't even have a photo of them."

"It's not like she's listening to this conversation." He paused. "But who doesn't have a photo of the person they're dating?"

"People cheating on their spouse."

"If that's what was even happening."

Kenna frowned. "Why would she have his stuff if they weren't dating?"

"If they were, why does he have zero calls or texts with her on his phone? Zero work emails, nothing in drafts—like when people try to hide stuff by not even sending messages. His messaging apps are clean. There's no evidence this guy was in a relationship with anyone other than his wife."

"Then he had a second phone."

"Too bad we can't ask him or his wife about it." Martinez sighed. "So are you coming here to talk to her, or not?"

Kenna lifted her chin. "I'll be there in an hour."

Bear ended the call. "How are you going to work this with two nonfunctioning arms?"

"I don't need arms to talk to someone." She looked at Ramon. "But I do need a ride."

Ramon set his bowl in the sink. "Let's go."

"I'll find Allie," Bear said. "See if she can do something about your hair."

"Come on. I can't possibly look that bad." Kenna glanced around.

Nora slipped off her chair and took the baby in the living room. Bear didn't look at her. Ramon disappeared, muttering something about finding his shoes.

Kenna sighed. "Allie, I need help!"

Chapter Twenty-Four

Kenna walked up to the entrance of the police department and clocked the button for the disabled entry, a square silver press button on a free-standing post just in front of the door.

She had her hands tucked in the sweater, in the long pocket across the front. Thankfully, it was November and cooler out, not a hundred degrees in summer. But she wasn't under any illusions that someone wouldn't call her on the fact she wasn't going to pull her hands out. Though, in a police station she probably wanted her hands where the cops could see them—just in case.

She leaned her elbow on the door opener. The fact she could gain entry *by herself* felt good, even if she couldn't lift a coffee cup.

Ramon grabbed the door handle, and it started to open toward him. He side-stepped the door and looked at her before going in.

Kenna followed him. "Thanks for driving me, by the way."

He glanced at her with a frown. "We're gonna do the pleasantries thing now?" He waited while the second set of doors opened. "You didn't talk to me the whole drive over here, but you want to do it now?"

"Forget I said anything."

Martinez waited for them in the lobby.

"No, I don't think I will." Ramon reached for her, then thought better of it. He neared her and spoke low, saying, "Did you call Maizie?"

Kenna pressed her lips together.

"What about Jax?"

He hadn't texted her today, but he'd filled her in yesterday. "He's on an operation," Kenna said. "He knows what happened, and we'll catch up when we have a moment."

"So, that's a no?"

"Can we not do this right now?" she whispered.

"You only want to *not* talk about it because you know I'm right and you're wrong."

"We're in a public place." She looked around. "We can talk later."

"It isn't me you need to connect with." Ramon turned and headed for the front desk.

Kenna blew out a breath.

A family sat in waiting area chairs on the left. On the right, an older man filled a tiny water cup from a dispenser. A guy in dark-green overalls pushed a mop back and forth, before squeezing the moisture into a yellow bucket.

Behind the desk, two officers—a man and a woman—noticed Ramon and Kenna. Ramon didn't talk to them. She lifted her chin in the direction of the man they'd come here to see.

It wasn't that Kenna couldn't have figured out how to call

Maizie with a few taps of her fingers. But the idea of talking right now made her want to lie down and cry herself to sleep. To say she was dragging was a mega understatement. She'd wasted most of the energy she had on drinking that smoothie.

She had time to talk to Maizie later and explain what was going on—which hopefully Ramon already had. Same with Jax, once his case was done.

Ramon seemed to think it was all a problem, but Kenna had the autonomy to choose how to react, process, and reconnect when she wanted to. Not on someone else's timetable of what they thought was appropriate.

Martinez pushed through a door, lifted his hand at the desk officers, and came over. "Did you get sick or something? It's been days."

"Or something." She wanted to shrug but kept her arms still. The cops here didn't need to know her struggles. She wanted to talk about Jacob, and what a colossal tragedy that was, or about Anthony and the fact he'd been arrested for no other reason than he'd been there. But she couldn't get the words out.

"Seriously, the officers who responded to that bridge incident said you wigged out."

Ramon said, "Anyone would react to having a cop point a gun at their face."

Martinez shot him a look. "They did their jobs."

Kenna didn't have the energy to squabble about whether his defense of them was valid or not. "Camra is here?"

Martinez nodded. Then had them check in.

Kenna managed to hand over her driver's license, which she had tucked in her pocket. The pain was an ever-present angry tension that made her want to bang her head into a wall. Usually, this was the point she'd take a full dose of ibuprofen, and she'd already taken the meds the doctor had given her. She didn't want to know what her arms would feel like if she hadn't taken anything.

"She's down here." Martinez motioned. "We kept her separate from general lockup, which is full right now."

"What happened?" Ramon stepped up beside them, holding the door so Kenna didn't have to.

The guy was turning into what she imagined an annoying older brother might be like. Having grown up as an only child, she didn't know how to react. Did siblings constantly hound each other with the idea they were doing things wrong? The back-and-forth was exhausting, and she needed to be fighting fit in order to figure out how to combat it. Not like she was right now, about to cave. She had to stay strong, or he would win.

Martinez glanced between the two of them. "Camra Tenison entered the PD lobby during an exchange between us and some local US marshals," he began. "The marshals were handing over custody of a suspect so we can talk to him. The door was open, and she snuck in during the chaos. She got all the way up to Major Crimes without being stopped. And at that point, she asked sweetly of an officer where to find the detective working this homicide.

"He assumed she was here for a meeting and walked her to my desk, at which point she grabbed a stack of papers and tossed them into the air. In the confusion, she started yelling."

"Good way to get yourself shot," Ramon said. "I'm surprised no one put a bullet in her."

Martinez stopped at the next door and hit a button. A buzzer sounded beyond the door. "She was, and is, unarmed. She didn't hurt anyone and didn't resist arrest."

Kenna said, "What did she do?"

The door clicked, and a light above turned green.

Martinez pushed it open and led them into a hallway with breezeblock concrete walls and far too much fluorescent light. "Screamed bloody murder about her boyfriend's death. How we're all sitting around, doing nothing evidently, and the killer is out there somewhere. Justice is too slow, she believes he's watching her. All of it was along those lines."

Kenna nodded. "I can see how she might think that."

"All of us have a time or two."

She didn't look at Ramon, or she would end up reacting to that comment. His tone sounded wistful. She had no idea what he was trying to do.

Martinez pretty much ignored both of them. He led them to the first cell, where Camra stood looking out a high window. Whether she could see a bird or plane from that angle, or nothing at all, Kenna didn't know.

"You okay?" Kenna asked.

Camra turned, a haggard look on her face that probably wasn't too dissimilar to the way everyone seemed to think Kenna looked right now. "Kenna, hey." Her voice was hoarse, probably from screaming it raw.

Kenna looked at Martinez. "Is there somewhere we can talk with Camra?" Not only because she needed to sit, but also because having bars between them would only make this woman feel like a suspect.

Martinez let Camra out of the cell. She walked with them to a conference room on the other end of this floor. "Take a seat."

He wasn't talking to Kenna, but she did what he said. Camra sat close, while Ramon stood by the door leaning against the wall.

"That's my associate, Ramon Santiago," Kenna said. "He's working with me on this case and a number of others."

Camra's assessing gaze took in Ramon. Maybe she had a

thing for guys with dark hair. Or guys that might be unavailable.

All Kenna could think was that it was a good thing Jax was blond. Not that he would ever meet this woman.

"Talk to me, Camra."

The other woman rolled her eyes. "You don't need to tell me I shouldn't have come here. I know that."

"Did you get the answers you were looking for?" Whether Camra considered this a success or a failure, Kenna needed to get her to decide if the method was worth the madness.

"I'm just so...frustrated sitting in my house doing nothing. Whoever shot Damien is still out there." Camra slumped back in the seat. Her visible exhaustion and the stress she'd been under didn't mar the natural good looks she possessed. But beneath all that, a person had to have substance. Otherwise, it was all nice packaging containing nothing.

"You mean, Damien and his wife."

"What?"

"I actually thought it might've been you who was one of the victims when I heard the news." Kenna paused. "It's a tragedy for sure, but at least they didn't have children."

Camra blinked. She seemed almost stunned by what Kenna just said. Even if they'd discussed it the last time, when Martinez and Kenna had interviewed her at the house. Effectively, what she'd done was put Camra's grief in its place. But this woman had to know that screaming at the cops, and being a nuisance, wasn't the way to find satisfaction.

Kenna continued, "The police are working the case, but it's not straightforward. Not that any case really is, but their deaths seem to be connected to another incident."

"What other incident?"

Kenna had thought she already knew, but said, "An attempted abduction occurred in the hospital during the same attack when Damien and his wife were killed. Do you know anything about that?"

"How would I?" Camra shook her head. "I didn't have anything to do with it."

"Do you know who might have had a reason to kill Damien, or his wife? Either of them could've been the intended target, or both."

Camra barked a humorless laugh. "Other than me? I know that's what everyone is thinking. I even had a reporter call me and ask why I did it. Why I killed both of them when I could've just killed her, and then he and I would've run away together."

Kenna frowned. "Wow, that's pretty forward. I'm sorry someone did that."

"I came over here right after." Camra sighed. "I wasn't thinking straight."

Kenna nodded. "That's understandable. You're grieving. It's okay to not think straight when you're under stress."

Or injured.

Maybe Ramon would hear that and get the concept that her actions didn't need to make sense right now. Not when she was in this much pain.

What she needed was a hug from Jax. Without any talking. Just a hug.

Kenna sighed.

Martinez's phone buzzed, and he looked at it. "I'll be back."

The door closed, and Kenna said, "What's going to happen next?" Maybe Martinez had already explained to Camra that she was getting a fine—or a ticket.

"I don't know. I guess the police aren't going to keep me updated now."

"But they're working to find Damien's killer."

"I hope so." Camra let out a breath. "The thing between us was just fun, you know? Sneaking around. Stealing time. There's a rush to it because it feels kinda wrong. Then you realize you fell in love. You didn't mean to, but it happened."

Kenna was pretty sure that getting involved with a married man *was* wrong, but she wasn't going to argue right now. And, what did her judgment matter? After all, the affair was over because the man in question was dead.

But why no indications they were in a relationship? No texts, phone calls—nothing.

"I know you cared about him a lot." Kenna paused, searching Camra's gaze. "But you can't take your frustration out on the police. They don't take it well when they're accosted. It could have gone a lot of ways today, and this was probably the best scenario. If they give you a ticket, I'd just pay it and go. Okay?"

Camra nodded.

Before she could say anything, Martinez stuck his head back in. "It'll be a while. Sorry. Just stay here."

Ramon shifted off the wall. "What's going on?"

"The guy the marshals brought in is dead. He just keeled over in his cell." Martinez shook his head, shock on his face. "You'll have to stay here until we get this figured out." He shut the door.

Kenna glanced at Camra. A flash of satisfaction washed over the other woman's face, disappearing almost as fast as it had come.

Before she realized she was moving, Kenna stood and the chair rolled back. She backed up a few steps, and Ramon moved in front of her.

He pinned Camra with a stare. "You did this."

"I don't know what you're talking about." The waterworks returned. "I did *what?*"

Ramon planted one hand on the table and leaned down, getting in her face. "Perfectly timed your entry so you could give the guy something that ended his life."

He'd said what her mind seemed to not have fully formulated yet. The fact Camra's presence here and the suspect's death were connected.

Kenna said, "An autopsy will tell the police everything they need to know about how that man died." She had to lean against the wall, but she couldn't be near Camra. Just in case. Ramon on the other hand seemed to be itching for a confrontation. Too many days watching a newborn? Maybe he was past ready to get back to his real work, and that was where all the frustration was coming from.

"I didn't do anything!" Camra protested.

Ramon chuckled. "No place like a police station to confess your crimes. You were the distraction, right? Maybe you didn't kill him, but it's no coincidence he's dead. You come in. He conveniently dies. The cops and the feds get nothing."

Kenna wanted to know who the dead guy was, and how he connected to all this.

"I didn't kill him."

"So you're the distraction," Ramon said. "Someone paid you to cause a scene while a killer did their work. Is that it?"

Kenna moved to where she could see Camra's face. That wasn't grief there—more like anger. Or frustration that she'd been discovered. The ruse was up.

It was time to come clean.

"I didn't have a choice," Camra said. "I'm not going down as a murderer!"

"Someone coerced you?" Kenna asked.

"I said I didn't have a choice."

Ramon stared her down. "Now say more."

Camra huffed.

"You were told to come here," Kenna stated. She needed to get Martinez in here to listen to this. She couldn't even pull out her phone, so she'd left it in the car. "You were told to do this, weren't you?"

Ramon shifted his stance. Alert. Ready for anything. "How did they pass you the instructions? Email, text, phone call...what?"

"A note in my mailbox." Camra sniffed.

"Where is it?" Kenna figured if they could get it then the police would want to use it as evidence. "What did you do with the note?"

"I burned it. I didn't even want to open it because I already knew what it was, but I had to see what this one said."

"You've had one before?" Ramon sank into the seat facing her, alongside the big table. He sat on the edge of the chair, nothing about his stance relaxed.

Camra nodded. "Instructions to do something, or else. And then it said to burn it."

"Why follow the instructions?" Kenna asked, already knowing there was an answer. "Just ignore it, and don't do what it says." But then, for all Kenna knew, it was Camra who had killed Damien and his wife.

"Last time I didn't do what they said, my mother was mugged outside the mall."

"So you were the distraction?" Kenna asked.

"I didn't kill him."

Ramon said, "Who are they?"

"I can't tell you that."

Kenna moved toward the door, to shift Camra's attention to her. "Yes, you can." She needed this woman to understand. "We've dealt with people like this before. If you do nothing, they'll never stop. And you'll never be free."

Camra sniffed and looked away. "We all sell our souls to something." She shrugged one shoulder. "Who knows, the next person who comes along could be worse."

"Who is it?" Kenna asked her.

"If I tell you, I'm the next to die."

Chapter Twenty-Five

Kenna slid into the car. She tucked her legs in, and Ramon shut the door. Her phone, in the cupholder, had a bunch of notifications. But she didn't tap the power button to light up the screen.

Ramon turned on the engine. "The killer works for the boss, taking orders and doing what they're told. Where have I heard that before?"

Kenna managed to smile. "It does seem a little Walter and Cecelia. Maybe they've seen all the news reports."

"It's good to be famous." Ramon knocked an imaginary piece of fluff from his shoulder.

Kenna shook her head. "It does make sense, though. The guy who hurt Reggie and stabbed Bear when he ran off is paid by the boss, whoever that is. Someone is calling the shots, and they've got more than just Landry on their payroll."

"Please tell me this is a 'cut off the head, the body dies' situation."

"You're not getting a sword."

"Party pooper."

"You did not just say that." Kenna shook her head. "You've lost your mind."

"We should head back to the house. The cops might want to be the ones who interrogate Camra, but we can tap our own resources." He pulled out of the parking space. "Maybe Nora."

"You think she knows who Landry works for?"

Ramon didn't answer her question.

Kenna tested moving her arms. They felt heavy and unwieldy. Like carrying two useless clubs instead of hands to grip things. She could swing her arms and whack someone, but the likelihood was that she'd do more damage to herself than them.

"When I woke up in the hospital—"

"I don't wanna walk down memory lane with you," Ramon cut in. "You're up and working. Your arms will improve, right? So let's keep moving forward. Work the case. Get this done. You can lick your wounds after."

She stared at him. "Fresh start?"

If he refused to even acknowledge the past, how was he going to make sure he didn't repeat a mistake he'd already made? One he should've learned from.

"As much as I don't want to feel like history repeated itself," Kenna said, "how can I not, when this is the same pain I've been battling for years? I'll always be fighting it. It's never going to go away. It won't heal. Not completely."

The fact was, she might have destroyed a good portion of the progress she'd made with her arm strength the past few years.

Done. Gone.

Ramon shrugged. "Guess you'll be stuck relying on other people for help." He sounded almost smug.

"I will need someone to carry my bags, and open doors for

me. How do you feel about coming on full-time as my chauffer?"

Ramon snorted. "Tell Jax. He'll probably retire just to take the job."

"Nope."

"So you don't let anyone in, because you don't want them doing what you think they shouldn't." He glanced over, taking a right turn. "Keep everyone at arm's length so they don't disappoint you."

"That isn't it."

Ramon was about to speak when his phone rang. He dug it out of the inside pocket of his blazer. Thumb swipe. Tap. "Hello."

"It's Maizie. What's going on? You're both out of the house, but the GPS I had on the car is fritzing." She sounded stressed out, worried and on the verge of something that could spiral out of control. "Like something is blocking the signal. It's intermittent at best."

"Everything's good," Kenna said. "There was a guy at the police department who was gonna talk to the police. But the bad guy paid Camra to distract them, and he ended up dead. We left them to figure it all out."

Silence filled the air in the car.

Ramon pulled into a pharmacy parking lot and found a space.

"I didn't know if you were okay."

"Can't lift my arms, Maze. Can't dial the phone with my nose."

Ramon said, "I feel like if you wanted to, you could figure it out. Or used voice commands."

"How to dial with my nose? Or allowing my phone to listen to me twenty-four/seven versus just tracking me every other way." She stared at him. "I can barely use the bathroom by myself. Do you know how much energy it takes? I feel like I need a nap after every time."

Okay, not exactly. But they both got the idea.

Maizie said, "Bear sent me copies of what he sent the doctor." Her voice was small, making her sound far younger than she was. "I showed them to Elizabeth. I hope that was okay. She's not that kind of doctor, but we looked up some stuff online. I hope that's okay."

"Maizie..." Kenna sighed, realizing the kid had repeated herself. "Do whatever you need to do. Okay?"

"You weren't answering your phone. Neither is Jax." Her voice shook.

Kenna closed her eyes. "I'm okay. Or I will be."

"I'm not giving you an update. I have nothing. I can't even think right now."

"Maybe you should go grab Stairns."

"He's mad at you because you haven't been answering the phone."

"I can't lift—"

"He said you could've figured out a way."

"She's been resting," Ramon said. "It was a bad night."

"I don't even know what happened."

Kenna took the phone from Ramon, dropping it in her lap because she couldn't hold it more than a few seconds. Just long enough to transfer it near her so she didn't have to talk loudly. "There was a kid. A young man on the bridge, looking for a way to end it." She sniffed. "I talked him down, but someone else intervened at the last second. We lost our balance, and the kid slipped. I spent too long holding on to him, gripping his clothes and straining my arms with his weight."

"And it still bothers you because that serial killer cut your tendons? They aren't healed, even though you had surgery."

Maizie paused. "Stairns told me what happened to you. More than what I knew." It might've sounded like a harsh way to say it, mentioning the man who had terrorized her, but Kenna heard the flat way Maizie said it. The girl was processing and trying to get a grip on the situation.

Kenna sighed. "They were surgically repaired, but it's never the same. I used them too much and strained them."

Thankfully, she hadn't simply torn them all over again, where they'd been severed before. That would have meant another surgery, not just waiting for the swelling to go down. Waiting for the injury to heal. Waiting for...she didn't even know how long it would take until she felt normal again.

She might never be back where she had been just days ago.

Tears gathered at the corner of her eyes.

Ramon pulled out and drove toward the house.

Maizie went silent for a while. Kenna, too, sat in the silence, looking out the window. Content to just be in each other's presence, even if it was only over the phone. Something she and Maizie did on occasion. One of them might fall asleep. One of them might put on a movie or play some music. They'd pick up the conversation eventually.

Ramon had said she was pushing them all away, by working the case herself. That she didn't want to change and have them be fully a part of her life.

But change wasn't always that obvious. Sometimes it was only tiny things, or incremental differences. The way she reached for her Bible these days. How she and Maizie spent time together, even from a distance. Jax, and this thing between them they were both wanting to explore. Even with all the unspoken between them, they knew how each other felt.

Even if they hadn't said it.

Because yes. She loved him.

Maybe Kenna hadn't ever admitted it to herself. She'd never said it to him. That kind of admission? It was huge. She'd never thought she would be here again in her life. Wanting to settle down with a man, and thinking about the future not just the next case.

How she felt was a simple fact, one single incremental change that had snuck up on her. Until she realized she loved him.

Just like that.

She would have to tell him. And let all of them in more.

Ramon wanted immediate change from her, the way he seemed to have bounced back from his past. But as far as she was concerned, she'd been making tiny adjustments this whole time.

"I used to live in New Orleans."

Ramon glanced at her.

"What?" Maizie said. "When?"

Kenna cleared her throat. "My dad took a case here. I was seven, and he paid the campground host to keep an eye on me. When he didn't come back, I stuck close to the trailer, but she figured out I was by myself."

"Did he get hurt?"

"It just took longer finding out what he needed to know, and maybe he got injured, but I don't remember." Kenna shook her head. "The campground host called the police, and social services got involved. They put me in a foster home. Here in New Orleans.

"I was here for three weeks, and I had the case evidence my dad had collected. He told me to keep it safe, but some bullies from the house followed me home from school. It was down the street from the house, and I had to walk back and forth."

Ramon pulled behind Preston's house and into a space but kept the engine running.

She continued, "There was this girl at the house. In my room. She was big, and all the boys were afraid of her. She saved me from them. She said I owed her, and one day she'd collect." She looked over at Ramon. "She's Anthony's mother, Leticia."

A knowing look crossed his face. "Martinez said the ATF had a person in the prison. Maizie found out Anthony's mother is incarcerated in the same place."

"What happened to your dad?" Maizie asked.

"He showed up a few weeks later. Maybe he'd been injured or captured. But he never told me." She bit the inside of her lip. "We just packed up and moved on."

"Like it never happened."

She glanced at Ramon. "People are how they are. It's just what I learned. How to keep going. How to push through and get the job done."

"How to ignore the obvious."

"How to be a stone-cold killer catcher," Maizie added.

Kenna frowned, but it was also a little funny.

"I'm sorry that happened to you," Maizie said. "But Elizabeth—and you—both told me that the things we live through make us who we are."

"So I'm a cartel enforcer?" Ramon asked.

Kenna leaned her head back on the headrest because emotions were exhausting. "No one is saying that."

"I'm just trying to figure it out," he said. "Like working with you and dealing with cops now."

"We all are," Kenna said. "What's nature. What's nurture. What God wants to wipe away and what He will use for His glory."

Ramon made a face, like he was unconvinced, but said nothing.

"Can He actually wipe it all away?" Maizie asked.

Kenna knew what the Bible said. "As far as the east is from the west. That's how far He removes our sins from us," she said. "Sometimes it seems hard to believe. Or we don't think we're that bad. What's the big deal? And everything in between. But what's true is just true. It's up to us what we do with it."

Ramon pushed out the car and headed for the house.

Kenna said, "Love you, Maizie."

"Love you too, Kenna."

She ended the call with a painful tap of her finger, slid it into her pocket and followed Ramon.

One of Bear's guys was in the back yard, a roving patrol. "I like how you shut the door with your hip," he called after her. "It was cute."

The humor was enough to cut through the tension of minutes ago, and he'd had no idea what they were talking about in the car.

She managed to laugh. "I aim to please." She kicked the bottom of the door with her boot, and Bear let her in. "Can't turn the handle."

He didn't lose the frown.

"What's going on?" Kenna kicked off her slip-on sneakers and glanced around. "Did something happen?"

He led her to the living room, where Preston sat in the armchair and Nora occupied the couch with Ellie. No one said anything.

"Bear?"

For once, he didn't look at her. He usually had the body language of a sibling toward her, but tonight he seemed cold.

"The crew hit another house tonight. It's all over the police band that a house got broken into. Trashed, and looted."

"Whose house?" Kenna asked.

Hopefully, no one was hurt.

"A friend of mine," Preston replied. "A judge who tries family court cases. Adoptions and such."

"Is anyone hurt?"

Bear didn't respond.

Preston shook his head. "All her case files were stolen."

Bear turned and left the room. Kenna followed him, slipping her hands in her sweater pocket. "Talk to me."

He got a water from the fridge but didn't open it. He squeezed it so hard it would probably explode in his hands.

"What's going on?"

"Allie didn't come back from the store yet." He glanced at the clock on the oven. "She should be back by now."

"You have GPS on her phone?"

"It says she's still there, but she isn't answering."

"So go find her," she said.

"I can't leave my detail."

Kenna spun to the hall. "Ramon!"

Chapter Twenty-Six

"There." Kenna pointed across the grocery store parking lot. "You see those flashing lights?"

Ramon steered the car toward the far side of the lot, where a black-and-white police vehicle was parked beside a gray sedan. "You think that's her?"

"I think we're gonna find out."

The grocery store was an upmarket chain, the kind of bougie place she usually steered away from unless she wanted something specific, and they were the only ones who carried it. It wasn't even about living frugally, but there was something about overly shiny shopping-mall-style grocery stores that didn't seem to be about food anymore. They were more about branding and lifestyles.

But then, it was also the closest one to Preston's house.

Ramon pulled into a space down from the police officer and what they hoped was Allie's car.

"You'll have to let me out."

Ramon glanced at her. "Why don't you let me handle this one? A single person is less suspicious than a pair."

Before she could argue the point, he climbed out and shut

the door. Which left her pretty much unable to do anything. Like getting out of the car. She figured if she had to, she could probably tug on the handle and then kick the door open with her foot. The problem was, any use of her hand meant that it would hurt more later. Not to mention stunt her recovery, or even risk her life at some point.

Just in case the worst happened, Kenna stayed where she was.

Okay, fine. She was mad.

But she didn't think he'd left her here out of spite, because the conversation with Maizie had turned to something spiritual.

Some people didn't want to hear about anything related to God, but she'd given up being offended by people's beliefs a long time ago. It wasn't too hard to leave people to make their own choice on what they followed. The same way she expected people to grant her the freedom to believe whatever *she* wanted to believe.

Kenna's phone rang.

But as much as she might want, it wasn't Jax calling.

It was actually Ramon's name that flashed across the screen. She managed to swipe across the screen with one finger and tap the speaker button before her hands flopped back into her lap.

She was going to ignore how much it hurt. Or how oversize her forearms felt—swollen and inflamed when they actually didn't seem much bigger.

The one thing she had learned was that however things were, it wasn't how they would always be.

Thirty feet away she could see Allie sitting in the front passenger side, her feet on the ground so that she was turned toward the officer. Kenna couldn't see any visible injuries, but that didn't mean she hadn't been attacked.

Things connected to this case seemed to be happening in rapid succession. Especially things that shouldn't be connected but apparently were.

At this point, Kenna wasn't even sure what the case was. The ATF was working on Momma Landry. The police were working on the crew of robbers breaking into people's houses. All she needed to do was make sure Anthony remained safe.

And wait for her arms to heal enough she could have basic functionality back. At that point, she would actually be able to drive her RV out of here.

Although, if she couldn't drive herself...

Maybe Jax could take a few days off and come over to help her get her RV where she was going. Like somewhere close to where he lived so she could spend a few days or weeks recuperating in a place she could spend time with him.

Through the phone she heard, "Babe, I was so worried," as Ramon closed in on Allie, and the police officer halted his questions for a second.

The uniformed man lowered his notebook and watched the newcomer with his victim. Assessing the situation, the way anyone who did this job tended to do without even thinking about it.

Ramon dissolved into Spanish, his arms going around Allie. "Just go with it."

Kenna was pretty sure she heard Allie chuckle. "I'm okay. I'm just ready to get out of here."

Ramon turned to the officer. "Are you almost done?"

The guy nodded. "Ma'am, are you certain you don't require medical attention? Even if you don't want an ambulance, it might be worth going to your doctor or urgent care and getting checked out. Just in case."

"I'll keep that in mind," Allie said. "Thank you."

The officer nodded and turned away, heading for his car.

Ramon said, "What happened?" He paused, then added quickly, "You should know, Kenna is listening from the car."

Allie glanced over.

Kenna would've given her a wave, but she settled for lifting her chin.

"I think I was followed on the way here. I was getting that vibe, so I took a couple of random turns. When I didn't see anyone, I just came here." Allie paused to catch her breath. "I figured I was just on edge because of everything going on. But then as I was walking into the store, someone popped up from between two cars and rushed me. They knocked me against the next car. I fought back, and I know I hurt them. But I think I passed out for a few seconds. When I came to, the store manager was standing over me with another customer."

"Did you get a look at his face?" Ramon asked.

Allie shook her head. "I don't even know if it was a guy. I think there was a flash of dark clothing. Something fluttering."

"Like a robe," Kenna said to herself.

"Do you think it was a robe?" Ramon echoed.

"I don't know." Allie groaned. "My head is pounding."

"I know you're supposed to get groceries, but maybe you should just head home. We can give you a ride if you need one."

"Yeah, that's probably a good idea." She started to get up out of the car.

Ramon caught her elbow and helped her stand. "Bear was pretty worried about you. He wanted to come himself, but he couldn't leave the detail."

"You don't need to explain it to me," Allie said. "I already know how this works."

Kenna's brows rose, but only because no one would be able to see her surprised expression. Unless they were creeping on her sitting in a car.

Allie followed Ramon over, then climbed in the back seat and let out a long breath.

"I might have some pain pills around here somewhere?" Kenna looked around, then twisted far enough she could look at Allie.

The other woman shrugged. "I'll be fine. I probably deserve to have a headache after I let that guy get the jump on me. The team is never going to let me live this down."

"And here I was thinking it was a good team." Kenna shook her head. "Those guys treat you like that?"

"It's just a saying. They'd give anyone a hard time for the same thing. It's not because I'm a Marine."

Or a woman.

Kenna chuckled. "Right. Wasn't Bear in the army, or something like that?"

"Yep."

Ramon shifted in his seat, turning far enough to hand Allie her car keys. "Can we be done with this conversation I don't understand so we can go?"

Kenna eyed him. "I was never in any military branch, and even I know they have a rivalry with each other."

Ramon only grunted and pulled out of the space, driving toward the exit where a Camaro pulled in. "So what do we think? Is this connected to Landry, and everything going on, or was attacking you about Preston?"

Kenna looked over her shoulder, far enough to see the expression on Allie's face. "Or something else entirely. But we don't have to talk about it now, if your head hurts too much."

Allie said, "I have no idea what it's related to."

"Given the clothing, I would lean toward whoever tried to kill Reggie and stabbed Bear." Ramon held the wheel with one hand, his other turning his phone on his leg. "Speaking of which. Did he even wake up in the hospital?"

Kenner shook her head. "We should find out, because I have no idea. And now I feel bad because I haven't made a point to check on him."

"Neither have I," Ramon said, "and I wasn't recovering from a major injury sustained in the last few days."

"If it was connected to your case, how would someone have known I was helping out you guys?" Allie paused. "They'd have to have followed me from the house—maybe because you were driving my car before, so they thought I was you. And if they did follow me then our safe house has been discovered. Which presents an entirely new problem."

"You're right. It does. And even if someone is trying to hit back at you guys because it weakens the protection around Preston, it's basically the same problem. They know where you are, and they're being strategic about attacking. Taking out vital team members so you're weaker."

"I'll text Bear, so we don't have to wait until we get back to the house before we fill him in." Allie shifted in the back seat, tapping on her phone.

"Good idea," Ramon said. "Because there's somebody following us, so we might not be back to the house for a while."

"Who?" Kenna looked at the side mirror. "How long have they been following us?"

"Probably since we left the grocery store. Maybe even before then, if they know where the house is." Ramon glanced in the rearview mirror. "I'll try and lose them."

"Just don't make it obvious that's what you're trying to do." The last thing they needed was to pull some high-speed maneuver and draw a bunch of attention to them. "If they've been following us this whole time, then the attack on Allie might have been designed to draw more of us away from the house. Now the real attack is going to come because they can ensure a greater result."

"That's a lovely thought," Allie said.

Kenna wanted to chuckle, but there wasn't really anything funny about this situation. With Allie and Kenna both incapacitated in different ways, it would be up to Ramon to take the lead in safeguarding all their lives.

"You know," Kenna said, "we could always just drive to the closest police station and get out and run inside."

Ramon glanced over at her for a second. "That's advice you give a single woman who needs to get herself to a safe place. I have a gun, and a grudge."

Allie snorted. "Are you sure you were never a Marine?"

Ramon chuckled, flashing a grin. "But going somewhere specific isn't a bad idea. They won't be expecting that."

"As long as it's nowhere near the house," Kenna said. Even if whoever was behind them already knew where the place was. "Although, if we're the distraction, maybe the attack is happening on the house right now and that's exactly where we're supposed to go."

"Bear said everything's good at the house."

Kenna glanced at Allie. "So we keep driving around until we lose them?"

"I might have already done it." Ramon checked his mirrors, then took another turn. "Just give me some time."

"We could hit another store," Allie suggested. "Do some actual shopping."

Kenna figured they might be better off doing grocery pickup than spending time walking around a store. But what did she know? "What about swinging by my RV so I can grab some things and check on the place?"

Ramon took another turn, waiting until the last minute and then swinging around the corner. "Let's do it."

At least it was something to occupy them with. Kenna didn't like this antsy, pent-up feeling of not being able to do anything. It wasn't just powerlessness, or not being the one who got to drive. It was the fact this pursuer hindered them from doing the work they needed to do. Then again, that put them in the framework of being an annoyance rather than a threat. And everything about this case so far said that these people were very much a threat.

Someone connected with Landry and her people was attempting to take them out.

They'd killed at least one so far.

Kenna wouldn't be surprised if someone took out a hit on Mama Landry and got another inmate to end her life.

They might even approach Lottie to get the job done.

"I think I lost them," Ramon said. "You still wanna go by your RV?"

"Yeah, just—" Her phone lit up in the cup holder. "It's Martinez." She answered it and just about managed to wedge the phone between her shoulder and her cheek. "Banbury."

"Hey, everything good?"

Kenna frowned. "Sure. Why?"

"Because I never know with you. But anyway, I was just calling to give you an update."

"Go for it." At least she could listen while Ramon did the driving.

"As much as we tried to get her to talk, Camra Tenison didn't give us anything. Whatever she told you, she wasn't willing to repeat it. Which means we only had your say so on what was said in the room."

"You cut her loose."

"Didn't have a choice," Martinez said. "She refused to say anything, and when we started talking about her flipping out at us, she said to just fine her or she'll get a lawyer and we couldn't hold her."

"You cut her loose because she wasn't worth the trouble."

"It was the brass's decision. They want everyone working on how this guy died in our custody. Not wasting our time with some nuisance woman."

Not how Kenna would've dealt with it, but she knew what it was like to have the higher-ups tell you what to work on.

Kenna said, "So how did he die?"

"I can't divulge details of an ongoing investigation."

That sounded about right. Enough Kenna wanted to roll her eyes. "Thanks for calling to update me. I appreciate it."

"Yeah, it sure sounds like you're full of gratitude." He chuckled. "Later."

The call ended.

Kenna leaned forward and dropped the phone on her lap between her elbows.

"Nice maneuver," Allie said. "And the way you dealt with that cop wasn't bad either."

"Thanks."

"Your arms hurt?" Ramon looked over.

Only all the time. "I'm not due to take more pills yet. But it's getting close."

"We should be good to head back to the house soon. I think I lost them."

Kenna thought about what Martinez had said. "We aren't that far from Camra's house. What do you say we swing by and find out what the police couldn't?"

Allie said, "I could do an interrogation."

"You can also stay in the car," Ramon said. "Both of you."

Chapter Twenty-Seven

"**D**id he just pick the lock, or did someone let him in?" Allie leaned forward to look between the front seats. So Kenna could look out the window at the house where Ramon had stepped inside.

"I don't know," Kenna said. "But I don't like this."

"He knew you were going to follow him in. He just wanted a head start."

"Sure, that's why he didn't open the door for me before he left me here."

Allie turned around. "You have a gun, right?"

"Check that duffel bag by your feet."

Allie rustled around, then got out. She opened Kenna's door.

Kenna got her hands in the front pocket of her sweater. She would do better with two slings to take the pressure off her forearms, or a way to bandage them against her front. But that would just feel way too much like a strait jacket. She shivered at that thought, not because of the cold. "You go first, since you're armed."

"Sure," Allie said. "Can't really see straight, though." But she still led the way to the front door. "Geez, my head is pounding."

"But you're alive."

Camra had been certain that if she spoke to the police, she would be the next to be killed. Kenna hoped that wasn't what had happened. Not just considering the fact Camra hadn't told the police anything. But also because too many people had lost their lives or been seriously injured in the last week or so, and they still barely had a clue what was going on. Let alone who might be behind it.

Kenna said, "Between the two of us, we almost make a whole person."

Allie chuckled, then stepped inside. "Call 'em if you see 'em."

As in, tell her where to shoot? "Got it."

Kenna scanned the inside of the house. Mostly listening for Ramon, and anyone he may have encountered. But also checking for the homeowner in any corner Ramon may have missed.

They didn't get far before he came down the stairs.

"It's clear." He looked at Kenna. "She isn't here, but you'll want to see this."

"Good thing we got out of the car, then."

He practically rolled his eyes and turned to head back upstairs.

Allie said, "I'll stay down here and hold the door."

"Good idea," Kenna said. Even though she'd rather lie down than climb a set of stairs that didn't even look that bad. "Start yelling if anything happens."

She followed Ramon up the tall staircase to the middle floor.

"What did you find?" She wasn't going to touch the breaking and entering part, if that was what he'd done. At least not until the police arrived and they needed an explanation for being in the house.

"Just go take a look." Ramon stayed in the hall while she entered the room.

Not the main bedroom, or even a guest room. This was more like storage given the tables along one wall, stacked with candles and paraphernalia.

"Is that voodoo stuff?" She wasn't really expecting an answer but needed to say it out loud anyway. "I'm guessing the stuff they collected from the mausoleum will turn up as being fake, and this is the same kind of things."

Or at least it was not the real stuff that a practitioner of that religion would use.

Some people might even argue that it wasn't a religion, even though it was. But Kenna didn't need to worry about semantics in the middle of a case.

She kept going, looking around the room. There was enough stuff in here for Camra to supply many murder scenes, not just the one Kenna had seen.

But if she had the stuff here, that meant she wasn't a victim. She was more likely someone behind it.

Or the perpetrator herself.

Kenna shook her head, trying to wrap her mind around it. If Camra was the person calling the shots here, then she had thoroughly pulled the wool over everyone's eyes.

She might even have been lying about the relationship with Damien. That at least would be one explanation for the lack of a digital paper trail on their affair.

Ramon walked down the hall, probably floating between her and Allie. Trying to keep them both within earshot.

Kenna kept moving around the room and found a stack of papers. She managed to shift some of them beside each other off the stack. Each one was a social services file for a teenager.

"Jacob." She spotted one for a girl she had seen at the hospital that day she walked by them talking in a group. "Anthony."

Kenna had seen enough. She caught up to Ramon in the hallway. "She could have those photos from work files that she brought home."

"I don't care if it's illegally obtained circumstantial evidence. The fact is, she isn't here. And she knows something she won't say."

"Any sign of how to find her?"

"The door was unlocked. But I don't think she's been taken."

Kenna shook her head. "We should call Martinez and tell him what we found."

"You heard him on the phone," Ramon said. "Did it sound like he wanted to work this case? Or did it sound more like the police are determined to cover their butts after someone was killed in custody?"

"Doesn't matter. We still need to tell him."

Ramon strode down the stairs and outside, where Kenna met him on his way back to her from the car. Allie stepped out onto the front porch and closed the door, wiping off the handle with her sweater sleeve.

He held the phone to his ear. After a second, he said, "No answer."

"Text him," Kenna ordered. "For all we know, Camra is the one giving orders to Landry."

Ramon lowered the phone. "Okay, what else do we need to do here?"

Kenna shrugged. "If we hit the house, what about showing Nora a photo of her? Maybe she can confirm if Camra is the one giving orders to Landry. Garth might've met with her."

Allie nodded. "And if she can ID her, then you guys can find her and your stuff will be wrapped up."

Kenna looked over. "In a hurry to get rid of us?"

"Sorry. My head hurts, but that was uncalled for."

"Believe me, I know what it's like to want a simple case instead of a big mess of things."

They got a photo of Camra from social media, and Allie sent it to Bear. Having him show the image to Nora was certainly the fastest way to confirm what they needed to know.

Within seconds, they had a response.

"Nora has seen that woman with Garth," Allie said. "But has no idea who she is."

"Does that even help us?" Ramon asked.

Kenna turned to him. "Call Anthony."

"You could probably just turn on that function on your phone where you tell it what to do," he shot back.

"As opposed to being your boss?"

He held the phone in front of her face, and she listened to it ring.

When Anthony picked up, she said, "It's Kenna. Is everything going okay?"

"Why, what happened?"

"I don't know yet. I'm going to send you an image of a woman, and I need you to tell me if you've ever seen her before."

"Okay." He didn't sound so sure.

"While you look at it, tell me if you've heard from your mom."

His voice sounded far away for a second. Then, "She called me yesterday. She said to tell you that you're definitely not square. Whatever that means."

"I owe your mom a lot." Kenna flexed her fingers in the sweater pocket. "She stuck up for me when nobody else did."

"You hurt yourself pretty bad on the bridge, right?" Anthony paused. "The cops wouldn't tell me what happened."

"They just let you go, right?"

"Told me if they ever brought me in again, I'd be going before a judge."

Ramon muttered, "Tell him to quit getting caught."

Kenna rolled her eyes. "Did you look at the picture yet?"

"Mm-hmm. Who is that?"

"Do you know who she is? Have you ever seen her before?"

"She looks like the kind of woman where you'd never believe what she does. All mild-mannered and stuff." Anthony huffed. "Meanwhile, kids like me get blamed for everything."

"That might be completely true. At least given what we're starting to learn about her. So do me a favor. If you see her anywhere, get out of there as fast as you can."

"Should I know who she is?"

"Don't worry about it, okay? Just lay low for now and keep to yourself. If anyone contacts you, give me a call and let me know. Got it?"

"Sure."

Kenna said goodbye and hung up.

"Okay," Allie said. "To recap, we were followed from the grocery store. We don't think this woman is a victim. We think most likely she's the suspect. No one we know can identify her as being behind it all. Anything else?"

"Yeah," Kenna said. "I need a cup of coffee."

"Let's go." Ramon motioned toward the car.

They got in, and he stood guard while they did. Once he had climbed in, Kenna said, "Back to the house?"

Ramon nodded. "We definitely need to regroup."

Allie said, "Bear wants me back at the house."

"Fine," Kenna said. "We can make a pot of coffee at the house."

Ramon chuckled. "Soon enough, you'll be able to drive again and you can go get as much coffee as you want."

"You'd better believe it."

En route to their destination, Ramon took one of the bridges over the Mississippi River. Just as they started up the incline of the bridge, he grunted.

"What is it?" Kenna looked at the side mirror. "Are they back?"

"They're not just back," he said. "At this time, they're not just following us."

A dark pickup truck—huge in the side mirror—came up behind them, shining blinding headlights in their back window.

Allie said, "Hold on."

"I would if I could," Kenna told her.

The truck behind them rammed the rear bumper of the car.

Kenna gasped. Ramon gripped the wheel.

A van drove alongside them, boxing them in, along with the truck.

"What are they trying to achieve?" Kenna wondered. Her mind couldn't compute the answer to the question.

"You don't want to know." Ramon hit the gas, pressing hard down on the accelerator pedal. The car struggled to go faster.

Kenna clenched down on her back teeth, every muscle in her body tight and sending pain up her arms.

The truck behind them rammed the car again. The van closed in on the left, crunching against the door. Metal scraped against metal.

She heard Allie in the back, frantically asking for the police and telling a dispatcher where they were.

Ramon's expression was stone-cold, the guise of a man who was almost certain he was not going to survive this.

Kenna stared out the front windshield and prayed, asking God for everything and anything she could think of that might help them. Nonsense sentences and snatches of ideas before she switched to something else. Her mind jumping from one thing to the next thing before she could grasp a single idea.

The van pushed them tight against the side of the bridge.

Behind them, the truck backed off.

"Here it comes." Ramon didn't let go of the wheel.

"If we go over," Kenna said, "we aren't going to survive hitting the water." She had no idea how far below them it was, or how deep. But slamming into it would be like hitting concrete.

"Then you'd better pray to that God of yours that we survive."

In the back seat, Allie said, "Please, Lord Jesus."

The truck behind them revved its engine. Ramon tried to speed up enough to get away, but it barreled down on them. Relentless as it rushed up and slammed into their back end.

At the same time, the van clipped at the front panel of the car.

Ramon lost control.

The car pitched off the side wall, bounced back, and started to flip over. Like a ball in a pinball machine, they bounced around, smacked off something, and lifted up.

The front end dipped, and Kenna saw only darkness in front of them.

They sailed through the air, down toward whatever lay below. Swallowed up in the night.

And then they hit the water.

A crash, louder than anything Kenna had ever heard. The airbags blew, and the front windshield shattered at the same time.

She jerked in her seat, crying out at the rapid deceleration of the car, suddenly having to fight against the dense water in their descent to the bottom.

Kenna tried to pull her arms from the sweater but couldn't move. She fought against the seatbelt with no effect.

The car plunged into darkness, and she could only hear her heartbeat in her ears over the sound of rushing water.

They were going to die down here.

Chapter Twenty-Eight

Kenna's body jerked. She gasped and swallowed a mouthful of water, then had to cough it out. Panic infused every inch of her. But with no strength to fight against it, she had to submit. A painful grip tugged her across the car and into the black expanse of water.

Her mind was a firestorm of panic. *Can't. Breathe.*

Ramon. It had to be him dragging her to the surface, where dim light shone in the distance above them. Kenna kicked with her legs, trying not to strike him. He did the same, holding on to her and using one arm to speed their way up.

Tipping her head back like that to look disoriented her, making her start to pass out. She had to look away from the surface, or she would give in before they even reached the air above.

Seconds dragged on.

He fought against the current pushing them up...up...

Her head broke the surface, and she coughed. Then sputtered, gasping and expelling water from her lungs. Great hacking spasms until she could take a real breath and get oxygen into her body and brain.

Ramon never let go. He held on to her, breathing hard but like he hadn't swallowed any water. He'd saved her.

Allie.

"Where's Allie?" She tried to look around, watching for the other woman to surface.

Ramon held her up while they both kicked their legs, treading water. He had a dark expression on his face. As if he considered the threat to be far from over.

Above them, people looked over the bridge. Traffic had ground to a standstill. Someone pointed, and she saw more than one phone out. *Guess we're live on social media.* Not the way she wanted to be remembered.

Kenna repeated, "Ramon, where's Allie?"

"She went up before us." He looked around. "She should be up here."

Kenna tried to turn around.

"Come on. Let's head to shore. We won't be able to tread water until someone shows up to fish us out."

She was about to point out she couldn't swim aside from just flailing her legs around when he just shifted her and started moving, one hand out in front of him, swiping through the water.

Some splashed in her face, so she turned her head to look at the blue sky. So innocuous looking when they'd nearly died moments ago.

"I'm guessing you were a lifeguard in the past."

He just kept swimming. Making decent time, actually. The guy was strong enough to hold up both of them, and she was pretty sure she wasn't going to give him a hard time for a while. Their brother-sister thing would be a little less antagonistic after this. She might even buy him a cup of coffee—or a cheeseburger. Mmm. That sounded pretty good.

"Still with me?"

"I'm thinking about cheeseburgers."

His body jerked, which she figured was a laugh. "Hey." He swam harder. "I see Allie. She's already over by the shore."

Kenna wanted desperately to see but had to wait. She prayed—a whole lot of thank-yous and praising God for the fact they were alive.

Finally, her feet touched the bottom. She scrambled for a foothold and managed to stand. Then tucked her arms against her front, crossing them as best she could.

Ramon held her elbows, his arm around her, and he helped her walk out of the water. "She's over to our right."

In front of them was a concrete wall, above which seemed to be some kind of industrial area. Warehouses. No people standing there, just the buildings. To the right was a break in the wall, and some concrete steps.

Allie stumbled across the pebbled shore, assisted by a woman. About eight feet of space before the concrete wall, which had moss up the side where the waterline had been at one point.

The warmth of the sun created a disparity that Kenna didn't like. It felt odd against the body-wracking shivers and dripping all over. She fought against the gravel for purchase.

"Go see if she's okay."

"We're both going," he told her.

They hurried after Allie and the woman, over to the concrete steps. Not rushing but wanting to move fast. Hoping Allie was all right.

"I can't believe we survived that."

"Are you going to tell me this means there's a God?" Ramon scoffed. "Like it was some kind of miracle."

"No, I'm going to ask how you can possibly believe there isn't a God when we just survived that. Because it's some kind of miracle."

He huffed, sounding amused and frustrated and exhausted—all at the same time.

They got to the steps.

Kenna hit a wall physically and emotionally. "Set me down." Her foot caught under her, and she stumbled.

Ramon helped her turn and sit on the steps. He knelt in front of her, scanning her. "You good? Injuries?"

"You should check on Allie."

"That lady is helping her." He touched her cheek, running his thumb over her jaw. "You're good?"

She frowned. "Thanks to you."

"I'm glad I was there." He shook his head. "I hope those guys come back. I want to throttle them."

"I would've died," she whispered.

She would never have been able to get out of the car, let alone swim to the surface. No chance. No survival.

Thank You. She hadn't been alone down there.

Ramon leaned over and kissed her. A soft, quick touch of his lips.

Kenna frowned, even though it was over almost as fast as it started.

His attention shifted. "Hey!" He scrambled past her and ran up the steps. Whatever that was about, she couldn't move if she'd wanted to go and see what he had.

All she was able to do was sit here and think about that kiss.

Sure, it hadn't been more than friendship. The relief of two people alive because they'd been together. It wasn't like the foundation of her life had just tilted off its axis, and everything would be thrown out of whack because he'd done that.

She was going to tell Jax. Otherwise, it would feel like a big secret, and she would get wound up and wound up tighter the longer things went on with him not knowing. Relationships were about honesty.

Had Ramon just been honest about how *he* felt?

Kenna shifted on the step and managed to turn around but couldn't see much. Then got up and trudged up the steps. Her clothes stuck to her. She had no idea where her phone was, or what she even had on her. Not a gun, or much in terms of weapons. There hadn't been much point carrying anything on her person when she couldn't lift it in her hand.

Who knew when she'd be able to hold a weapon...or even a fork.

She slipped her hands into her sweater pocket, shivering against the cold even though her face felt flushed. Her braids were probably dripping also.

At the top of the steps, she spotted Ramon running away from her along the street between two warehouse buildings.

Ahead of him, she could see a white panel van.

He stumbled, slowing as he came to a stop. The van turned the corner at the end, and he watched until it was out of sight before turning and striding back to her. His longer legs ate up the feet between them.

Ramon called out, "That woman stuffed her in the van!" He was breathing hard. Moving fast, coming right to her. He slid an arm around her waist again.

Sirens screamed in the distance.

"What do you mean stuffed her in there?" She had so many questions. Or should, but her brain didn't seem to want to function. "Who was it?"

Ramon walked with her, both of them moving slowly.

A cop car turned the corner at the end, and then an ambulance.

"We need a...a phone," Kenna sputtered. "We need a description of the car, and the woman." She forced her thoughts into some semblance of linear ideas. "Maizie. We need Maizie, and we need to call Bear."

"Our phones are in the Mississippi River."

The cops got out, and the EMTs came over to check her vitals.

Kenna felt like she was swept up all over again, swallowed by all that water, but it was questions from the cops. Explaining what happened.

Ramon looked over from talking to the cop, just a few feet away. "Don't touch her arms."

The EMT reached for her elbow, and she glared. "Don't touch my arms."

He flinched.

Okay, so she'd yelled that.

"It's a preexisting condition that has nothing to do with the river." Kenna looked at the cop. "We need a phone, so we can call people that we know who can help find the woman who just got abducted from right here. She was with us in the car when we went over."

The cop told her to take a breath and try to calm down.

"Martinez," she continued. "Call Sergeant Martinez. Tell him I need his help. And the ATF, whoever those two agents were from the briefing." Sometimes there were just too many names to remember, and it wasn't like she'd ever see them again.

Ramon looked like he wanted to give her a hug.

"Get help here," she warned. "Or leave us alone."

"Kenna."

She shook her head. "Who cares that my car and all our stuff is in the river when Allie just got abducted by a woman!" She pinned Ramon with a stare. "It had to have been Camra Tenison."

The cop made a note on his little notebook—logbook—whatever they called it.

"Yes," Kenna said. "Write that down, and everything else. But *get help* here!"

He lifted a brow. The guy had some miles on him—the kind of body language that told her he'd been doing this long enough he thought he'd seen everything. Maybe he had. "Are you telling me what to do, ma'am?"

"Yes!"

Ramon turned to the cop. "She's understandably upset. We appreciate your help."

At least he didn't tell the guy she was on her period, like he had at the courtyard with the food trucks. That felt like weeks ago, and it had only been days. Bounty hunting for a solid paycheck and some well-rounded skills Ramon could add to his already wide skillset. And as always, it had led to this.

Murder.

Abduction.

Tears filled Kenna's eyes. *Lord, keep her safe.*

The EMT said, "I'd like to look at your arms, even if it's preexisting. Can you take off your sweater, maybe?"

Kenna shook her head. "I'll go in and get checked out by a doctor. My physician can send over information so they know what's going on."

"Figured you'd object to even that, so all right. Let's get you to the hospital."

"I can walk."

"I'm sure you can," the EMT muttered.

Ramon went with her, climbing in the ambulance. "You're late on pain meds, right?"

"I don't want to pass out right now. I need to be lucid."

"Even if the pain is so bad you're screaming?"

She pressed her lips together.

The EMT had her lie back on the bed. He asked her a few questions about what she was taking, and when she'd taken it. After radioing in to the attending ER doctor, he gave her a shot.

"I better not go to sleep."

The guy pretty much ignored her. She couldn't be the worst patient he'd ever treated.

"Ramon, what did you tell the cop? Is Martinez going to meet us at the hospital?"

The EMT was checking his vitals now.

Ramon leaned away from the guy and whispered, "He'll meet us there."

That was the only way she relaxed. "We need to call Maizie and Bear. Or get Maizie to tell Bear. There's no time to waste. Every second could mean the difference between finding her alive and her ending up like Reggie."

Ramon's expression shifted.

"What?"

His Adam's apple bobbed with a swallow. Finally, he said, "You were out of it after the bridge. I didn't want to upset you."

"That's why you came in and had it out with me about ignoring you."

"Reggie passed away. He succumbed to the severity of his injuries, and there was nothing the doctors could do to save his life."

Kenna stared at him, her eyes burning with unshed tears. "That isn't going to be what happens to Allie."

"You're assuming it was malicious," the EMT said. "Maybe whoever put her in that van took her to the hospital."

Kenna looked at him.

"They weren't rescuing her," Ramon countered. "It was an abduction."

The EMT said nothing, raising his gloved hands.

Ramon lifted his chin. "Let me borrow your cell phone."

"I'm not supposed to do that," the other man said. "Your cop friend is meeting you at the hospital, right?"

"They can use mine!" the other EMT called from the front—the driver of the pair. "It's in the cabinet above the insulin."

The EMT nearest Kenna frowned. "You aren't supposed to—"

"Bro, just let them use it." He said his PIN number, and Ramon reached over, digging out the phone.

The EMT didn't look happy, but Ramon moved quick. Too quick for him to object much beyond muttering.

"This is life-or-death," Kenna said. "And we appreciate your help."

"Hey, Maze. It's me." Ramon dipped his head and explained. "Call Bear. Tell him what's happening so he can get on this. We'll work our angles." He paused. "Okay, got it. Yeah, she's good. We both are."

Kenna managed to relax a tiny bit, but maybe that was about the shot she'd been given. She found she was actually able to think beyond the pain.

Martinez could help. Bear and his team might have a way to locate Allie—like if she had some kind of tracker on her. Maybe Maizie could track the van and find a location.

The ambulance stopped.

Both EMTs moved. A door slammed. Another opened, and the bed she lay on started moving.

Kenna sat up because she refused to be helpless when a woman was out there, suffering who-knew-what. She of all people understood that cold, paralyzing fear. All she could do was pray. Allow others to help her—the way Ramon had pulled her from the water.

Allie had gotten herself out of the river. She could survive this.

Lord, help her hang on.

The medical staff pushed the bed through the halls of the emergency room, into a bay surrounded with curtains. Metal swooshed against metal as the nurse drew the drape closed.

Ramon opened it a second later and stepped in. He sat on the end of the bed, facing sideways so she could only see him in profile.

She wanted to reach out and take his hand, but there was no way that was happening. "We'll find her."

He stared at the monitors. "I hope so."

Chapter Twenty-Nine

Martinez had shown up wearing street clothes, which should've made him look younger even with the badge on his belt, but the worry lines on his face had the opposite effect. He stood at the end of Kenna's bed, and his gaze strayed to the bandages on her arms that covered her wrists and looped around her thumb. It wasn't a forever solution, but for now it actually helped—or just made her feel better.

The nurse had even added thick tape, effectively immobilizing Kenna's wrist and thumb so she would think twice about moving anything. She'd told Kenna a story while she worked about how she'd done sports med for a while in college and one of the football players on their team had participated in the entire game with two fractured wrists, insisting he continue to the end. All the while, Kenna had glanced at Ramon, then Martinez, then Ramon again.

"Earth to Kenna." Martinez shifted his weight but didn't wave in front of her face at least.

She blinked. "Sorry. What were you saying?"

"I've got a pair of detectives, the ones you met actually.

Byrd and Fisher. They're working this case, so they're on the vehicles that ran you off that bridge." He blew out his cheeks and exhaled. "You guys almost died."

"And a woman is still in danger."

Martinez nodded, glancing at Ramon. Probably wondering how he could say that and look completely impassive. "We're tracking down the vehicles and running the plates based on witness testimony."

Kenna managed a smile. "Thanks."

"You figure it's Landry?" Martinez said. "Or whoever is calling the shots has other people on their payroll?"

She couldn't help thinking about Camra. "Has anyone located Camra Tenison?"

Martinez shook his head. "We have a BOLO out, but no one has seen her. It's looking like she went to ground, or she ran. Are you sure it wasn't her who kidnapped your friend?"

Kenna looked at Ramon, because he was the one who'd been close enough to see the abductor.

Ramon didn't shift out of his stance, arms tight by his sides. Feet apart, giving him a hip width base he could move from in a second. Like when someone walked by the curtain. "It was a blonde."

"She could've changed her hair," Martinez suggested.

Ramon shook his head. "I swung by the fourth floor on the hospital"—he looked at her—"when we traded out. I took a look at the woman with the bronze blouse. Just in case it was relevant."

Kenna nodded. She would've done the same.

He looked at Martinez. "It wasn't her. This woman had longer legs, and they were toned. And I doubt Camra could have subdued a Marine, even one that just swam out of a river. She had no muscle. She was just skinny."

Martinez nodded. "Okay."

"Why do you ask?"

Before he could answer Kenna's question, the curtain whipped open. A nurse stopped, holding the curtain back. "Right here." She didn't look happy but turned and walked away.

A guy in bike shorts and a tank top appeared, a messenger bag on one hip. The strap across his chest to the other shoulder. Baseball cap. Bicycle gloves. "Kenna Banbury?"

She nodded. "Yes?"

He dug in the bag and pulled out a padded manila envelope, which he held out to her.

Ramon grabbed it. "Thanks."

"Thanks," Kenna echoed. "I appreciate it." Whatever *it* was.

The courier headed away again, leaving the space where the curtain had been open for her to see the busy emergency department hallway. Staff. Other patients. A phone rang.

Ramon tore the envelope open. "It's a burner phone."

"Maizie?"

Martinez said, "Who?"

"My office manager." She could get on board with it sounding like her business was bigger than it was, especially when they didn't know who was involved in this and who wasn't. To Ramon, she said, "Call Bear."

They'd already tried from Martinez's phone, but Bear hadn't answered.

"It's turning on." Ramon tapped his foot while the phone screen flashed.

Kenna asked Martinez, "Why were you asking about the abductor being Camra?"

"Just thinking something through." He glanced at Ramon. "We got DNA back from the mausoleum murder scene."

"You got a match?" She'd still hardly processed the fact that Reggie was dead.

Kenna hadn't even known him that well. And yet, he was gone, because she'd entered his life. The inevitable had happened.

Far too many people she'd met in her life were now dead because of her.

One was too many.

She'd lost count of the true number.

"I can come back later." Martinez eyed her. "You're not okay."

"Just talk." She sniffed. "I want this over, and that means finding Allie. Finding the killer. Finding Camra, or whoever Landry took orders from."

"DNA from the scene in the mausoleum came back as a familial match to Camra Tenison."

"And you think that's who abducted Allie?"

"It's a stretch based on nothing but instinct, but it's certainly possible."

"Even if it means someone else is out there." She figured they'd already known that, though. "So, she has a sister...or a cousin?"

"Sisters would make sense. According to the techs." He paused. "I ran her. She has no siblings. But I did discover she was adopted. I can't access any of the records because it was all sealed, except the fact that Judge Sandra Watts tried the case. She's a family court judge, does adoptions and all that kind of stuff."

Kenna bit her lip. Why did that sound familiar?

Martinez added, "She's the most recent victim of this breaking and entering crew."

"Preston's friend."

He frowned. "Who?"

"Don't worry about it." She shook her head. "So this lady is connected. Maybe even chosen as the latest victim for a reason...because all her case files were stolen, right?"

"How do you know that?" Martinez shook his head. "Never mind, I don't want to know."

"So she presided over Camra's adoption? Maybe her parents know if she has a sister."

"Parents are deceased," Martinez said. "They died a few years ago. Maybe she has a biological sibling, though. A sister she's made contact with."

The phone rang.

Ramon tapped the screen. "Yeah?"

"It's Bear. Maizie got me up to speed. What's the latest?"

Kenna shifted forward in the hospital bed. She needed dry clothes because she'd soaked through the mattress and hadn't wanted to leave in a gown—or be admitted overnight. "The cops are helping us."

Martinez stepped closer to the bed but didn't say anything.

"She's a blonde," Ramon said, holding the phone up to his mouth. "We think she might be a birth sibling of Camra Tenison."

"I'll pass that to my office," Bear said. "Everyone in Miami is on this."

"Do you guys have trackers?" Kenna asked.

"In our phones and on our person. But with the dip you guys took in the Mississippi, it's dark. Our techs are working on rebooting the one on her person, but it's a long shot. We need to go old-school to find her." Bear paused, then said, "As soon as we get a lead, I'm gonna need you guys here so my people can get Allie."

He wanted them to take over for the team and watch the house? That made Kenna wonder if this was by design. If the point of taking Allie wasn't to pull the team away from the house so they could get to the people being protected inside it.

Ramon looked at her. "We'll be there."

Kenna would want to rescue her friend herself, so she understood Bear's need to get out there. "As long as you know I'm effectively useless. Ramon will have to cover us all."

"Noted. Anything else?" Bear asked.

"I just need to call Maizie. Get her to dig and find Camra's sibling." She glanced at Martinez. "In completely legal ways, of course."

He shook his head.

Over his shoulder, Kenna spotted a familiar figure pass the opening between curtains. What was Anthony doing here?

Was he looking for her?

Bear said, "Keep in touch."

"Will do." Ramon pocketed the phone and turned to her. "What?"

"Anthony." She lifted her chin, then scooted off the bed.

Things were happening at a rapid pace right now. It couldn't be a coincidence that he was here, but still, she was glad they were dealing with everything one at a time. First Camra's sibling—a sister? Then Bear and the hunt for Allie. Safeguarding Preston, Nora, and Ellie.

Now Anthony.

She stepped into the hall, her clothes feeling stiff and cold. Damp in a way that would lead to uncomfortable chafing soon enough.

Anthony turned the corner down the hall, deeper into the hospital.

A nurse appeared in front of her, motioning back to the bed. "Ma'am, you need to return to the bay until the doctor can see you."

"I'll be back. I need to catch up to my friend." Plus, her legs worked just fine—except the chafing.

Kenna ducked around the nurse and jogged down the hallway, even though it jarred her arms. Martinez and Ramon trailed her.

Anthony disappeared into a side room. The door shut before she got there, so she waited for her backup to catch up.

She nodded at the door. "He went in there."

Martinez frowned. "Supplies?"

Kenna shrugged.

Martinez drew his weapon.

"Put that away." She shook her head. "You don't need it."

"I get to be the judge of that." Martinez twisted the handle and pushed the door open, but stayed where he was. Gun in view.

Anthony turned around to them and dropped what he was holding. *Busted.* A box of gauze spilled on the floor, and packets went everywhere. His gaze darted between them.

"What's going on, kid?" Martinez held the gun by his side. "Looking for something?"

"I was just…"

"Don't bother," Ramon said. "Just tell us what's going on."

Anthony looked at Kenna.

"Is somebody hurt?" she asked him.

He wavered, his jaw shifting, but he said nothing.

"You didn't mention anything when I talked to you on the phone." Another thing that happened recently, which felt like days ago.

"You just told me to look at that picture," he muttered.

So he hadn't volunteered information. He'd played it cool and kept his composure. "What's going on, Anthony?"

Same thing Martinez had asked.

But this time, the kid answered, "One of my friends is hurt."

"So bring him in."

Kenna couldn't smack Martinez, so she kicked him. He frowned at her. "Let him talk."

Anthony shrugged. "That's it. One of my friends is hurt."

"Who? Where are they, and how bad is it?" She stepped into the storage closet and motioned for him to go ahead of her out of the room.

He looked her up and down. "Why are you all wet?"

"Went for a swim. Don't ask me to use my arms anytime soon." Kenna followed him out. "What happened?"

"We were running," Anthony explained. "He got hit by a car, and the guy just drove off. He didn't even stop."

And whoever *we* was, they hadn't called the police. "You're getting supplies?"

"I need medicine, but Nesta didn't know how to get in the pharmacy cabinet. She just told me where to find bandages and stuff."

The girl who'd gone to floor four, knowing exactly where she needed to be in the hospital.

"Her mom was a nurse here before she got shot in the ER."

Martinez frowned. "I remember that. She was a nice lady."

Anthony looked at him.

"You can trust us." But she wasn't going to promise he wouldn't get in trouble.

Anthony leaned against the wall with his upper body bent forward. As if he could no longer carry the weight of it. "He did get hit by a car, and the driver just drove away. She didn't even look back."

That piqued Kenna's interest.

"She?" Martinez repeated.

"I didn't see her face or anything."

"Let's get help for your friend, first." Kenna glanced at Martinez. "Then we can track the car." She faced Anthony. "Your mom asked me to protect you, so that's what I'm gonna do."

His expression gave nothing away. She had no idea if he believed her or not. "I can take you to him." He cleared his throat, looking a lot younger than he usually did in that moment.

Kenna would've squeezed his shoulder but had to settle for a nod. "A friend of mine got kidnapped just a couple of hours ago. We think whoever is ordering around this crew of thieves is the one who took her. Too many people have died already...and I don't want that to happen to my friend, or yours."

"So if you know who it is," Martinez warned, "or you have any idea where this woman—our kidnapper—might've taken her, then we need you to say."

Anthony's expression shuttered.

"We do need your help," Kenna said, trying to salvage the situation. "I can't find my friend, but we can help yours. Martinez wants the person in charge taken down, and any information you can give us would be helpful."

"Tit for tat. Isn't that the saying?" Anthony glanced around, a hard look on his face now.

Ramon sighed. "It's how life works, kid. Trade for favors and do what it takes so you end up on top. Kenna can help you figure that out, but you'll be on the right side of the law *and* ahead. Not ahead and on the run from the cops." He paused. "You get the difference?"

Anthony nodded.

"Let's go." Kenna tipped her head down the hall. "Take us to your friend."

Chapter Thirty

"Why'd you call them?" Anthony stood in the hall of the house, which had a foreclosure sign on the front lawn and clearly hadn't been lived in for months. Maybe years. The kids seemed to be using it as a place to squat. Hang out.

Kenna was surprised drug users hadn't taken it over. Or, if they'd tried, the kids had claimed it for themselves.

She glanced at the EMTs now working on the kid. He was a mess. "It's a miracle he survived this long. You guys did really well keeping him alive."

The girl who'd been with the injured kid came out, worrying her phone in her fingers. Flipping it over and over. "Will he be okay?"

Kenna managed a shrug. "If he recovers, it'll be thanks to you guys." But still, they needed to accept the alternative if that's what happened. "If he doesn't make it, that won't be your fault. You did everything you could. Everything you know how to do. Now the EMTs can do what *they* know how to do."

She stared at Kenna. "I know you. You were at the hospital, right?"

"Nesta?" When the girl nodded back, she said, "I remember you from the elevator."

The girl's expression shifted.

"And you were listening when the doctor was discussing Damien's prognosis with Camra Tenison."

Nesta almost smiled—almost.

"Did you know that woman?" Kenna asked. "The one in the hallway."

Nesta shook her head.

"Had you ever seen her before?"

"Uh-uh. What does she have to do with anything?"

"I'm not sure," Kenna said. "I thought she was involved, but it might be someone else."

Ramon and Martinez wandered out of the living room, over to where Kenna stood with the kids. Anthony didn't look super happy with how things had turned out. But the reality was, he was twelve, and he'd reached out to her for help. That help was going to come in the way Kenna knew how to give it. The rest they would figure out together, and she was more than happy to be an advocate for him in a world where kids like this rarely had someone take their side and be supportive.

"It looks like he might be okay," Martinez said. Reluctantly, by the look of him. "But he'll need surgery probably because he has internal injuries."

Which meant they were seriously lucky the injuries hadn't been worse. That the impact of the car hadn't ruptured something. Otherwise, this kid would probably be dead by now.

"They're taking him to the hospital?" Nesta asked.

"They're getting him ready to go. There isn't any time to lose."

"I want to go." Nesta started to move.

Martinez lifted his hand. "I need you and your friend to stay here and talk to me. I have questions, and you're the only ones who can give me answers."

"Am I being arrested?"

Kenna shook her head before Martinez could say whatever he was going to say. "No one is arresting you."

"Seriously, Kenna?" Martinez pinned her with a stare. "They've been robbing people. Someone wound up in coma."

"You stole files." She shifted, and it hurt. Plus, she shouldn't have said that out loud necessarily. "Anthony, can you tell me about the last house you and Nesta did? The one the other night?" She had no concept of when it was. Or how Anthony managed to act like everything was okay on the phone when she'd spoken to him. She'd sent him Camra's photo. The convo hadn't been super relaxed, and it had sounded like he was in the middle of something. But still...

"What about it?" Anthony said.

Kenna tried to get her thoughts to coalesce. "You hit the home of a local judge."

Nesta nodded. "The judge who declared my auntie unfit. She put me in a home."

Kenna glanced between the two teens as they stood facing each other on either side of the hallway. "Were you instructed to remove case files from the house?"

Both kids shifted. Only a slight movement, but Kenna clocked it. She knew Ramon and Martinez would have also. Just a tiny note of defiance.

"It's time to start talking," she said. "Before you get in over your heads with this thing."

In front of her, Martinez seemed to be gearing up for something.

Probably something along the lines of how they were already in over their heads.

The EMT appeared behind them—one of the pair. "We're headed out."

Kenna nodded since she was the only one with the guy in her line of sight. Martinez said, "Thanks."

"Yeah." The guy disappeared, moving quickly. So they could get their patient the critical care he needed.

"Someone is telling you what to do," Kenna said. "And it ain't me. I'm the one who's here to help you out, to tell this cop in front of me that you guys need an advocate. Someone to stick up for you when you wind up in front of a district attorney. Or in court. You need someone to argue for you that you were coerced. That you're as much victims as you are the perpetrators."

Maybe these kids didn't need to know all that, but she hadn't been able to keep the words in. She had no filter right now with the way her arms felt and how tired she was.

"Look, I know you don't think you need help." She paused. "Maybe you think you've 'got this' and you think you're in control."

Nesta definitely thought that.

She couldn't tell about Anthony from his expression.

"But you're not." Ramon stepped forward and tugged down the collar of his still-damp shirt. The two of them probably smelled like the Everglades.

"See this?" Just under his collar bone, someone had taken a literal branding iron and superheated his skin, carving a W into him. "This is what happens when you get in over your head. You do a few jobs here and there at first. Time goes by, and you realize you're working for them all the time. Doing things you would never have done a few years ago. Then it's all-in. 'Do this for me. Prove your loyalty.'"

Nesta shifted her stance.

"You were in a gang, or what?" Anthony said.

Ramon let go of his shirt collar. "This kind of gang is in Mexico, and they distribute drugs and people across the border. I was supposed to be undercover. I cut some corners, did some things I'm not proud of. Then I got burned, and I had no choice. I thought I had nowhere to go. This was my life now." He looked at Kenna then, with the same expression in that second before he'd kissed her. "And then she showed up. Got me out."

She didn't know if it was affection, or appreciation, or both. Maybe he'd reacted to the adrenaline of survival. Either way, she was pretty sure he knew nothing was going to happen between them.

Anthony glanced at her. "You did that?"

She nodded. "As often as I can when I meet someone that needs help. It's what I do."

"Maybe we need help."

Nesta gasped. "Tony!"

"You heard them. This might be our only shot."

Martinez said, "Your shot at what, kid?" Thankfully, he'd softened his tone.

Anthony said, "She tells us whose house to hit."

"Not all of them," Nesta said, wrinkling her nose.

Anthony nodded. "At first, it was just us. We were blowin' off steam, rippin' people off. They can afford it, ya know. They just claim on their insurance...or whatever. Who cares?"

To his credit, Martinez said nothing.

"Then...," Anthony continued, "I guess she figured out it was us. She told us who to hit next. Paid us extra to do it. But that guy wasn't supposed to be home."

"And the judge's house?" Kenna asked.

"She said, 'Take the files and get rid of 'em.'"

"Did you?" Kenna's instinct said maybe not. Their friend had been injured.

"Nah. We have 'em."

Nesta let out a breath through pursed lips.

Anthony said, "I'll get the bag."

Martinez followed him into a room down the hall. Kenna glanced at Ramon. He nodded, then followed the guys. Because she wanted him to keep an eye on Martinez, but also because she wanted a minute with Nesta.

"Is it true? Everything Anthony said."

Nesta looked at Kenna. Trying to figure out how she knew?

"Talk to me, please. Let me help you."

Kenna had so little strength right now that this kid could shove her and she would go down. This teen could make a run for it. Live free—on the run from the police. But when they caught her, it would be so much worse for her.

"The choice you make right here, right now, is going to determine the rest of your life," Kenna said. "Make the right one."

"It wasn't our idea. Breaking into those houses. It was always hers."

"You've met her?"

Nesta nodded. "She comes to the house to see Mr. Wilson when Mrs. Wilson is at book club. They go into his room, and they don't come out. They make...noises."

Kenna wanted to throw up.

"I'm not an idiot. I know what they are doing."

"Then I guess I'm not an idiot either," Kenna said.

Nesta almost smiled. Then the amusement disappeared, and she made a face. "It's so gross. He's...gross. And he smells like Cheerios all the time."

"And the woman?"

"She's pretty, but my mom called clothes like that 'trashy.'"

"I think your mom and I would've been friends," Kenna said. "I'm sorry for what happened to her."

"She was the best."

Kenna gave her a moment, then said, "Do you know what the woman's name was?"

She shook her head. "I was taking the trash out one night, and she talked to me. On her way home or whatever. Then I saw her talking to Colton and Petey. Then they had the idea to start breaking into people's houses. It was like a game, waiting until no one was home and then getting inside."

Kenna nodded.

"She used us, and we fell for it."

"I think that's true, yes. People think kids won't figure it out, but I guess you did." Because Nesta had to believe she had some power over what happened to her next.

Martinez stepped into the hallway, holding a backpack. He leaned against the far wall where Anthony had stood before. The teen boy and Ramon were just inside the doorway. "If I show you two some photos, can you tell me which one is her?"

"I already looked at the one Kenna sent." Anthony shrugged.

"You can gather mugshots"—Kenna glanced at Martinez—"but we need a way to narrow it down. Like bringing in Mr. Wilson. Asking about his girlfriend and leaving all the breaking and entering stuff and all the kids out of it."

"You know as well as I do that we can't just let them go."

"You can find a social worker who is competent and compassionate, a couple of ATF agents who are looking for the big fish, not some kids who got caught up in it, and I can get these guys the best lawyer in New Orleans." Kenna lifted her chin. "But they aren't getting arrested. They'll come voluntarily."

And if they didn't like that idea, she would convince them it was what they needed to do. So they had a chance of getting past this.

"Won't Mr. Wilson see us if we're at the police station?" Nesta asked.

"I'll make sure he's taken somewhere else," Martinez replied. "Or I can have you guys brought to somewhere other than the police station. Since you're not being arrested." He shot her a look like he wanted to throttle her, but she wasn't going to back down.

This was about trust.

He had to build some with these kids, or he wasn't going to close this case.

"I heard some guy got assassinated in lockup at the station." Anthony bristled. "So I don't wanna go there."

Behind him, Ramon grinned.

Then his phone—her phone—rang, and he moved out of sight.

Kenna wanted to connect with Maizie, so she hoped that was who was on the phone. Even though she wanted Maizie working to find Allie, helping Miami Security International with the hunt for their team member, she could use Maizie's help getting a photo of the woman Nesta had seen in her house.

Could Maizie find Camra's biological sibling?

"Any leads on Camra, or Landry?" she asked Martinez.

He shook his head.

"Kenna." Ramon shifted Anthony out of the way and

moved into the hall where he could stand right by her. "Bear said they found Allie, but they have to *go*."

"Good. They should get her back."

And the quicker, the better. Before the worst happened.

"That means we have to go." Ramon winced. "We have to get back to the house to relieve the team, and we need to go *now*."

"Right." Kenna looked at Anthony. "I have to—"

Before she could finish, he shrugged. "Go. Whatever."

"This is about saving someone from getting killed."

He softened a fraction, but not much. In his world, his thing was the most important thing happening. Kids usually did, until they experienced more of the wider world—or they never grew out of it and became self-absorbed adults.

She stopped in front of Martinez.

"You don't have to say it. I'll take care of them." He tossed his keys to Ramon. "I'll call Fisher and Byrd. Her sister is a victim's advocate."

That was good. "You take care of them like you'd want a cop to do if they were *your* kids. Got it?"

He nodded. "Got it."

Kenna raced for the door, where Ramon was already getting in the driver's seat of Martinez's car. He leaned over and pushed open her door.

She eased in. "Let's go." As he leaned over and pulled her door shut, she let out a sigh. "Not sure how much help I'm going to be if someone shows up at the house."

He glanced over. "Bear needs to get Allie back." Then he hit the gas.

Kenna pressed back into her seat and kept her mouth shut.

"Besides, I think you'll do just fine helping me keep Nora and Ellie safe. And Preston."

"We do make a pretty good team of platonic coworkers." Ramon chuckled.

After a few minutes of silent rally car driving through residential streets, he said, "You're praying for Allie, right? That she'll be okay?"

"I haven't stopped."

Chapter Thirty-One

"Anything?" Kenna shut the back door and managed to lock it.

She'd done a full walk around the perimeter of the house, setting up cameras since there were only two of them. Well, Preston claimed there were three of them here to protect Nora and Ellie, but she had no idea his skills.

"Nothing yet." Ramon walked down the hall toward her, carrying a rifle. "Maizie is hanging in the background, so we should have word as soon as Bear and his team find Allie. She's also digging up sibling information on Camra."

Which meant hacking government databases, or so Kenna figured. She wasn't going to ask. She'd assume Stairns had that covered and he'd explained to Maizie what was legal and what wasn't—or how to not get caught, at least.

Right now, she couldn't worry about it. She'd had to have Nora help her change into dry clothes. And she needed something to combat her exhaustion. Far beyond what coffee could achieve.

"I found this." Ramon lifted the gun, which had a strap

attached. He dropped the strap over her head before she could say anything.

She slipped her arm through. "I can't fire it."

"The squeeze doesn't take a lot of pressure. You won't be able to control the kick, and I doubt you have a chance of hitting your target, but you look threatening enough it might be a deterrent."

"Spray and pray?"

"Works for you, doesn't it?"

Yes, praying worked for her. "I guess it's better than nothing."

"Preston is working on the rest of his arsenal," Ramon said. "He's determined to pitch in to protect Nora."

"And what if the guy who is gunning for Preston shows up? Is Preston going to fight him, too?" Kenna didn't like the idea of having to watch both of their backs and split focus between the two. "He should just go in the panic room with Nora and Ellie."

"Maybe we can convince him if something does happen. There could be time when we go to the study and tell her it's time to duck in there and hole up while we take care of the problem."

Kenna shook her head.

"I know." Ramon came over and squeezed her shoulder. "We'll figure it out. We'll adapt, and we'll take care of this."

She nodded. "Right."

"Makes you wish you were the kind of person who drinks those giant energy drinks, right?"

She chuckled. "I'm gonna take more meds."

"Good idea."

As she passed the breakfast bar, the burner phone rang. She used her left hand to answer it, since she might need the other to fire a gun. "Kenna Banbury."

"It's Detective Byrd. Your young friend Anthony just got a call from his mother. She's got information from Landry."

"Okay." Kenna leaned her hip against the kitchen counter. "Go ahead."

The line fuzzed a little, like the phone being handed over. Then Anthony came on. "Kenna?"

"Yeah, you heard from your mom?" She wanted to ask him how things were going with the police, and getting everything squared away, but the sense of urgency wouldn't let her go. As if instinct was aware of something impending. About to kick off.

"Uh-huh. She said she talked to Landry."

"Already? That was fast."

"I know," he said. "She got one of her crew to fake a hit, and Mom stepped in. Pretended to save her. In return for protection, Landry told her about the woman who ordered her people to kill Damien and his wife in the hospital."

Kenna's brows rose. "Wow, that's amazing."

"Detective Byrd said you'd want to know, because she said you seemed so interested at the Broadway Hotel when they were interviewing her."

Kenna blinked. "The hooker?"

"Her name is Sharee Delights." Anthony cleared his throat. "I looked her up on her website once."

"Dude."

"Pfft, whatever. I was just looking."

Kenna shook her head. "So this Sharee person is the one who orders Momma Landry around?"

"Apparently Camra Tenison is her sister. That's what Momma said."

And both of them had inferred they had a relationship with Damien, in spite of his wife. Maybe neither did, although Sharee didn't seem to be too discerning what with Mr. Wilson at the group home as well.

"Did you recognize her as the woman Nesta said visits her group home?" Kenna asked.

"Yeah, that's her. Mom said that Landry told her that she's crazy. Crazier than Momma."

But was she crazy enough to wear a robe and kill a man in a mausoleum, make it look like ritual sacrifice to some dark spirit? That was business Kenna didn't want to mess with, so she was very glad it wasn't real.

"Great," Kenna said. "Any idea how to find this woman?"

"Landry told my mom that Sharee probably has all Momma's guys that aren't in jail on her payroll right now. I don't know how many, but it could be a whole army."

"That's what I figure." Kenna didn't like the sound of it, but if the baby was payment for a debt, who knew what Sharee was thinking. Did she want to take the child, or kill everyone in this house?

Or was Allie her whole focus right now and they would be safe here?

"Thanks, Anthony."

"You, too."

Kenna said, "Yeah?"

"We're doing okay. I never thought I'd say this about a cop, but Detective Byrd is pretty cool."

"That's good." They said goodbye, and Kenna waited for him to hang up first so she didn't have to use her finger. She turned to Ramon. "I guess Maizie can quit searching for the next of kin. We should tell her this woman's name."

Ramon nodded. He was about to say something when brakes squealed outside. There was a crash, the sound of glass shattering, and a small explosion.

Kenna raced down the hall to the sitting room at the front

of the house, beside the front door. On the other side was Preston's study. He filled the doorway, staring into the sitting room.

Flames licked up the couch, and smoke filled the air.

Kenna shut the door so the fire didn't spread as fast. "Call 911, Preston. *Now.*"

"Then get in the panic room with Nora," Ramon said.

Kenna looked at him, her back to the wall beside the sitting room door. "Ramon, what's going on outside?"

He tapped the power button on his small tablet. "They're not approaching the front. They're coming around the back. I'll head them off."

"I'll get Nora settled."

Kenna ran for the room upstairs where Nora was staying with Ellie, the door slightly ajar. She kicked it wide. "Gotta go. Time to hunker down."

Nora moved immediately, swinging her legs off the bed and standing with Ellie in her arms. She rushed to the closet in the corner and pulled the door open, used one arm to shove back the hanging clothes, and revealed the door.

"Preston taught you the code?"

"He had me change it so no one knows it but me. Not even him."

Kenna looked away and heard the series of beeps that told her Nora typed in her code. "That's good."

The door clicked open.

"Everything is going to be okay."

"For me and Ellie, maybe." Nora stepped into the small room, barely the size of an elevator. But it had some supplies, a toilet, and a phone that used the internet to call out. Preston had even set up the connection so that even if someone cut power and communication to the house, it would still work.

"What about you?" Nora said.

The baby started to fuss, and Nora shifted her. Patted her back.

"Don't worry about us," Kenna said. "Just stay safe, okay?"

Nora nodded.

"You have to shut the door."

After a brief moment of hesitation, Nora pulled the door shut. It clicked, and the lock engaged.

Kenna heard a crash downstairs, and a thump. She went to the window and looked out, unsure really why she chose to do that when the threat would be coming up the stairs soon enough.

A van had parked at the rear of the house, barely visible from this side window.

Kenna saw a blonde standing by the vehicle. Before she could get a good look at the woman, she moved out of sight.

Time to get to work.

Gunfire broke out downstairs.

Last time she'd been near Preston, months ago, he'd been shot in the neck. Hopefully, he had a bulletproof vest on now so he was at least covered over his vital organs—the way Ramon and Kenna had chosen to prep for this. She didn't want Preston to get hurt again.

Her thoughts solidified into a cold resolve.

She crept to the door and looked out.

No one came up the stairs. Kenna took the opposite direction down the hall and used the tiny staircase that led to the kitchen, probably what servants had used a century or two ago. Her boots hammered on the bare wood steps, no matter how quietly she tried to move.

Kenna had the gun in front of her, the strap heavy on her shoulders.

Lord, I don't know if I can even fire this.

Maybe she wouldn't have to.

Kenna eased the door open with her foot and looked into the kitchen. A guy in a T-shirt and jeans, a full beard and facial piercings, turned to her.

Gun.

She squeezed the trigger, and her weapon sprayed a grouping of bullets in his direction.

He fell back, stumbled, and went down. Hopefully, if not dead, then dazed enough she could get by him. All they had to do here was keep the situation as contained as possible until officers arrived to assist them.

But a whole lot of chaos could happen in a matter of minutes.

A buddy of his came in. The guy immediately spotted her and swung around. Gunfire blasted down the hall and caught him in the back. His expression flashed with surprise, and he went down.

Preston stepped into the room, breathing hard. Sweat running down the sides of his face.

"There's another—"

Preston twisted to the man she'd downed and fired a single shot.

A weapon clattered to the tile floor.

Kenna kicked the door shut behind her. "How many?"

"Too many. Ramon is outside."

The woman. "The boss is out there as well."

Her phone rang on the breakfast bar, stopping her from saying more. She looked at the screen and realized that was Jax's number. She couldn't answer it right now.

"Go," Preston said. "I've got things handled in here."

Kenna moved through the kitchen. "How about you go out front and wave down the cops when they get here?"

"Nora's okay?"

She stopped right beside him. "Holed up. Safe."

Preston nodded.

"Go." She repeated his order back to him and headed for the back door.

Sirens sounded in the distance. Help was on the way, but that didn't mean she could be complacent.

The door started to open, coming inward.

Kenna waited a couple of seconds, lifted her knee and kicked it hard. She put all her strength into that kick, confident it would be far more effective than anything she could do with her hands right now.

She heard a yelp, and someone hit the ground.

More would enter. She couldn't kick them all. Nor could she fight them off with her hands.

She needed the element of surprise.

And just a little crazy.

The next guy shoved the door open. She stepped into view and squeezed the trigger of the gun, knowing it wouldn't last long. Maybe her finger would do her a favor and cramp up firing so she couldn't stop.

His body jerked, and he fell back. The bullets kept coming, hitting the man behind him. He went down as well, falling with his arms pinwheeling around as he tumbled down the stone steps to the path that led down to the gate.

She managed to shift her finger, and then moved the gun to her other side. Left-handed firing would be worse than right but would save her dominant arm. Just in case.

Kenna took cover behind a huge terracotta plant pot.

A woman screeched.

Sharee Delight.

If she was here, then at least she wasn't terrorizing Allie. But did that mean it was Camra that was the killer of the two of them, or someone else?

Kenna yelled, "Give it up! You'll never get Nora and that baby!"

"Get her!" Sharee screamed.

Someone fired.

Kenna peered up far enough she could see the gunmen who'd run through the stone archway jerk and go down. "Ramon!"

"Yeah!"

"Thanks!"

He fired again, downing more men.

When no additional men came in for a second, Kenna yelled, "Cover!"

"Copy!"

She got up from behind the pot and raced down the path. No way was she going to let Sharee get away. The cops were almost here, but she had to make sure this woman was locked down. Otherwise, it was all for nothing.

Kenna hit the side wall of the arch, forced herself to stop, and looked around.

A bullet whizzed at her. It snapped past her face, nearly taking her out.

Game over.

Should've told Jax how I feel.

She got her weapon up, in front of her. Took a breath. Rounded the corner.

An engine revved.

Kenna ran to the van, but didn't see anyone inside. An SUV that'd been parked behind it backed up, fast. Sharee sat in the driver's seat with a feral look on her face.

A cop car pulled in at the end of the lane behind the houses.

Sharee barreled the SUV into the side, pushed past it onto the street, and turned. She gunned it and drove away.

Kenna let go of the gun so her arms didn't have to hold it. The weapon hung by the strap in front of her.

A cop car buzzed past the end of the street, lights and sirens. Going after Sharee.

Kenna ran to the officer whose car had been struck and saw him clutching his head, shoving at the airbag. She knocked on his window. "You okay?"

He nodded. "I will be when they get that woman."

"I have to check on the house." When he nodded again, she raced back to find Ramon on the phone. "What is it?"

He turned to her, a sickened expression on his face. "They found Allie."

So why did he look ill?

The ambush had only been a distraction so that Sharee and her people could hit the house and try to grab Nora and Ellie. Right?

"What's going on?" Kenna asked.

"She's dead." Ramon swallowed. "She was dead when they got there."

Chapter Thirty-Two

Ramon opened the back door for Kenna. She'd ditched the gun but not much else. There were cops and crime scene people all over the house. Which, considering the amount of deceased persons in here, wasn't all that surprising.

She watched Bear's team—minus the man himself and Allie—trudge up the stairs. "Hey."

The guy who'd complemented her on using her hip to close the car door came in first. "He won't leave her, but he ordered us back here." He glanced around and found Preston in the kitchen. Nora was packing her and Ellie's things. "Wheels up in forty minutes."

Preston nodded. "I'm ready. I'll give Nora a hand with her bags. Ramon?"

"I'll help." Ramon followed him out of the room.

Kenna turned to Bear's team, surveying the haggard looks on each of their faces. "I'm so sorry for your loss."

The guy who'd come in first nodded. "Her parents are flying in from Kansas."

"That's good." Kenna had to clear her throat. "Any resistance when you breached the residence?"

He shook his head. "It was like she wanted to be killed." He pulled out his phone and showed her a photo.

"Camra Tenison. She's the one who did it."

One of the group said, "Why do you think we killed her?" and stepped between Kenna the other man, then disappeared after Ramon.

Bear's number two guy sighed, scratching his jaw. "We're taking Preston, Nora, and Ellie to the Washington Coast house so he can help them get settled. Not sure after that."

Kenna nodded. "I'm sure you can all use some downtime."

Each of them needed to rest...and grieve.

"What about the other one?" he asked. "The sister?"

"The ATF is working with New Orleans PD, and they are going to raid several locations simultaneously. Ramon and I are going to oversee it, just so we know it's over. You know?"

"Good."

Nora appeared, holding the baby.

Kenna said, "Washington?"

The young woman shrugged. "It'll be good to get away, even if it's cold and gray all the time there. Preston said it has a huge fireplace and he'll teach me how to light it before he goes to his other house."

"What about Garth?" Kenna asked. "I can pass on a message if you want."

Nora shrugged. "I'll write him a letter. He'd better behave and get out quickly, or Ellie isn't going to know him."

Kenna figured that was a solid plan, even if the danger had passed. What did the new mom have here to hold her to Louisiana?

Preston came back in. "I gave Ramon a set of keys to the house. I'll lock up when we leave. Let yourselves back in so you can grab your things, and he will set the alarm when you guys go. Doesn't matter when."

Kenna nodded.

He gave her a hug, even though she couldn't return it. "I'd like to say it was good to see you. And it was, but..." He let out a sigh.

"I know. You, too."

Preston smiled, mostly sad but also affectionate. "Don't forget about my London trip in the New Year. At least think about it."

"I will," Kenna said.

Especially now Bear's team had been rocked. They would be missing a dear friend and vital member of their group from now on. No new hire would fill that hole.

She glanced around at them. "We'll see how my recovery goes, and then we can talk about what you need me to do."

Preston said, "It's not what I need you for." Then he walked away.

Kenna frowned at his back.

Ramon came in. "What now? It's nearly time to go."

"I know." But she couldn't let go of the fact that Preston's words indicated there was something for her in London.

What could that be?

And why not just tell her the real reason she would be going?

"Come on." He nudged the back of her shoulder. "We don't want to miss them catching Sharee—or whatever her name is—and nailing her to the wall." He opened the door.

Kenna stepped through. "Or they could, you know, arrest her."

"Whichever is good with me."

He drove them to the house where Martinez was part of

the raid, an upper-middle-class neighborhood that surprised Kenna. The whole place was white picket fences and the kind of streets where kids should be riding bikes down the sidewalk or swinging from tires.

She turned to Ramon. "You ever live in a place like this?"

"Why would I?" He snorted. "These people think they're better, but I prefer neighborhoods where folks know they're messed up and they're not trying to hide it behind plastic veneer."

So cynical. "Maybe you should buy a cabin in the woods. Or a bar in the bayou. That one we went to might be for sale."

He chuckled. "Let's go see if they found her."

"Sure, right as soon as you open my door."

Ramon rounded the hood of the car to do just that. "Milady."

"Shut it."

He laughed and slammed the door behind her. "If you weren't in so much pain, it might be funnier."

"I need to collapse on my bed and—"

Ramon caught up to her. "Sleep for eighteen hours. *I know.*"

Kenna rolled her eyes. "Do I need to thank you for everything you did earlier?"

"No."

"Are you going to tell Jax that you kissed me?"

"Already did." Ramon shrugged. "He called back earlier, when you were in the RV, taking a shower."

He'd sat outside on one of her lawn chairs.

Kenna glanced at him. "What did Jax say?"

"He was getting on a plane. I told him you were good, and it was almost over."

"Oh."

"There's Martinez." Ramon pointed.

A SWAT van was parked in front of two SUVs. And a black-and-white cop car blocked the drive where the same SUV that had sped away from Preston's house had been parked.

Sergeant Martinez spotted them and strode over. "The ATF have her. Shot a couple of guys who were in the house, the last of Landry's men. They're going to bring her out in a minute." He rocked back and forth on his heels. "Even the commander is here for this one."

He pointed behind him, toward an officer Kenna had seen in the PD conference room.

Two ATF agents she had spoken to at the prison walked out of the house, a cuffed blonde woman between them. Sharee screeched and hollered no matter what they did.

One of the men winced. "Shut your mouth. You aren't doing yourself any favors."

She had pristine white running shoes on, yoga pants, and a tiny crop top. Pretending she'd been working out, rather than ambushing Preston's house. It was the woman Kenna had seen outside the house, through the window. She was also the hooker that Detectives Fisher and Byrd had been interviewing the day she'd gone to the Broadway Hotel to see Preston.

Kenna shook her head. "She was Camra's biological sister?"

Martinez nodded, shifting around to watch the agents walk her toward the cop car blocking the drive, where an officer stood waiting to load her in the backseat. "They met online a few years back, apparently. Sharee had been running scams with other foster kids, picking up ones who were malleable. Creating different crews she had working for her.

Funneling money back. All the while, she's playing the part of local small-time hooker."

"Smart."

Kenna and Martinez looked at Ramon.

He shrugged. "What? She gets others to do all the work and keeps most of the money. It's basically how capitalism works, isn't it?"

The special agent touched Sharee's head, so she could climb in the car without hitting herself on the doorframe. She turned and tried to bite his hand.

Martinez hissed.

Kenna had more questions. "What about Wilson? The kids are going to get new guardians, right? Someone who actually treats them well and will take care of them."

He nodded. "There's a couple at my mother's church who run a group of homes a little out of the city. Faith based, and with plenty of fun. Plus, they help out on the farm, and they can either homeschool, do online school, or catch the bus to their local school. Very individualized, and they have a therapist on staff. As well as a resident pastor—he's a retired missionary."

"That sounds great."

"All the kids are going to be given the choice. Detective Byrd's sister is sticking with them like glue. They're getting processed with the district attorney, and he's talking about community service for the ones not involved in what happened to that Damien guy. When it all shakes out, there might be a couple who do some juvie time. But those records will be sealed. And when they get out, we're all going to make sure none of them fall through the cracks."

Kenna could've kissed him. But unlike Ramon, she didn't go around expressing her gratitude like that. "Thank you."

"I didn't do it for you. Those kids deserve better."

"Yes, they do." Each of them hadn't always made the right choices, but with the support of adults in their lives, they could learn new skills—new ways to make decisions and discover the lives they really wanted.

Everyone had choices.

Some people just had to be shown in a way that they believed it.

Martinez put his arm around her shoulder and gave her a side hug. "Thanks, Kenna." He shook Ramon's hand.

"You're welcome. Thanks again," she said. "And have Anthony call me?"

He nodded. "I'll pass that on. I think he's doing all right."

They walked away from the black-and-white, where Sharee pounded on the window and screamed at the cops.

Ramon looked over at her. "I'm surprised you didn't offer to adopt the kid."

"It's not like I didn't think about it." Kenna thought about a lot of things. Didn't mean they were good ideas. "But he probably doesn't want to live in Colorado with Maizie, and Stairns and his wife while I'm on the road all the time."

Not that she hadn't thought about settling down at some point.

Finding a home base, and a way to continue to do the work she loved. Maybe raise a family of her own and adopt a bunch of rescue dogs so they always had happy four-legged friends around.

Ramon said, "Back to the house?"

She nodded, leaning her head back on the seat. He closed her door.

She closed her eyes. And must have fallen asleep, because the car stopped and she realized they were back at the house. "Looks quiet."

All the parking spaces were empty.

The team was gone, taking Preston, Nora, and Ellie with them. Bear was with Allie's body, probably at the morgue by now. She should stop by...but she didn't know what to say to him. Once she'd given him some time, she would find him and make sure he was doing all right.

"All quiet," Ramon said. "Except the back door is open."

He raced around the car, doubled back to pull her door handle, and then ran to the path that led up the back.

The technicians had cleared out hours ago. Who was here?

She got the door closed and headed for the back, her limbs far heavier than they should be. Feeling the weight of overexertion, fear, and grief all rolled into one.

She expected to see Allie out here, but it was only the memory of that woman that hung around like Halloween pumpkins. Left discarded and forgotten.

Kenna wasn't going to forget Allie—she was going to find a way to honor her.

Before she even got to the door, Ramon appeared with his duffel slung over his shoulder. "I'm taking the car those Miami guys left us."

"What?"

"There's someone inside waiting for you."

Kenna couldn't even ask who before he was off, striding to the car. She frowned and picked her way up the stairs. It felt like heaving her body inside, and she wondered what on earth Ramon thought she was going to do with herself now.

Wasn't he supposed to set the alarm when they left?

Then she saw him.

Jax stood by the breakfast bar with a small suitcase beside him. "My case is done."

At that, her pain should've become a distant memory

along with all the fatigue. The grief. But it didn't. Tears filled her eyes, and spilled over onto her cheeks.

"Hey." He pushed off the counter and came toward her.

Kenna tried to talk. Nothing came out but a hiccupping sob.

Jax wrapped his arms around her, strength and gentleness at the same time. Keeping her safe. Holding her up when she needed it. "Sounds like you had a rough week."

She laughed, but it came out more like a sob. She wanted to wrap her arms around him in return but didn't have the strength to do even that. Let alone hold on.

She wanted to hold on.

"I love you."

He tensed. His head moved alongside hers, and she looked at him, which should've made him wince. She probably looked like a drowned puppy. "What was that?"

Kenna scanned his face. The expression in his eyes, part nervousness, part affection. A whole lot of hope. "I love you," she repeated.

"That's good." He cleared his throat. "Because I love you."

Yeah, she'd pretty much figured that out.

Kenna ducked her head and buried her face against his shirt again, even though she was getting it all damp.

They stood that way for a while. Him rubbing his hand up and down her back. Kenna enjoying having him here for the first time in a while.

Eventually, he said, "What do you need?"

"Other than this?" She heard his chest rumble under her cheek and gave herself a moment to enjoy it. "Can you drive my RV back to Phoenix? I think I might hang out near you for a while." She leaned back and looked at the satisfied expression on his face.

He kissed her. "Do we need to swing by the courthouse on the way?"

Kenna laughed. She bit her lip, then said, "Maybe I should meet your mother first."

"Whoa." He blinked. "Now I know you're serious."

"I guess you'd better get used to it."

Jax chuckled.

Kenna looked around. "Let's get out of here."

Keep Reading For...

- Where to find more great Lisa Phillips books.

- How to sign up for Lisa's newsletter and get a FREE book.

- Where to find Lisa on social media.

About the Author

Find out more about Lisa Phillips at her website, where you'll discover more romantic suspense fan-favorite series and heart-pounding thriller novels.
https://authorlisaphillips.com/

If you loved this book, please consider sharing about it on social media. Or leave a review at your book retailer website, on Goodreads, or on Bookbub. Your review will help others find great books to entertain and encourage them!

Signup for Lisa's newsletter by scanning the QR code below to stay updated on sales, new releases, and recommendations for your TBR pile. New Subscribers even get a FREE book!

Find Lisa on Social Media!

facebook.com/authorlisaphillips

instagram.com/lisaphillipsbks

bookbub.com/authors/lisa-phillips

Also by Lisa Phillips

Find out more about Brand of Justice at my website:

https://authorlisaphillips.com/product-tag/brand-of-justice/

Book 1: Cold Dead Night

Book 2: Burn the Dawn

Book 3: Quick and Dead

Book 4: Over the Limit

Book 5: Skin and Bone

Book 6: Dust and Ashes

Book 7: Long Road Home

Book 8 : Dead to Rights

Book 9: Fear No Evil

Book 10: Out of Time (January 2025)

———

Other series by Lisa:

Last Chance Downrange

Chevalier Protection Specialists

Last Chance County

Northwest Counter-Terrorism Taskforce

Double Down

WITSEC Town (Sanctuary)

Numerous other titles including several with *Love Inspired Suspense*, find the complete list here (or scan the QR code):

https://authorlisaphillips.com/all-books/